MW00943683

BOUND

Vijaya Bodach

ISBN: 9781983227417

Cover Design and Logo by Derrick Alderman
Cover Art © Rudall30/Shutterstock
Cover Texture © K. Ruslan/Shutterstock
Author Photograph © Max Bodach

For any inquiries about this book, please email:
vijaya_bodach@yahoo.com

For more information about the author, please see:
https://vijayabodach.com or **https://bodachbooks.com**

+JMJ+

This book is dedicated to the memories of my mother, Malati, and my auntie, Saraswati.

The air thrums with talk of parties this last day of school, but I won't be going to any.

"One more year," I whisper into my empty locker, closing it shut.

When I turn to join the mass of high school humanity making its way out, Colleen Mendoza steps beside me, her smile so wide she'd explode if she didn't spill. "Kurt Thompson invited ME!"

"Where?"

"At his farm!" Colleen squeezes my arm. "Come with me! It'd be fun to go together!"

My glasses have slipped down my nose but I don't push them up. Instead I look at Colleen over the top with my no-way-am-I-going look. "My dad…"

"Yup, you need to get permission." She pushes the glasses up my nose. "For me. It's not like I'm friends with any of them."

"And I am?" I laugh.

"But you … you take classes with them and everything so it's different."

As though that's a valid reason. "I have to get up early to go to Seattle for the laser treatment." I'm hoping she'll take pity on the way I look, like an old worn-out patch-work doll.

"So? You use your scars as a copout," Colleen says, slugging my arm gently.

She's right. I do this all the time, isolating myself from the world at large. I should be over it after six years, but a severe

1

burn lasts forever. I hardly remember who I used to be before the burns. People say not to judge a book by its cover, or it doesn't matter what you look like, but the sad truth is that people naturally assume the outside reflects the inside, and unfortunately, I feel ugly on the inside as I am on the outside.

"I'm just so relieved to cocoon myself at home," I tell Colleen.

She sighs. "I'd probably want to be a cloistered nun in your shoes ... I mean, skin."

We both laugh because she has Kurt on her mind, not the rosary.

We wend our way down the stairs and finally emerge into the bright summer sunshine. Cars rev up in the parking lot and everybody mills about, not wanting to say goodbye. A few kids wait for the bus. Colleen and I pick up the pace, eager to get home.

"We should've driven," she says.

"It was your idea to walk," I say.

"Because it's the only exercise I get. But if I'd known about the party earlier, I'd have driven. Remember, exceptions!"

I should be happier for her. A pang of jealousy pricks at my heart knowing no boy will ever ask me. Not even Sheldon Williams, my best friend until that almost-kiss six years ago.

We walk the two miles home, talking about the things that lie ahead for us this summer.

"I'll work all day at the fabric store and spend my evenings looking at the stars with Kurt," Colleen says.

"The sun doesn't set till nearly nine," I say. "Maybe you'll have to go to the movies."

We giggle because our little college town practically shuts down in the summer.

"And you'll recover beautifully from the laser treatment, with new skin to show off in the fall," Colleen says, dreaming for me.

"Like a phoenix rising from ashes."

We part ways at the corner. Colleen gives me a quick hug. "If you change your mind, call me."

But we both know I won't.

I go straight to my room, pulling up the sleeves of my pink Oxford shirt. It's pale against my mostly chocolate skin and the ropy scar that entwines my left arm. Damn keloids. Kneading my fingers into the rough edges, I will them to melt into my skin.

I strip off the shirt and run my right hand to my left shoulder, feeling every indentation. This is who I am. Rebecca. The girl who played with sparklers, the girl who burned, the girl who lived. Except I distinctly remember my sparkler dying out that inauspicious July Fourth when I nearly kissed Sheldon. I have reconstructed the past based on what others have told me. I know it's normal not to have total recall of traumatic events, but it's unsettling to have these large gaps in my memory.

I push my thick black hair away from my face and trace my fingers along the curve of my jawbone. Concentrating on the corrugated parts of my face, I think how gullible I've been all these years rubbing expensive lotions into my body. Except for keeping my skin moist, they've not made any difference. Plain old petroleum jelly would've done as well. But fractional laser treatment looks promising. In essence, I'll be burned again—the thought gives me chills—but the new skin that will grow back will be smooth. I pick up an old copy of *Glamour* magazine on my nightstand that showcases twenty-one-year-old triplets who survived a fire as babies. The scar reduction was dramatic. Even Dad agreed.

3

It's hard not to dream of looking like a normal girl, of walking about, hair up in a ponytail, arm straight down instead of bent, and not being stared at. Of short sleeves and short skirts. Swimming.

I've learned to ignore the comments, the mothers shushing their loud children who ask, "Mommy, Mommy, did you see that?" Not even *her*, but *that*. Like I'm not even a person.

Melody rubs up against my leg and begins to purr. I pick her up and nuzzle her soft fur until she protests. She digs her claws into my tank top. "I love you, too," I croon, disengaging from her. She lands softly on my discarded shirt. Before she can settle into it, I slip it back on. Mel immediately curls towards me, chirps a funny *mrreow*, and begs for more cuddling.

Mel supervises me as I fill a duffel bag with books, billowy Indian tops and long cotton skirts. I take a last look at the cupboard full of creams and decide to take the largest tube of the tropical moisturizer. My skin is perpetually dry and itchy given that I hardly have any sebaceous glands left.

Melody follows me to Joy's room, circling the suitcase I wheel out of the closet. When I hoist it onto the bed, the lid falls open and a bunch of stuffed animals stare at me. I add them to the pile of toys against the headboard and pack the suitcase with Joy's clean clothes, enough for a week. I'm making a mental checklist of what else she might need when I hear a car slowing down, a dog's bark, and Joy's shrieks.

I peek out the window. An unfamiliar car speeds away, and Joy urges the neighbor's dog to fetch a ball. She sounds exactly like a ten-year-old. "Fetch the ball, Lucky. No, Lucky. Fetch the ball, Lucky. No, Lucky." Except Joy is nearly twenty-three and Lucky always runs past her with the ball. Even the dog doesn't respect her.

When Joy kneels down on the grass, Lucky barrels into her, knocking her over. He stands over her, his body nearly folding

4

in half with furious wagging. Joy laughs uncontrollably. Thank goodness she's wearing shorts instead of a skirt, the way her legs are flailing. I don't want people to gawk at her. Joy finally tosses the ball in the air. Lucky's off and running to fetch it.

I return to packing the clothes when Joy bursts through the door, all hot and sweaty, bits of grass still clinging to her clothes. "All I want for Christmas is a dog, dog, dog," she sings in the squeaky voice of the Chipmunks.

"Be thankful Dad lets you have Mel," I remind her. Dad can't stand animals shedding fur everywhere, but he especially cannot stand dogs. He thinks they smell.

Joy picks up Melody and plants kisses on the top of her head. "I have to change."

"What for?"

"Folk dancing!" Joy does a little Irish jig.

"Why don't you finish packing," I tell her. "I'll get us something to eat."

I leave her looking at the pile of clothes.

The first thing that catches my eye on the kitchen counter is the package of flat bread— naan. I survey the contents of the fridge and decide to make two little Indian pizzas with the *naan*. I slide them into the oven.

When I return, Joy is in her underwear and bra, rifling through the suitcase. She picks out the bright red skirt I just packed. Why she can't wear one that's hanging in the closet is beyond me. Joy takes her time choosing a blouse. It always surprises me she doesn't try to hide her nakedness. Even though she's not obese like Mom was, she's got a three-inch roll on her stomach when she bends over.

Joy selects a yellow blouse with embroidered red flowers. She tucks it into the waistband of her skirt and goes to the mirror, shrugging one shoulder, then the other, while I refold the clothes she messed up. Then she pulls the smocked neckline down, and still farther down, until it rests below her deltoids, revealing round caramel shoulders, and the beginning of her cleavage. She could be a Bollywood starlet.

"Stupid bra," Joy says, tugging at the white strap.

"You need it for dancing," I tell her, acutely aware that I don't have breasts or nipples and will never need a bra. My burns were severe enough to warrant removal of my breast buds. When I began high school, Mom and my doctors assured me I could have implants after I'm done growing if it still mattered. Seeing Joy's skin stretch smoothly over the exposed mounds makes my own chest constrict.

I pull the blouse back over her shoulders. "There. That looks better. You don't want everybody seeing your Mumbai mangoes."

Joy giggles. "Mumbai mangoes" was a phrase Mom used.

"I miss Mommy," Joy says softly, her eyes wet, where moments before she had laughter.

"I do too." I envelop her in a hug. Joy has the same softness as Mom. I doubt my bony frame is any comfort, but we stay enfolded for a little while, leaning on each other. I hold back my tears. No matter how hard we try, we haven't been able to patch the ripped fabric of our universe ever since Mom died from a massive coronary last year. She was the sun in our lives; without her we seem to live in eternal darkness, just floating through space without any direction.

Joy pulls away. "Come folk dancing with me."

"Nope. I need to get everything ready for tomorrow." I can't even think of all the things that need to be done. Mom always took care of everything. "Do you know this will be the first time we'll go to Harborview without Mom?"

"I'll hold your hand," Joy says, taking mine into hers. "I'll never leave you."

That's what I'm afraid of sometimes. I don't want us to be like a binary star system, circling each other forever.

She pushes the hair from the left side of my face and runs her fingers along the scars. "You're still pretty. The doctors will make it nice."

I wish I had Joy's confidence. When over half your body is burned, all of you pays the price. I can almost envision the new me. "Let's finish packing. Otherwise, no folk dancing."

Joy pouts, but places a coloring kit, her favorite stuffed animal, a wolf she named Buck, and various bits of gaudy jewelry into the suitcase.

I add a windbreaker for cool nights. She picks high-heeled sandals.

"Those aren't practical," I tell her, packing her sturdy tennis shoes. "You'll want something comfortable for walking around."

"We're *driving* to Seattle," she says, rolling her eyes at me.

"Yeah, silly, but what if Dad takes you to the zoo or the Japanese garden?"

"He will?" Joy gives a huge smile.

"Maybe." I hope so, while I go for intensive physical therapy after my laser treatment.

We finish packing, with Melody weaving in and out of the clothes, finally settling on top of the suitcase.

"You want to come too, Melly?" Joy's eyes brim with tears. "Why can't we bring her?"

"Colleen will take good care of her like she always has, and Mel will be happier here than in the hotel. Besides, she'd hate being in the car for six hours."

"That's not true. Melly could sit on my lap." Joy picks up Melody and lets her settle in the hollow of her crossed legs. "See?"

"She's staying here," My patience is suddenly running thin. I'm tired of being her personal chauffeur. "It's almost time for folk dancing, unless you want to skip it."

7

"You're mean." Joy makes a face at me, and scratches Mel's chin until we can both hear her motor. She has the loudest purr of any cat I know. "I'll miss you so much, my smelly Melly."

Joy chuckles at her cleverness, then demands to eat.

"Oh, no!" I gasp.

I run to the kitchen, Joy following closely behind. I put on an oven mitt and take out our little naan-pizzas.

"It's terrible," Joy says, looking at the charred bits of onion and zucchini.

"Ugh. Sorry. I forgot to turn on the timer." I can't believe how careless it was of me; the whole kitchen could've been set on fire. I test a piece of sausage. "Not too bad."

The two of us gnaw on the leathery naan and its burned toppings. I toss the remainder in the garbage and hustle Joy into the car.

I hop into the car and drop off Joy at Smith Gym. "Have fun! Catch a ride home with Hilde, all right?"

I head home, thinking how both Joy and Colleen want me to spend the evening with them doing something fun, and how responsibilities weigh me down. I don't know how Mom took care of everything and still managed to have fun with us. What's wrong with me? Tears prick at my eyes and I don't try to stop them. When I turn into our street, I drive on the wrong side, stopping briefly to grab our mail. Buried with the grocery coupons and other junk is a large packet from Wayne State University. I let out a squeal.

Freedom!

~~~2~~~

I tear into the envelope and flip through the glossy magazine depicting campus life. Hah! I know people dream of going to Yale or Princeton or Stanford, not some podunk school in Detroit, but odd as it may sound, it's what I've been dreaming of. It's the perfect place for me—far from here.

I pile Dad's stuff on the kitchen counter and toss all the junk mail into the recycling bin. It still hurts to see mail addressed to Mom, especially when it says: *Mrs. Vidya Joshi or Current Resident.* As if Mom were replaceable.

I put aside the glossy Wayne brochure. The plainer booklet, detailing the program for a bachelor of science combined with a medical degree, is what really interests me. It's an eight-year commitment. Scholarships are available. Yes! I think about the coursework, what I'd like to major in. Chemistry or Microbiology? I'm intrigued by the smallest creatures. They ravaged my body after the burns, ruining the skin grafts. How can something so tiny destroy so quickly? Then I think of mighty oaks toppling over from a mere fungus, and the bodies of men and women eaten from the inside out from various viruses. I think about my skin—the largest organ in my body—how it still protects even though more than half is ugly and fragile.

~~~

I don't hear Dad until he's right in front of me. "What's this?" He plucks the booklet out of my hands.

"Dad! I'm reading it." I can't believe he's so rude.

9

He scans the page I was studying, then flips to the cover. "Hmm. BS/MD program. You can't do this." His round brown face shows a trace of pink.

"Why not? If I get in, I'll have a guaranteed seat in medical school. Guaranteed."

"It's in Detroit."

"So?" But what I really want to say is: That's exactly why. Because it's far away from sleepy little Pullman, home of Washington State University, Joy, and Dad. "It'll be just like going to WSU. Get it? Same letters." I cough out a laugh. "Only I'll be a Warrior, not a Cougar."

"You belong here." Dad rips the booklet in two and chucks it in the recycling bin.

I'm up in an instant to retrieve the halves. How dare he? "I'm also checking the program in Missouri." And just to drive home my point I add, "Florida too. You can't stop me."

Dad puffs out his chest as though he's in a classroom making a proclamation. "Your mother is gone and Joy cannot lose you so soon after. Don't you understand?"

I knew he'd bring up the real reason soon enough. Dad *needs* me because I'm doing everything Mom used to do for Joy. He can't be bothered about his own daughter. Why should he? He's a very practical man, my father, *Doctor* Shiv Joshi. Only he's not a medical doctor, but a Ph.D. getting accolades for his pioneering work on prenatal genetic testing. Couples come to him to discuss possible genetic abnormalities in their unborn babies. That way they can be sure they'll have a perfect baby to haul around in their Lexus. I was perfect once too, but people don't remember anymore.

"We discussed this," he says calmly. "The matter's settled. I forbid you."

"What? When?" My voice is shrill. "It's not fair to make me stay in Pullman for Joy. This isn't India."

"I said forget it."

10

"Is that why you adopted me? So that I could be stuck with Joy?" The words tumble out before I can take them back. My ears grow hot. I've even become the primary liaison with Joy's social worker, Tessa. Why me? Why not Dad?

I hear myself take shallow breaths, my heart beat, and the whispering of the curtains. Dad speaks after a long silence. "Is that what you think?"

"Wouldn't you?"

I think about how it must've been when they discovered that their precious Joy, their miracle baby, wouldn't really grow up. They couldn't hope for another little miracle, so they packed their bags and went to India to find an unfortunate infant. They'd be doing a good deed, giving a poor orphan girl a privileged home. Everybody must've lauded them for their charity. Only they didn't think that this infant might grow up and want to do something else besides take care of her adoptive, delayed sister.

"We've denied you nothing, Rebecca." Dad waves his arms about. "Everything we've done, we've done for you and Joy."

He lifts my chin and I stare into his dark brown eyes. "Joy wanted to adopt all the children at the orphanage. But she chose you because you were like a fairy child, with big black eyes that wouldn't leave her face. She loves you. I love you." He lets go of my chin and shakes his head. "We hire sitters and therapists, doctors and nurses. Not siblings."

"But we pay the price," I say, thinking how he's exacting it from me now. He checked out after Mom died and doesn't seem to be aware of the burden of having a daughter who is like a child.

"We all pay a price. Society pays a price. This is why I do the work I do. To alleviate suffering. Look at you! Isn't this why you want to be a doctor?"

11

I don't have to look to feel the scars on my arm, my neck, or my face. My chest, stomach, and back are a constant reminder of what I am—a burned girl. I nearly died. For all practical purposes, I did, because what they resurrected is not the original me, but a caricature of my former self.

I remember being engulfed in flames, screaming and rolling. Memories of the pain afterwards come crashing through. The agony of discovering my charred body, sliced open, my innards draining away. I lived. I was only eleven.

"A miracle child," Mom used to say. That's when she held my bandaged hands and told me I survived as a newborn in a cardboard box left outside a church. Someone, a street sweeper or even a priest, found me and took pity on me before I got devoured by wild dogs, before I died from hunger and thirst. That person saw my humanity, my worth.

"Rebecca darling," Mom used to say, "you are a beautiful and beloved child of God. Never forget that."

I'd wail about why something like this would happen to me. Hadn't I suffered enough? Mom tried to soothe me.

"I don't know why terrible things have to happen. All I know is you must have a great purpose in life to be spared from death," Mom used to say.

Dad wants to make Joy my purpose. But don't my wishes matter?

"You don't know what it's been like for me," I finally say. "I've given up a lot of friends for Joy. Even before I got burned, I was shunned because of her. I will not give up my dreams and my future. I want to be a doctor. You know that. I'm working towards that. Why forbid me?"

"Nobody is asking you to give up your dreams. You can go to school here. Wayne State isn't any better than Washington State. Staying here will give Joy the stability she needs. After four years, you can apply to medical schools anywhere in the country."

"Why is it always about Joy?"

"Just a minute, Rebecca. You might not realize this, but since you were burned, it's been all about you. Six years! We were taking care of you, sacrificing everything so that you might live. How many times have we gone to Harborview for reconstructive surgery? You think it's all free? Your mom and I worked hard to make sure you wouldn't be disabled as you grew. Aren't we spending thousands of dollars on this new laser treatment so that you can have a chance at having smoother skin? It's purely cosmetic."

I want to pummel his chest. It's not like I'm trying to get wrinkles removed or fix my sagging left eye. I have keloids— huge lumpy scars. It's as though the grafted skin doesn't know when to stop growing. Some scars, like the contractures I develop in my joints, restrict movement. I remember having the neck of a ragged old woman. I didn't even have a neck but a mass of flesh connecting my chin to my chest. The doctors *gave* me a neck by releasing that contracture. That's the first so-called cosmetic surgery I had. At age eleven-and-half. Yes, sir. Cosmetic. Because nobody ever died from looking hideous.

I thought I'd die from the procedure. They placed a tissue expander in my cheek. A little silicone balloon was inflated under my skin so that it would stretch and grow over a few months. The excess skin was used to fashion my neck. But until then I looked like a mutant.

But the words are trapped in my throat and I can only whisper, "You don't know what it's like. You don't know anything." Tears threaten to spill out of my eyes but I refuse to cry. I shove my hands into my pockets before they do something stupid, like smash the happy family photos hung on the wall.

"No I don't. But we all suffered with you. Especially Joy." Dad's eyes grow moist as they rest on the pictures. I didn't realize that he's like me, choking back his grief because Joy feels Mom's absence so acutely. She cries every night, even now. I push all the missing and grieving away and turn my attention to the torn brochure—my life preserver.

"Why don't you concentrate on what's offered right here, right now?" Dad says softly.

This family—my family—saved my life, not once, but twice. Now I owe it to them, to Joy. Or do I?

"Just let me dream, okay?"

"Don't go," is all he says.

I walk away from him, leaving him to his pile of mail. And before I know it, I'm in my Honda, pealing out of the driveway. I take the steep road down Pioneer Hill and the highway towards Lewiston and the Snake River. The town of Pullman in the rearview mirror makes me happy. I pretend I'm driving all the way to Detroit since this would be the first leg of the journey.

But I get sidetracked before I even get to the scenic part.

~~~3~~~

The Thompson farm comes into view with its rusted-wheel fence. An ancient green tractor stands guard. I slow down, looking for Colleen's dented Prelude. I've been in it a thousand times and always feel like it's going to fall apart with all the rattling noises it makes. The passenger door doesn't latch properly either and it'd just be my luck it swings open on the curvy road when I'm in it. Thank God the seatbelt still works.

Colleen's car is parked near the front. I have to drive nearly a quarter of a mile before I can pull over to park. She'll be surprised to see me. Disobeying Dad. I realize I forgot my cell phone on the kitchen counter. It gives me a perverse pleasure to know there's no way for Dad to contact me, ordering me to come home. I sit in my car and debate going to the party. Colleen won't be the only one surprised. Everybody else there will be too. They'll look at me. Talk about me. But I'm here. Colleen will be so happy. A long time ago, I discovered the best way to get rid of sad-mad feelings was to do something nice for somebody else. And so I read to the little kids at the burn center at Harborview, sang songs and drew pictures. I made up silly stories with happily-ever-after-endings.

I walk along the road wondering again whether the others will think I'm crazy for coming to a pool party. Me. Ugly as sin, in a bathing suit. How I wish I had Colleen's two piece suit she made for me last year for my birthday. The snug shorts cover most of my thighs and the top goes past my waist. Colleen designed it so my good shoulder is bare, but the scarred one has a sleeve. The dark brown material blends with my skin and the sparkly red and gold accents make me feel interesting. I look almost normal, except when I pull my hair back in a ponytail.

I summon courage as I open the gate. A metal weathervane with a rooster squeaks in the slight breeze.

Music blares from the back of the house, so I don't bother going indoors. But the moment I step around to the side, the smell of beer and vomit makes my stomach churn. This is what people call fun? I wonder how many girls get knocked up at these parties. Well, no danger for me, but still, how could I be so stupid to stop by here? I'll be trapped listening to kids who only talk about getting out, but have no prospects. They will thresh wheat or work at the university or the drug store. They're going to be stuck here forever.

I could turn around and get back on the road, but now that I'm here, I might as well make Colleen happy. I suck in the stale air and march to the back patio.

I don't see a single friendly face, lots of skin, though, beautiful white skin, some golden. My brain screams that I don't belong here, but my heart won't let me leave. Rocco, my former biology partner, is at the bar, making drinks.

"What are you doing here?" he asks.

"I'm not sure," I say. "Have you seen Colleen?"

"Over there." Rocco points across the pool. I push my glasses up my nose to get a better look.

Kurt and Colleen are talking like old friends. When she drains the last of her drink, Colleen turns her back to Kurt. He unzips her dress and she steps daintily out of it, revealing her body in a one-piece sea-foam swimsuit. When she bends over to untie her sandals, Kurt moves closer.

"Oh, no," I whisper.

Kurt wraps his arms around Colleen. She twists around and kicks off her sandals. Their torsos press. They laugh. Colleen

16

drapes her dress over a nearby chair. They walk hand in hand into the pool as though they've been doing this forever.

"Strawberry margarita for you, señorita?" Rocco asks.

"Sure," I say.

"Don't spike it," says a high male voice I'd recognize anywhere—Sheldon's. I swivel around. His shorts are dripping. "Hey," he says.

"Hay is for horses," I say automatically.

We laugh. My mom tried to break this casual greeting habit of ours, but the reference to the horses became a code of friendship instead.

"I see you've been swimming." *Shut up*, I tell myself. *Quit pointing out the obvious.*

"The water's great. I just came to get a drink." Sheldon holds up his can of Sprite. It slips out of his hands. Everything seems to.

"Me too." I smile at Sheldon's awkwardness.

Rocco slides a strawberry margarita towards me. "*Virgin*, just for you."

"Thanks." I have no idea if it's spiked or not.

After Rocco leaves us, Sheldon says, "I didn't think I'd see you here."

"Me neither. Kurt invited Colleen and I ended up here because I was just taking a drive to let off steam."

Sheldon shakes his head. "Your dad?"

I tell him about applying to BS/MD programs and how mad Dad is, and Sheldon agrees it makes no sense to hold me back here.

"Oh, I'll make an application here as well, as a back-up, and the University of Washington, but it would be so nice to start a new life elsewhere."

"It's been that bad?" Sheldon asks.

"Not until last year," I say. "Without Mom …"

I let the unspoken thoughts linger.

"Yeah, it'll never be the same," Sheldon says. He should know. He's been motherless for a long time; she left her husband and three sons when Sheldon was only six or seven. Now it's just him and his dad, and pretty soon Sheldon will leave as his brothers did. "Everybody takes their own separate way, like planets moving off in a straight line when the sun dies out."

Does this boy download stuff from my brain?

"That's exactly what I was thinking," I say. "Mom was our sun."

"I think mine was more like a comet, the non-returning type," says Sheldon.

I wonder how hard it must've been to have a mother who chose to divorce herself from her family. "Do you miss her still?" I ask.

"Nope. I did, in the beginning, when she left. We visited a lot, but weekly visits became monthly and after a while, with all of us busy playing sports, she just sort of disappeared. She moved away to Chicago for a better job I guess. Last I heard, she has a new boyfriend."

"I assume you're not interested in a stepdad."

"Exactly. Who needs that? My dad's the best. I'm not even sure why she split because I don't remember any fighting. Dad said she fell out of love. It's bizarre." Sheldon sips his Sprite.

"Maybe it wasn't love?" I wonder aloud.

"I don't know," says Sheldon. "How would you know if it's real?"

"True love lasts through everything, like with my mom and dad. He may have his faults, but he loved Mom. He flirted with her!"

"That's cool," says Sheldon.

"And Mom didn't think twice about herself. She always wanted to do what was best for us. I wish I'd been nicer to her."

"But no kid ever thinks about that," says Sheldon. "Hey, you want to swim?"

"I don't have my swimsuit."

"There's a bin of extras. They always have guests who forget to bring a suit."

We rummage through the suits. Lots of boys' shorts. A few bikinis and one-pieces. "No way, Sheldon. Sorry to be so cliché but I'd stick out like a sore thumb."

He holds up a sun-screen shirt and shorts, both meant for boys. "It is a pool party. You'll blend in better with these instead of in jeans."

"Good point." I change in a little cabana while Sheldon waits for me. When I emerge, he laughs.

"It'll do," I say. I look silly in too-big clothes, like a little girl playing dress-up.

We walk over to where Colleen has her stuff and she waves to me from the pool. She breaks into a quick crawl and rests her elbows on the edge.

"Jump in!" She squeals as Kurt pulls her toward himself.

I add my pile of clothes to her chair. I take a long drink of my strawberry margarita and place my glasses in the center of the table.

I walk to the edge of the pool and test the water with my toe. Nice and cool. Suddenly I'm in.

"Oh, you rat!" I sputter and gasp.

Sheldon laughs beside me. "You never did learn to jump right in."

"Ugh. I hate it."

But now that I'm over the shock of the coolness, it feels great. We swim in lazy circles and splash one another. Without my glasses the world around me disappears and it's just Sheldon and me, like when we were kids.

"So what are you doing this summer?" I ask.

"I have an internship at Cal. Tech." Sheldon's chest puffs out a bit. "Signal transduction lab."

"Oooh, nice. I've always thought it was neat that cells have their own Morse code to send messages to one another."

"Me too. Actually, your dad put me in touch with the lab down there," Sheldon adds.

This is a surprise. Bitter jealousy rises in my throat. Dad is so eager to help others in their careers—he holds court with his students—but when it comes to me, it's not about me at all, but what I can do for him. And right now, that's taking care of Joy.

I take a deep breath, duck below Sheldon and swim underwater to the other side. I don't want him to see me hungry—hungry for what he has—freedom.

I come up for air and he's already there, grinning.

"That's another reason I'm mad at Dad," I say, my words tumbling out in a rush. "I wish I had an exciting summer project like yours that would help me get into medical school."

"Sorry."

"Oh, it's not your fault. Besides, I already have a job shelving books at Holland Library." I try to sound light. "I couldn't have gone anyway. I'm having laser treatment next week."

My hand automatically goes to my face to feel the scars Sheldon is looking at. With my hair slicked back from swimming, he can see the bumpy skin covering my left cheekbone and ear, and how it makes my eye droop.

"I hope it makes the skin smooth again," I say.

"Good luck," he says, never taking his eyes off me.

"Thanks. You too."

We tread water in the deep end, and it reminds me of the time we were kids, taking swimming lessons together at the outdoor public pool. The other kids would goof off and play, but Sheldon practiced his movements, getting his side-stroke just right or just frog-kicking to make sure he had enough power in his legs.

"You should do some of your fancy dives," I say.

Sheldon hoists himself up and heads to the diving board. I swim on my back as I watch him dive. Even without my glasses I can tell when it's his turn, because he always waits a breath or two longer than the others. I still don't know how he allows himself to hurtle towards the water. He falls with his arms outstretched like Jesus on a cross and then up and over his head as he makes contact with the water.

Later he twists and somersaults. Effortlessly.

Everything is easy for Sheldon. He's smart and nice and people naturally come to his aid. I can just imagine what my dad said to him. *Oh, yes, absolutely. Let me give Harry a ring. I know him. He'd love to have you work with him this summer.* Did Dad ever once think maybe I would like to do this too? I've worked in a few labs in the summer, washing dishes, making stock solutions, helping with data collection, but I've never gotten to work on my own project.

It would be fun to work beside Sheldon, washing gel plates, developing autoradiograms in the dark room, poring over data. It'd be how Mom and Dad worked together before Joy came along. There was always a bittersweet tinge to these stories Mom told. I can't imagine what a sacrifice it must've been to reorient her life to focus completely on Joy, but she never let us believe we were a burden. She took pleasure in all our accomplishments.

I come back to the present with sounds of clapping and cheering. "Go Shellllllldddd!"

Other boys jump off the board as well, diving, cannon-balling, belly-flopping. Shouts of approval go up for each and every one of them.

A hand snakes around my foot. "Stop that," I say, kicking.

"Don't you want to dive?" It's Kurt.

"No."

"Oh, don't be a chicken," Kurt says. Then he cups his hands around his mouth and shouts, "Chicken! It's time to play chicken!"

A whole bunch of girls jump into the pool screaming, "Chicken!"

Colleen swims furiously towards us. Kurt ducks under as she climbs on top of his shoulders. Madison clambers upon Sheldon. He hangs on to her ankles.

Even with my blurry vision, I can't watch. I swim to the edge and scramble out.

I change back into my own clothes and head over to the bar to get a drink of water.

"Have this instead," says Rocco, pushing lemonade towards me.

I take a sip, and almost spit it out. "It's awful."

Rocco shakes his head and drinks it himself, without a single grimace. "It's a party."

I want to get out of here, but Colleen isn't ready to leave. She must've been here for several hours already. But she's having too good a time with Kurt. So I sit and watch and wait, fuming over everything. How could Dad help Sheldon and not give me a passing thought? And why is Madison still on Sheldon? Doesn't she have a boyfriend? Why can't she sit on *his* shoulders?

I snag a bag of chips, grab a water bottle, and console myself that I'll be going away in just one more year. I leave the pool area and meander through the vegetable and flower patches. The smell of sweet pea blossoms reminds me of Mom. She'd braid them into her hair, and when Joy and I asked, into ours.

I pick several flowers to take home with me. No one tends our backyard garden anymore now that Mom's gone. The weeds have overtaken the small vegetable plot we used to have. Volunteer squash shows up. I observe what's growing well here—tomatoes, beans, peas, beets, corn. I see lots of summer squash as well. They also have roses and sunflowers. I like how the flowers and vegetables are all mixed in, a true kitchen garden. I resolve to revive our little patch, for Mom and for Joy.

When I return to the patio, it's different. The pool lights bathe everybody in it a blue glow, and my classmates are somehow calmer after all the chicken-play in the water. Only the occasional splash punctuates the murmuring and laughter. People lie on the lounge chairs staring up at the moon.

I look for Colleen, but she's nowhere to be found. Neither is Sheldon. I ask Rocco, but regret it immediately. He's drunk.

Finally Colleen emerges from the house. She staggers towards me, with Kurt right beside her. She laughs hysterically. "Did you see the statue in the bathroom?"

"No."

"It's pissing!" Colleen cackles again, and slips her arm into mine. "Come with me. You should get a tour."

"No, we should go home."

"No way!"

Maybe I can sober her up a bit before going home. I shove a water bottle in front of her. "Here, drink this. You'll feel better."

"Strawberry margaritas taste better." Colleen turns those amber eyes of hers to Kurt and he's off to the bar to make her another.

"You're drunk," I whisper.

"You're ugly."

I'm stunned into silence. I know she's behaving like this because she's drunk, but it's not easy to have the truth flung in your face. I fiddle with my hair, still damp from swimming. I tell myself it's the chlorine from the pool that's making my eyes burn.

23

"And it's all my fault." Colleen buries her face into my shoulder and sobs.

My body instantly stiffens.

"Why?" My voice is barely a whisper.

But Colleen snuffles harder. She knows something I don't and I hate that. I must uncover the secrets shrouding the day I got burned.

Kurt returns with another margarita.

"She's had too much," I tell Kurt. "I'm taking her home now."

"She can stay here," says Kurt. "And so can you. Sheldon's spending the night." He winks at me.

Heat suffuses my face.

"We don't spend the night with boys." I take Colleen's arm.

"Aw, don't be such a drip," says Kurt. I've been called worse and I don't care anymore.

Colleen flings the sandals over her shoulders and we begin the long walk together to my car. Colleen's half-asleep and she puts one foot after another automatically. I notice how quiet it's gotten. Only a few kids remain, either talking or sleeping on the lounge chairs. And it's a mess with all the beer bottles, chip bags, clothes, and towels strewn by the pool. Only the pool looks pristine.

"Wait!" Sheldon shouts from behind. He has no trouble catching up with us. "What's wrong?"

"Can you help me get her home?"

"Sure. We can take both cars, so she won't have to come back to pick it up. But I'll need a ride back here," Sheldon says, taking Colleen's other arm.

"Why do you stay here?" I ask. "Do you see what Kurt did?"

"She wanted to drink, too, so don't blame Kurt." Sheldon is quick to defend his friend. "He's kinder than you think."

"Name one nice thing he's done for anybody."

"I stay with him every time my dad has to leave town to help one of my brothers move," Sheldon says. "And when Dad had to be taken to the hospital in the middle of the night for pneumonia. I can always count on Kurt."

I didn't even know his dad was sick. We've drifted so far apart. We keep our pace, Colleen in-between us, still sleep-walking.

I apologize.

"Don't worry. Some people only show their exterior." He stops walking when we get to the gate. "Like you," he adds.

"I know." I keep thinking how good it is to talk to someone who really knows you. "Listen, Colleen said that it's her fault I got burned. Do you know anything?"

Sheldon looks hard at Colleen. "She's drunk. It was an accident. We were careless."

"Yes, but I remember my sparkler going out."

"So, it's my fault," Sheldon says softly.

"No, no, no! I'm not accusing you!" I say. I know he didn't set me on fire. "We *were* careless. But I don't remember everything."

"She wasn't even near us. You never would've ..."

"... tried to kiss *you*."

"Right." He blushes, but he doesn't know I can see him clearly in the moonlight. He picks up Colleen and places her in the passenger seat of her Prelude. I kick the door shut.

"Keys?" he asks.

"Oops! I think all her stuff is still probably out on the patio."

"I'll get it," Sheldon says, ever the gentleman.

But I wish I'd gone instead because Colleen barfs all over herself. There's nothing to clean her with so I take off my shirt and wipe her mouth and chest up without throwing up myself. At least I have my tank-top.

Sheldon returns before I'm done. "Gross."

"I didn't realize she'd get sick like that," I say.

Sheldon hands me her keys. "Sorry that you have to drive her home."

"I'll keep the windows down." I give Sheldon my keys. "My Honda is parked a ways up. I can drive you."

"No thanks. I'll walk."

I do a U-turn, heading back to Pullman.

This is exactly why I want to get out of this town. There is nothing to do except drink and drop dead. Even Colleen succumbed. Her parents will be so mad to see her in this state. What will I say?

Mrs. Mendoza saves me the trouble of talking. She thanks us for bringing Colleen home and tells us to get ourselves back home as well. I look back at Colleen, held in her father's arms, and know she's safe.

"I've got your house keys; don't you give a second thought to Mel. We'll take good care of her," says Mrs. Mendoza, giving me a quick hug. "I'll pray for a fruitful treatment."

~~~

Sheldon and I are lost in our own thoughts as I drive him back to Kurt's. But I don't want to lose this opportunity to say what I've been wanting to ever since Colleen blurted out that she was at fault. I clear my throat, and my words sputter like a car backfiring. "I don't blame you, Sheldon. Do you know every year fifty thousand kids get burned? Kids are especially vulnerable because well … they're kids. They play with matches and sparklers and get too close to the stove and tip over boiling water on themselves. I never knew any of this until after I became a statistic. But let me be clear. I don't blame you or Colleen or anybody else. I just want to fill the gaps, that's all."

"I'm just glad you made it," he says simply.

"Hey," I say. "No hard feelings. Have a great summer at Cal. Tech."

"Hay is for horses."

~~~

It's nearly midnight when I creep into the house. However, when I peek into Joy's room, it's empty. Where is she?

Finally, as the grandfather clock finishes gonging, Joy twirls through the front door, shaking her peasant blouse loose. "I want to be a Jew!" she says. "They have the best songs." She takes a step forward, back-tracks and swirls. Her skirt flares out. Last week she wanted to be Macedonian.

Mom got her involved with the folk dance group at the university a year before she died, and Joy loved it from the very beginning. Mom encouraged me to come along, and I did a few times, and even danced because the music is so infectious, but when you live with Joy, you want your own space. Besides, they were all a bunch of misfits. Hah! I should talk. But once in a while I'd join Mom and Joy on Friday nights and everybody would be thrilled to have an extra set of feet. Besides, that's one thing I can do—dance. Even though I went sporadically, I picked up the footwork quickly. All because of Hilde. She could break down the most complicated Bulgarian dance into component parts. I also have my summer job because of her. Hilde works in acquisitions at Holland Library and asked if I'd like to work the summer with her. The perfect job, because if I couldn't be a doctor, I'd be a librarian, tucked in amongst the books.

"How come you're so late?" I ask now. "You know we're leaving first thing in the morning." I know I sound like Dad but I can't help it.

"We went for ice cream," Joy says, licking her lips. "I had raspberry swirl."

Oh, how I wish Colleen had something simple like this.

27

"Let's get you ready for bed." I should've stayed home and picked her up earlier myself, but then again, Colleen might be stuck with Kurt. I should be grateful Joy has friends who are willing to give her rides or take her out for an unexpected treat on a Friday night.

Joy hums a haunting tune, most likely an Israeli folksong. Melody settles herself right on top of Joy, adding her purr in perfect harmony.

"Goodnight, sleep tight," I say, kissing the tops of their contented heads.

~~~

I flip through the now-taped BS/MD brochure from Wayne and try to capture my dreams again. They're no longer sweet.

I've wanted to be a doctor since I was a little girl, before I was burned. Joy wanted to be a vet. I don't know how she managed to find injured birds and squirrels so often, but she did and we'd squirt them with water and baking soda, or rub Neosporin on them if they stayed still enough. It's a miracle we were never bitten by all the critters we've rescued. Now she works at the Animal Care Center at the university. A real job with benefits.

I sometimes wonder whether Joy kindled my love of human medicine. Treating neighborhood kids was just the next step after fussing over hurt animals. I loved spraying on the disinfectant, peeling the backs off Band-Aids and carefully applying them to the scrapes and scratches kids got.

But I'm done playing. There are consequences if I don't do the things I need to do to assure myself a place in medical school. Getting burned was a huge setback. I missed a year in junior high, but Mom homeschooled me and I came back stronger academically. I know there will be obstacles, but they're less likely if I'm away from here, from Joy.

Joy. Oh, I love her. And I will always make sure she's taken care of, only I don't necessarily want to do the caring.

Dad should be doing it now. I know after he dies, I will be the only family left for Joy. Because who will marry a developmentally delayed girl like her? And she'll be my only family as well. Because who will marry a burned and damaged girl like me?

The next morning, Joy barges into my room, holding out CDs, providing a running commentary on each of them.

I'm not even dressed and although Joy has seen my patchwork of a body, I grab my towel to cover myself.

Joy prattles on. I don't care about the Chipmunks or the soundtrack from *Evita*.

"Just pack whatever you like," I say.

"Can I pick more than six?"

"Yessss," I hiss. "Just put the extras in the CD rack. Now let me get dressed!"

As soon as she leaves my room, I drop the towel and lather on moisturizer. I slip into a long brown skirt and white blouse. I choose a scarf with orange swirls. Although it takes me less than five minutes to be dressed, Dad glances at his watch when I come into the kitchen to pour myself a bowl of cereal.

"You girls had a late night," he says. "We'll be lucky to get out of here by ten. I'll start packing the Pilot."

"Yay! We get to ride in the Pilot!" Joy says. "It's a funny name for a car."

"Especially since it can't fly," I add.

Joy loves Dad's Pilot because it holds six compact discs. Plus the speakers are much nicer than in Mom's Civic, which is what I drive. Joy loves it all, from the chanting of monks to the screaming of Van Halen. My favorite has got to be Bach. I've picked an album with music for four hands and two pianos—the music must surely come from the heavens.

Dad and I take turns driving. I need the practice, especially on the highways. The landscape is golden with the wheat undulating. Mom had once said it was like a woman's body, with curves. I feel more like a butte, with bones jutting out at sharp angles.

"You're going too fast. The speed limit here is only sixty-five," says Joy from the back.

Damn. She's right. It's hard to watch the speed on this endlessly straight road. The heat makes it shimmer as though there's a lake far ahead.

"Use cruise control," says Dad, his hand near the steering wheel pointing to the buttons. "Slow down and as soon as it reaches sixty-five, push *set*."

"But I want to be in control," I say.

"Use cruise control. It could save you a speeding ticket."

I bring my hand away from the two o'clock position to set the cruise control button when the speedometer says sixty-five mph. Now my foot doesn't know what to do. I have to concentrate to keep it still on the floor of the car.

"Can I drive?" asks Joy.

In my rearview mirror I see her pouting.

"There's nothing to it," says Joy. "Just push the pedal. It's not fair Daddy won't let me drive."

Joy pushes my seat with her feet.

"Daddy, Daddy can I have a turn?" Joy can be relentless.

"No," he says, turning around. "And put your feet down."

"Daddy, it's not fair. I have a learning permit."

Dad turns around again. "I said no and that's final. Your permit expired long ago. What you have is an ID. You are incapable of driving. Accept it."

"If I practice ..." Joy's voice is small.

Dad turns around. "Stop arguing right this minute. It's finished. Let Rebecca concentrate."

"You know I'm slow," Joy says.

We've always encouraged her to keep working hard and not give up by telling her it takes her a longer time to learn. But I'm not sure she can accomplish some things, no matter how hard she tries. But I bite my tongue and stay out of this conversation.

I wouldn't trust my life with her behind the wheel even if she did pass the test.

Joy sniffles in the back seat.

I have to hit the brakes hard because I've caught up to a slower-moving truck. Cruise control made me lazy. "Should I pass it?"

I've passed cars before, but a semi is so long.

Dad shouts, "Go!" and I press the accelerator all the way to the floor until I'm practically in the truck before going into the other lane, the lane where oncoming traffic would be coming. It's clear. I'm flying. I am even with the truck and want to get away from the roar of its engines.

When I see the truck in the mirror, I slide into the right side of the road but I end up on the shoulder.

"Easy, Rebecca, easy." Dad's voice is soft.

I swerve and manage to get back on the road, dust flying behind me. But my entire body is tense, from the tips of my fingers to my toes.

Minutes later, a cop screeches behind me. Shit. Shit. Shit.

"Slow down, Rebecca, and pull over," I hear Dad's voice but can't seem to think what I need to do.

Joy screams, "The police! The police!"

I get ready to hit the brakes.

"Just take your foot off the gas," says Dad.

I do as he says. The car slows down. Finally my brain begins to function as I press my foot on the brake and the car slows down enough for me to pull onto the gravel. Another car whizzes by as I kill the engine. I can't stop trembling, terrified

32

that my license is going to be taken away. Dad mutters about cops making trouble and creating mountains out of molehills.

The police officer knocks on the window. I fumble forever to find the button that makes the window go down. Okay, push. But it doesn't work. I have to turn the key to power it on.

The window purrs on its way down.

"Driver's license and registration please." I look at the perfect teeth of the policeman as his mouth moves. The ugly side of my face is reflected in his shiny shades. I wish he'd take them off.

I slide my license from my wallet and give it to him without a word. Then I fish around for the registration. Dad finds it in the glove compartment.

"She was speeding, wasn't she?" Joy shouts behind me.

"Miss Joshi," says the cop. "Do you know how fast you were going?"

"No sir," I say. "I was passing that truck and, and..." I gulp.

"And you forgot to slow down." The cop must've heard that a hundred times. "This happens to beginning drivers. Mr. Joshi, were you aware of this?"

"Not really," he says. "But when I realized she was driving too fast, I didn't want her to hit the brakes, so I told her to step off the gas."

"That's not true," says Joy. "It's *after* you flashed your lights at us." Joy is a stickler for the truth and this time, she's taking perverse pleasure in all this. I can hear the smirk in her voice.

"Well, yes," says Dad. "It all happened so quickly."

"I clocked you at ninety miles per hour. Do you think that's a safe driving speed?"

"No sir. I'm sorry, sir." A dam of tears is waiting to burst through and I'm shaking, but I manage to add, "I'll pay more attention."

"Daddy told her to use cruise control, but she didn't," Joy adds.

I turn around. "I did, you … you … nincompoop!" I wish she'd shut up.

"I'll let you all go this time. But remember to watch the speedometer *and* the road." The cop smiles a perfect smile as he hands me back the papers and my license. They slip out of my fingers onto the floor of the car.

"Mr. Joshi, keep an eye on things."

"It's *Doctor* Joshi," Dad mumbles beneath his breath. "These people don't know anything."

As soon as the cop leaves, Joy asks, "Now can I drive?"

"Shut up!" says Dad. "You never, ever open your mouth to talk to a police officer. Rebecca could have gotten a hefty ticket."

"But she was speeding," says Joy. "She *should* get a punishment. Everybody should get a punishment. You are all so mean." Joy is screeching now. "I have a learning permit, but nobody will let me learn."

I will strangle her if I don't leave this car.

I slide out of the Pilot and into the heat of the desert. People think Washington is the evergreen state, but that's only a small sliver of it. Eastern Washington is more like a desert. I walk into the sage brush, stretching my arms up and bending side to side. I pluck a dusty leaf and crush it in my hands. The smell is lemony. After a while I realize Dad's calling me. He's out, stretching his legs as well and waves to me.

"Coming," I say, plucking a few more sage leaves and some chamomile.

I take a step back when I see Joy is in the driver's seat. No way!

Joy grins and honks the horn.

"Out! Now!" Dad barks, holding the door open for Joy.

Joy climbs over the center cubby and plops into the passenger seat. Dad pushes the seat back and slides in. I get into the backseat.

"Everybody buckled up?" Dad asks as he glides smoothly on the road. I watch how easily he passes cars and sets the cruise control so that he will not get a speeding ticket. He doesn't fall asleep even though the droning of the sitar makes me doze.

I wake up to Joy poking my leg. "What do you want to eat?" she asks.

"You pick," I say. It doesn't really matter to me. Ellensburg has a long road full of fast food restaurants, gas stations, and boring shops. Joy points to a little Mom and Pop shack that's selling tacos. Dad pulls in.

I adjust my scarf and hair, taking care that the scars on my face and neck don't show. It's impossible to hide my hands, so I don't worry about them. I smooth down the loose-fitting top over my skirt and step out into the dust and heat.

"Rebecca! The man wants to know what you want," Joy says. "I'm having a plate of food, not just a taco."

I stand in the pull-out shade of the shack and the wonderful smell of sautéed garlic and onions reminds me how hungry I am. I look at the options and choose *carnitas*—braised pork—with Spanish rice.

"That's our specialty," says the man. He prepares them, squeezing fresh lime juice on top.

When I reach to the counter to take my plate, the man asks, "What happened to you?"

"Fourth of July accident," I say, irritated that people notice me just for the scars.

"Sorry about that. My father, he got a gasoline burn on his leg."

My hand goes limp around the plate of food. "How is he doing?"

"Oh, he's fine now. It happened a long time ago. But his leg will never be the same."

"Half my body was burned," I whisper. "And it's only been six years for me. What's it like for him?"

"Oh, that's tough. My dad can walk and still do all the things he used to." He leans forwards. "You're doing great. Hang in there."

"Thanks."

Yes, I will be fine. All I have to do is think of the horrible fate of the young Indian brides who do not come with enough dowry, or do not produce a son, and are subjected to "accidental kitchen fires" or have acid thrown on their faces, with not much medical treatment past critical care leaving them permanently disabled, I know I'm lucky to have had reconstructive surgeries to make my body more functional.

My hands have retained their dexterity. I roll up the corn tortilla around the meat and salsa. I bite into it; the sweetness of the fresh tomatoes complements the tartness of the lime and blends perfectly with the pork. Joy prattles on about how Mom's homemade salsa is better. I tune her out. This man at the taco stand gives me hope. His father is okay. I wonder if my scars will smooth out as I age, the pain and tightness disappearing eventually.

"Rebecca?" Dad dangles the car keys. I don't take them.

Dad doesn't say another word as he climbs into the driver's seat.

"I'll sit in the front seat," says Joy.

I am content to sit in the back and watch the scenery as Joy talks nonstop about the mice and rats and guinea pigs she cares for at work, as though they are her close personal friends.

Golden wheat fields gave way to sage brush on our drive here, but now the majestic Cascades loom ahead. I want to drive through the pass, so I tap Dad on the shoulder. "I'm ready."

Dad takes the next exit so we can switch.

"It's just like musical chairs," says Joy as she climbs into the back seat.

We cut through the Cascades, the sun low and orange, casting a glow over the trees. But as we get closer to the city, the number of cars increases, I get hot and nervous. "Dad, there's no place to pull over."

"Just drive," says Dad. "You're fine. I'm here to guide you."

Dad is the best navigator. I do as he says without thinking—change lanes, take a left, stop there—and only focus on driving and not hitting other cars. Dad knows the city so well he doesn't even need a map. Someday I want to be able to drive like that.

5

We swing by Harborview Medical Center to register, then head to Nautilus Bed and Breakfast. The owner of the B&B has graying hair, pulled tight behind her head, giving her face a pinched look. She ushers us in, but puts her hands to her face when she sees my extended hand. "Oh my!"

"It's not contagious," I let her know. She'd faint if she saw my crazy-quilt torso.

"Oh, no, I don't think that sweetie! You look great. It's been many years. I'm Mrs. Paulick." She crushes me in a hug as though we're long-lost friends. She releases me to greet Joy in the same manner.

"You remember me and Rebecca?" Joy asks with wonder. Oh, good, I'm not the only one who has no memory of this nice old lady.

"Of course," says Mrs. Paulick. "Your mother stayed here all those months to be near Rebecca. Where is she?" She looks to our car where Dad is unloading our luggage.

Fat tears roll down Joy's cheeks.

"She died last year," I say, wondering why it is that the entire universe does not know this fact.

"Oh, honey, I'm so sorry." Mrs. Paulick pats Joy's shoulder. She blubbers even more. "There, there. Let's get you settled, then you can tell me everything."

Mrs. Paulick wipes her own eyes before leading us upstairs to our rooms. It's actually one room, very pink and flowery with twin beds. "I thought you girls would like this. Just don't whisper all night long."

Leave it to Dad to try and save a few bucks. He crams Joy and me into one room, never considering that I might want my own space.

An orange tabby slinks past me into the room. Joy scoops her up, dropping her stuffed wolf Buck. "You can sleep with me," she coos to the cat.

I pick up Buck.

"Let me know if you need anything. Cookies and tea—I remember you all love tea—are ready downstairs."

Joy drops the cat and follows Mrs. Paulick. I unpack a bit, transferring the Wayne State brochures to the backpack I'll take to the hospital. I can't risk Joy seeing them. I won't tell her about Wayne until it's a sure thing.

Dad brings up the suitcases. "I'm going to rest for a bit," he tells me.

When I go down to the kitchen, Joy is dipping almond biscotti into her tea and talking nonstop about how much she loves animals, and how she takes care of mice at the university. Her voice is filled with pride. I know for most, this would be a menial and undesirable job, but Joy gets a huge sense of accomplishment from cleaning cages of lab mice.

"Joy is a natural with animals," I say, and Joy gives the hugest smile.

It makes me feel good to pay compliments, so I continue. "Our mother would've loved this biscotti," I tell Mrs. Paulick, dipping it into my cup of Earl Grey. "I can't remember a single dessert she made without almonds."

"God rest her soul," says Mrs. Paulick, her eyes welling with tears. "She suffered so much, but always, she placed her trust in God. We prayed and cried together many, many times. She kept in touch – sent me a Christmas card every year."

I hold on to my teacup, letting the smell of the bergamot soothe me. I let this cozy little nook of the kitchen, with paintings of sunflowers, daisies and roses, ensconce me in its warmth.

"Was she sad?" I ask. It occurs to me I never spared a thought for Mom while at Harborview. I was either comatose, furious, or resigned.

"Oh, no, dear. She was happy at every little thing that went well. She thanked God all the time. But there were setbacks, especially in the beginning, and it was very scary." Mrs. Paulick frowns momentarily. "We worried together. But I made sure she had a good time too. We went out walking, watched funny movies together, ate lots of chocolate, and laughed."

"I never realized. Thank you for taking care of Mom."

"Your mom was an amazing woman, and it was my privilege," says Mrs. Paulick. "Here, have another cookie."

Finally, in an effort to lighten the mood, I say, "Mom said that almonds would make us smart."

Joy manages a smile. "It worked on Rebecca. She's going to be a doctor."

I smile and refrain from saying anything about the BS/MD programs. I sip my tea, imagining myself as a country doctor, driving a Jeep, or even flying in remote parts of Alaska. I should learn to fly.

"It'll be good to have a doctor in the house," Dad's voice booms, interrupting my fantasy. "I won't have to worry about calling mine for my chronic aches and pains."

I bristle at the thought of being a doctor just to care for *his* bad knees and high blood pressure. What if I want to do trauma or plastic surgery?

"You'll have to listen to me," I say. "You can't eat too many sweets."

"Well, we old people have to have our vices." Dad rubs his round stomach and reaches for the tray of cookies a third time.

"Sweets are mine. These are terrific, Mrs. Paulick. You should give Joy the recipe."

I roll my eyes. Another recipe for Joy to collect so that she can pretend that she's a great cook.

Mrs. Paulick laughs and promises to pack some to take with us when we leave after our stay is over.

~~~

Dad takes us to a fancy Indian restaurant that night. We start with samosas, a deep-fried pastry filled with spicy potatoes and peas. We never make this at home because it's so time consuming. Besides, I will never deep-fry anything. Too dangerous.

Next comes lamb curry, tandoori chicken, okra with tomatoes, lemony rice, and naan. Joy eats half my dessert of dumplings in cream. One day she's going to be obese like Mom and die from a heart attack. For her sake, I should finish my own bowl, but I will explode if I have another bite.

We take the leftovers to our B&B and order extra samosas to go. When it comes to food, Dad always splurges. We don't get to eat this kind of food in Pullman unless we cook it ourselves. There is no Indian restaurant there, even though Indians are everywhere. The nearest one is in Spokane and that's an hour-and-a-half away.

Joy watches TV with Mrs. Paulick and chats about everything, while Dad and I go to our rooms. He'll probably work a bit. I browse the magazines in the magazine rack—*Seventeen, Redbook, Woman's World*—but nothing interests me. I look through my *Glamour* magazine and the Wayne State brochures and dream of a normal skin and life. Without Joy.

~~~

Sunday morning, Joy begs and begs to go to St. James Cathedral. Mom had brought us there a couple of years ago, and we had loved the singing of the choir and lit a candle at the

41

feet of Mary and admired the gold-leaf burning bush. But Dad doesn't go to churches. He was raised Hindu, but the truth is, he doesn't worship any God. He's his own god.

He said, "I went to church for my wedding, your baptisms, and your mother's funeral. That's enough." It's strange that our mother, who was so devoutly Christian, the daughter of an Anglican priest, would've married my father, but it was a love-marriage. Disapproved by both sets of parents.

They said, "No wonder they have no children!"

Mom told me all these stories, how hurt she was, but all was forgotten and forgiven once Joy arrived after fifteen years of marriage. However, once they discovered her mental and developmental delays, it was back to how inauspicious this marriage was. Over time though, Mom said, the comments disappeared. Joy was accepted as she was.

~~~

I am not comfortable driving in downtown Seattle, otherwise I'd take Joy to the cathedral, so Joy pesters Dad to take her to the zoo. He gives in. I hang out at the university bookstore near our B&B and pretend I'm a student there. I get some stares, but people are so much more mature. They look away. Only the children gaze unflinchingly. They know I'm not normal.

I sit in the shade of a cedar tree and soak up the atmosphere. White clouds scud across the sky and the air is just at the perfect temperature. Bright red rhododendrons bloom and brighten the area. I flip through my new purchases – memoirs, medical texts, and a gorgeous book about baby animals photographed locally that I'll give to Joy for her birthday.

When I get back to the B&B, Mrs. Paulick isn't home, so I poke around the kitchen and make myself a cup of tea. I'm sure she won't mind if I help myself to a couple of peanut butter cookies from the jar. I walk around looking at the family pictures. Happiness radiates from the faded photographs. I suppose once upon a time our family was happy too, but it seems so long ago.

That evening, while Dad and Joy scarf down spaghetti and meatballs, I nibble on a spinach salad. Joy's exuberance grates on my nerves. She talks about lions, tigers, meerkats, penguins. I'd expect even an eight-year-old to be less self-centered.

"Can I have your nuts?" she asks.

I push my plate towards her. My stomach tightens with anticipation.

Tomorrow.

It'll be better tomorrow.

~~~

Early Monday morning I wear a soft hospital gown and get prepped with an IV, pillow, blanket. I've already dozed off from the sedative when a nurse returns to wheel me to the treatment room. Everything is sterile white. Joy holds my right hand. It's soft like Mom's but smaller. I miss Mom. This is the first time I've been through a procedure without her.

It's very noisy as the laser is calibrated, but I have a hard time keeping awake. Dr. Martinez extends my left arm onto an adjoining table. I see his crinkly eyes and know he's smiling beneath his mask.

"Okay, sleepyhead. If you need something, speak up or raise your hand or foot, that is, whatever limb we're not working on. Okay?"

"Got it."

"Only small parts of your body will be uncovered at any point, okay?" Dr. Martinez says. "We'll begin with the left arm."

A nurse has already anesthetized it topically. I look with interest as the laser is positioned over my arm, and I fight to stay awake. It's hard to see without my glasses.

The smell of smoke makes me panic. That's my skin that's burning. I should get out of here, but when I try to get up, I realize I'm strapped to the gurney.

"Are you okay?" the nurse asks, as she dabs my cheek with a warm washcloth.

I must've cried out. I suck in a breath. "Smoke does that," I whisper.

She nods in understanding.

It's ironic that my skin has to be burned again for it to be healed. I close my eyes but the smell of burning flesh—mine—brings back so many memories that I can't contain them. Joy prattles on. I get only snatches. "Sparklers. Flames. Screaming. Burning. Dunking. Bathtub."

I don't remember anything Joy remembers. I recall a dusky Fourth of July, sitting on a bench next to Sheldon. We were eleven. I wore my daring pink cat dress leaving my right shoulder bare. Ruffles zigzagged diagonally across my body and over to the left shoulder. We had a box of sparklers between us and we were lighting them one after the other, writing our names, making patterns in the air, laughing.

"Save some for when it gets dark," I told Sheldon.

We decided to light one last pair. We joined our sparklers together, making the sparks even more brilliant. On the bench our pinkies touched and he interlaced his with mine. Light and dark. So perfect together.

I watched my sparkler die. I turned towards him and he turned toward me and I wanted to kiss him. I could've. Instead, I was on fire and Sheldon pushed me off the bench. I remember screaming and blackness.

When Joy mentions the bathtub, I have a vague memory of thrashing in water, my mom's face white with worry above me.

When I woke up, I thought I was dead. No, worse. In hell. My whole body wracked in unbelievable pain, as though a thousand needles were jabbing me repeatedly. I heard my name from afar. Before I could ask any questions, I was gone.

I don't remember how long I was in that comatose stage. Machines kept me alive. But I wanted to die when I got a glimpse at my body for the first time. Doctors had sliced my charred skin to relieve the pressure of the tissues that swelled beneath.

Later, under total anesthesia, they removed it all because I was in danger of getting a massive infection. Instead I was covered with dead skin. Someone else's. A cadaver. Or maybe a pig. I must've known it was something awful because I told them to get rid of it. They said it was for retaining fluids and maintaining body temperature. I wanted to tear it off, but my hands were bandaged because they suffered second-degree burns when I tried to pat the fire from my chest.

I screamed. I wanted to hit my mother for saving me, for turning me into this monstrosity. Every day was a torture – the bathing, the bandaging, the infections that would ruin the grafts from skin cultures grown in the lab from my own skin. Later, I was even more grotesque with tissue expanders in my face, right shoulder and calves.

When I was out of danger, Mom drove me crazy with her talks about purpose, God's plan, and miracles. That's when I learned the truth about my beginning: I was left in a cardboard box on church step as a newborn.

Revolted by the reality of being unwanted and uncared for, I heaved and threw up on my fresh bandages. I had to undergo a thorough cleaning to make sure I didn't get an infection. I wailed at the injustice of my life.

Later, when I had no more tears left, I asked, "Why? Why me? It would've been better to die in that box."

"The ways of God are mysterious," Mom said. "I wish you hadn't suffered, nor your birth mother, but you are alive for a reason, and you must trust in Jesus."

"Where was your precious Jesus when I was in that cardboard box?" I lashed out at Mom. "And when I got burned?"

"He was right there with you, weeping." Mom tried to kiss me, but I pushed her away.

When tears filled my mom's eyes, it made me feel good. I wanted to hurt her, too.

~~~

And here I am, missing Mom, enduring yet another procedure. For what? Smoother skin, thinks Dad. It's so much more. It's a chance to let people see the real me, one who isn't defined by scars. Tears seep out of my closed eyes and into my hair, leaving a trail of hope.

~~~6~~~

Surprisingly, I'm not in pain. This laser treatment took time because I have so many scars to "iron-out" but I'm thrilled with the disappearance of the keloids. My days are spent mostly in intensive physical therapy. They admonish me for not keeping with the daily protocols, but also praise me for coming along as far as I have. Harborview feels like home—the bright colors, the other patients, the humming and beeping of instruments. In my free time, nurses direct me to other burned children who could use some company and encouragement. I read them books, show them my scars, and they are impressed at how good I look. Hah! It's all relative.

If I went to the University of Washington next year, I could get a job here at Harborview Medical Center. I know lots of people. Maybe Colleen and I could room together. But will I be far enough away from Joy? She certainly can't come here on her own, and Dad only makes trips across the state if they're necessary. I wonder how often they'd come to visit. Monthly? Vacations? Unannounced? I shudder from the thought I'll never be free of Joy, that she'll always intrude upon my life. It'd be great to have a complete break as I begin a new life as a college student. Plus to have a guaranteed seat in medical school is no small thing. That is why I must stay focused on the BS/MD programs and not let other things distract me.

Mrs. Paulick prepares a separate room for me so that Joy can have the kitty in hers. While my new skin grows, I need to avoid dust, dirt, and sunshine. Also pets. I'm grateful for the quiet after the long days at Harborview. Dad brings doggy bags filled with food I especially love— roasted Greek lamb with potatoes, spicy Vietnamese beef soup, and samosas. I can never have enough of them. I don't mind having to stay indoors given the state of my skin. It's splotchy, red and weepy. Ugh. But in a month, it will be beautiful.

~~~

A week later, we're back at home, laden with goodies from Mrs. Paulick's kitchen—almond biscotti, chocolate chip cookies, raspberry tarts. And recipes. When Mom was alive, she would experiment in the kitchen with Joy. Now there aren't ever new treats to gobble up after school.

Both Dad and Joy have returned to work; I still have another week before starting my job at Holland Library. I wear loose Indian clothing to protect my red and peeling skin. I miss having Mel curl up with me. But the new skin that is growing back is smoother. I worry that the keloids will return after the healing is complete and I'll always be a Halloween nightmare.

I never ever dressed up for Halloween after I got burned. One year Mom and Joy went trick-or-treating while Dad was travelling, so I passed out candy to the little fairies and ghosts and pirates that came to our door. The kids shrank back from me. I was the monster.

In India, there are still freaks of nature at the circus. People with claws for arms. Poor thalidomide babies all grown up with flippers coming from their torso. A bearded woman. We paid money to see them before I got burned. They laughed and made lewd jokes. Even though I was repelled by them, I wanted to watch them do the most basic things like picking up a pencil. They'd scoot on their backs or roll on a dolly, grinning, as though their deformities were nothing. If I were in India, I'd fit perfectly in their show. I wouldn't have surgery upon surgery to fix my body. I can imagine the banner: *Girl Born from Fire*. My crooked, contracted limbs, my grotesque

48

neck, my mouth grinning like a fool, drooling, but paying my way for food and shelter and protection. I wonder what kind of life they lead. I suppose all the family they have are other freaks. Like Joy and me.

Except Joy looks normal. Mom and Dad even talked about placing a matrimonial ad online, but they never did. Too risky. People could take advantage of her. Heck, they've never even let her date.

What would we put down for Joy besides "voluptuous Indian beauty," alongside the fact that she's a citizen? Would a desperate Indian man, looking to come to the US, marry a girl like her? I know Joy would make someone—someone who'd like a youthful and fun loving wife—a great wife. She is affectionate and spontaneous. She cooks a few things. She cleans. She even holds a job. Oh, how she loves working at the Animal Care Center. We are really lucky to have a social worker like Tessa, who found this job for her.

I can't wait to start mine. It's a bore staying at home all day. I mostly read and sleep. When Dad and Joy get home, I begin cooking so that Joy can help. Poor Mel. She meows to be let in my bedroom since she knows I'm here, but until my skin is healed all the way, I have to keep everything scrupulously clean. She can't be napping on my bed, with all the litter she tracks in her paws.

Thank goodness Colleen is coming over after her shift at Fabrics and Fashion. She loves her job there. And she's got the staff excited about offering a no-sew sewing class. I laughed when she told me.

"It's a class for people like you," she said. "We'll use a hot glue gun."

She's so talented with her hands; she paints, draws, sews, and puts together things that I'd throw away, like a photo frame or a centerpiece that anyone would be proud to display. She's making fancy pillowcases for Joy's birthday.

Finally, Colleen walks into my room, letting in Mel. "You really should lock the front door. Who knows what riff-raff is walking around the neighborhood." She grumbled about the fact that people still think her dad's the hired help just because he's Mexican.

"But you are so fair, like your mom." I wouldn't have known she had Mexican blood if I hadn't seen her dad.

"Without the freckles. But I tan easily. Look how brown I get in the summer." Colleen shows me her arms and they look like burnished gold.

I grab Mel and put her outside my door, closing it shut. She follows us to the kitchen. Colleen unfolds the cloth she is holding on the counter. Tiny black felt mice fall out.

"They're so cute." I rub them; the felt is as soft as fur. "Joy will love it."

"Joy is the only person I know who won't freak over mice or spiders. How old is she going to be?"

"Twenty-three," I say.

"Hard to believe," says Colleen, arranging the mice in a circular pattern. "Think she'll be able to keep this job?"

We both know things are unpredictable for Joy. When Mom died, she was just getting started with work. Tessa tried different things: working at the library (except Joy spent more time talking to patrons than emptying out the trash), at Dissmores Grocery (except Joy spent more time talking to shoppers than bagging groceries) and at Paradise Farms (except Joy spent more time playing with the animals than cleaning out the chicken coop). Tessa finally hit upon the perfect job at the Animal Care Center at the university. Joy cleans cages. She talks to the mice and rats all she wants, and nobody minds.

"She's had the job since this spring and no one has called to complain."

"I'm glad," says Colleen. "I'd hate for the pillowcases to remind her of those cute little mice if she lost her job."

"I'm surprised she hasn't asked to have a cage full of her own pet mice at home." I know how persistent Joy can be when she wants something, but there's been no talk of pet mice.

"She probably knows Mel would give them a heart attack," Colleen says.

"Besides, Dad would never go for a rodent."

Colleen embroiders bits of grass and little flowers around the mice. She takes a break to pop spoonsful of spicy chick peas into her mouth. "They're hot, hot, but I love them." She gulps water. "Oh, make a mango smoothie while I stitch the last of these mice."

I pull out the tub of yogurt and blend mango juice with it. I pour it into two glasses. Colleen and I both say, "Heaven!" when we take our first sip.

We drink our mango lassi and talk about the classes we're going to take for senior year. We'll definitely take Spanish. It's a no-brainer for Colleen, who speaks Spanish with her father, but she says it's always the grammar that gets her. I want us to take another class together but she's not so interested in world literature.

"I'd rather take creative writing," she says.

"But you're always doing all these creative things. Take World Lit. with me instead." I try to make puppy dog eyes at her but she is unmoved. "Please?"

"I tell you what," she says. "Why don't we take both?"

"But I'm not creative," I say. "You've even had to teach me finger painting."

"Exactly. If you take it, you'll learn. Your creativity is so buried, we need to coax it out."

"If we do both, I won't have a free period to do my homework."

"So? Big deal. Come on, Rebecca. This is our last year to take classes together. After this we'll only see each other in the summer and some weekends. You know I'll be in Seattle at the Art Institute."

"Not if I go to the University of Washington."

"But what about Joy?"

Shit. Shit. Shit. Even my best friend thinks more about Joy than me. She can't even squeal in happiness at the possibility of the two of us sharing a little apartment. Nope.

"What about her?" I look up to see whether the next words will have any impact. "Actually, maybe I'll only see you summers; I'm thinking of moving to Detroit."

Colleen sputters. "No way! Why would you want to be so far away?"

She doesn't get it. What my life has been like since Mom died.

"I have dreams too, you know? Apart from Joy." I turn away from her and rinse the empty lassi glasses.

"I didn't mean it like that." Colleen comes after me. "What's in Detroit?"

"Medical school."

"They've got one in Seattle."

I roll my eyes. "You sound just like Dad. There is no guarantee I'm going to get in. Okay?" Why do I have to defend myself to my best friend?

"Look, thanks for coming over, but I don't have time to explain everything right now. I've got to pick up *Joy* at work."

"Don't be mad." Colleen gathers up the pillowcases. At the door, she pauses. "You can tell me tomorrow when we finish up the embroidery. Okay?"

"Okay." I bolt the door behind her, fuming at Colleen. Why doesn't Dad teach Joy to ride the damn bus?

~~~

I'm behind Heald Hall in less than ten minutes. There are just a bunch of dumpsters here. Joy sits on the steps, chatting with a guy who's spitting periodically.

Joy talks some more and I end up waiting for her, the Civic idling. I wish Dad wouldn't work late so much. After last Christmas, he began working all the time. I wouldn't mind doing the same instead of having to deal with Joy. Oh, well. Once school starts up again, we'll be on a stricter schedule and Joy will be coming home with Dad.

Joy finally opens the door of the Civic and slides into the bucket seat. She rolls down the window. "Bye, Nick. I'll see you tomorrow." She waves. He grins, then spits again.

"Sorry I'm late," I say, reversing the car out of the parking lot. Nick disappears into the building.

Joy opens the palm of her hand and pops a sunflower seed in her mouth. "Oh, don't worry. I was just waiting with Nick. He comes down to get mice for the summer biology class." Then she makes an O with her mouth and lets the husk shoot out.

"Did Nick give you those?"

"Uh-huh. He's really nice. He likes the mice too. Once he …" Joy stops. "I don't mind if you're late."

"What did he do once?" I prod Joy given that stopping mid-sentence is not at all like her. She can't keep a secret. Even when she buys a present for me, she's got this huge grin on her face and she can't wait to tell me. I have to tell her not to spoil the surprise..

Joy giggles. "Once Nick took a mouse. It was so scared, it peed and squeezed a poopy right on his hand." She chortles and the sunflower seeds scatter into her lap. "Nick jumped and the mouse ran up his arm. But I am fast. I picked the mouse off his shoulder." She laughs like a monkey and I can't help but join her.

"You'd better not lose any mice."

"Never," says Joy. "Even if I take a mouse out just to pet it a little bit, I always put him back in the cage."

"You know you're not supposed to do that. What if you get them mixed up? Or lose one?"

"Never," says Joy. "The mice love me and it's because I pet them that they're so happy. Mrs. Peznokatz says I do the best job."

Does she know what happens to those mice? Has she ever wondered why they never come back?

Joy jabs at the air towards me with her pointing finger. "I've been here since Easter. And I love it. And my mice are very happy."

I try to apologize but Joy hardly takes a breath. "Why are you always worried about this and that? I don't tell you how to do your job properly. I wish I could drive. Then I wouldn't have to listen to you give me a lecture about my job. You and Daddy are always saying 'don't do this' and 'don't do that'. Only Mommy believed in me." She slams her hand down on the dashboard.

It's true. Mom's patience with Joy was heroic.

"I'm sorry." I reach out to hold her hand but Joy slaps it away. "I know you do a great job and the mice are lucky to have you. It's just that sometimes I worry."

We're both silent. When we get home, I remind Joy to wash her hands. I bite my lip and brace myself for another outburst.

"I'm not a baby! Everybody treats me like a baby. Everybody, except Nick! You don't think I know to wash hands? I was the one making sure everybody was washing their hands when they came to visit you in the hospital so that you wouldn't get germs." Joy scrubs her hands with soap, rinses them, and then flicks the water on my face.

"Sorry. I deserved that." This might be the perfect time to bring up riding the bus. "I know you're frustrated. I am too.

With Mom gone up to heaven, I feel as though I have to take care of everything."

"Hah! I cook all the good food. You order pizza or throw something in the microwave. That's not cooking. I take care of all the important things."

I neglect to point out that every time we cook together, I'm the one that ends up doing the bulk of the work. She's the great recipe collector.

"Listen, since you want to be independent, why don't I teach you how to ride the city bus?"

Joy considers this. "What if I get lost?"

"You won't. I'll show you where to get on and off. And you'll learn to read the schedule. You'll be able to go all over town by yourself."

Joy gives me a wide smile. "Can we do it tomorrow?"

"With me looking like this?" I'm all red and splotchy, with uneven pigmentation.

Joy pouts. "It's never going to be the perfect time."

She's right. "Okay, okay. We'll start tomorrow."

~~~7~~~

We take a front seat because this is where I want Joy to sit—near the bus driver. "This is so much fun," says Joy. It's anything but. I have to endure the stares of all these kids on the bus who are going downtown to hang out. I hate the whispering. I look terrible right now with my peeling skin. Worst of all, I can't cover it up as I usually do because it's so sensitive and everything irritates it. I am most comfortable in the sheer muslin Indian tops, but you can see through them.

We'll get to downtown Pullman soon enough and all the brats will be gone.

I show her the map. "See the three bus routes. A, B, C." I trace the route with my fingers on the map, showing her how easy it is. "The A bus makes a loop around the high school and the university. The B bus makes a loop around the other two hills. The C bus goes to all four hills."

"It's too confusing," says Joy.

"Only because it's the first time."

When we arrive downtown, I take her hand and try to lead her. She won't get up.

"I don't want to change buses." Joy refuses to budge even though I'm standing up. "I will only take the C bus so I never have to change buses," Joy says.

I'm proud of her for recognizing this. We should've gotten up earlier to catch that one.

"Not this time, Joy. Otherwise, you'll be late for work. It will be faster to take the A bus because it goes to the university first. Just come with me." I smile at her.

"Don't leave me," she pleads, squeezing my hand. It hurts just a little bit.

"Don't worry," I assure her. "I promise we'll do this many times together. Okay?" So what if I get stared at? This is more important, especially if I get accepted to Wayne.

We step onto the A bus. I push Joy ahead of me.

"In a couple of weeks, you'll be able to go around Pullman all by yourself. Trust me."

"I don't know." Joy's voice is soft and pensive as we sit together in the front again.

"Remember I had to trust you when you taught me how to ride my bike? Now it's your turn to trust me."

"I gave you a big push and told you to pedal," says Joy, smiling. "Don't stop!"

"And you ran beside me because every time I stopped, I nearly fell over."

"I told you to put your foot down," says Joy. "You did it. In two days, you were riding your bike."

"You've taught me a lot of things." It's a sudden revelation for me.

Joy laughs. "Without me, you'd still be on a trike. You'd color outside the lines. And..."

"...have Velcro on my shoes." We both laugh remembering how hard it was for me to tie knots. Joy never gave up. She's the most patient teacher I've had.

"This is the first time you're teaching me," she says.

"Yeah." It's sad. I haven't really taught Joy anything. Mom always did. We were great playmates when I was little, but once I surpassed her, I didn't teach her a thing. Nothing.

A couple of blocks before the hospital comes into view, I tell Joy to pull the string. "That way the driver knows to stop."

Joy pulls the string, and when the little bell rings, she pulls it again.

"Just once," I tell her.

The driver gives me a grateful smile. I know the temptation is great for Joy, the way her hand inches towards the string.

When the bus stops, I say, "I'll see you after work here. Opposite side of the street."

I watch her walk up the hill as the bus pulls away. She's comfortable on campus so I don't worry. She knows where to find Dad and she likes going up to the Cub, the student union building, or to the Bookie, the student bookstore, to get a treat.

Except for the driver and me, the bus is empty on the way home. I transfer downtown and think about how I take all this for granted. Just like I want to be able to drive in Seattle without a map, I want Joy to be able to get around Pullman without one. She'll never drive and she hates to walk; this will give her some independence after I leave. I'll just have to work with her really hard this year to show Dad she can do it.

~~~

Dad is surprised that Joy doesn't want to ride with him in the morning. "I'm taking the bus," she tells him.

"Really?" he asks. But then he pats her head and goes to work. He has no clue what an achievement this is for her. I hate it when he doesn't acknowledge her accomplishments. Not everybody is cut out for a Ph.D.

~~~8~~~

On Thursday, Joy is giddy at the bus stop when I meet her. "I'm going to a movie tomorrow night with friends from work!"

"What about folk dancing?" I ask. She hates to miss it.

"Oh, I do that every Friday."

"Will you need a ride home?"

"Nope," says Joy.

I'm relieved. I have so much to do and going back and forth on the bus is eating up precious time. I want to get my application to Wayne in good shape before I start work at the library. All these essays to compose, notify people who will need to write letters of recommendation, and I'm sure I've forgotten a dozen other things.

"*Julie and Julia* is playing," says Joy.

"It's all about cooking. You'll love it. Come straight home."

~~~

Friday morning, when I come downstairs for breakfast, the kitchen stinks of something sickly sweet. "What is that?"

"Anais-Anais," says Joy, as she pours Cheerios and blueberries into a bowl. "It's Mommy's."

I sniff her arm. "Oh, Joy, you must only put on a drop. Not spread it all over like lotion."

"I like it," says Joy. "It has to last all day so that I smell good for the movie tonight."

"Huh?" I don't get it.

"I don't smell so good after cleaning cages," says Joy. "I want to smell like flowers, not mouse poop."

"Make sure you come home right away, okay?"

"Okay, okay." Joy slurps the rest of her cereal. "I want to go on the bus by myself."

I didn't think she'd be ready so soon. "Have a great day," I tell her as she walks out the front door, her mirrored bag swinging jauntily by her side.

~~~

Dad is flustered when he gets home. "Hilde called me. Joy wasn't at folk dance," he says.

"Oh, I forgot to tell you. She went to a movie instead."

"You forgot? Do you know how worried I was when Hilde called? She's concerned too. I'd better call her and let her know." He punches the buttons on his phone and fills her in.

Next he calls Joy. "We need to keep better track of Joy. What if something happens?" Dad says.

"Relax, Dad. I just forgot to tell you, that's all. Besides, Joy's got a cell phone." I'm trying to convince myself as well. It's been well over an hour since the movie ended and she should be home by now.

"Well, she's not answering, is she?" Dad paces the living room. "She needs to be supervised."

"Then you do it," I snap. "You expect everybody else to keep track of her while you work. I'm not her keeper."

"You know that's not what I mean. We need to account for her time, what she's doing."

"She's with her work friends. Maybe they went out for a bite to eat." I'm trying to talk myself into not worrying. "Joy needs to be able to do things with her friends. She's going to be twenty-three years old! Give her some independence, Dad."

"I suppose you're right." Dad scratches his balding head. "I'm going to hop in the shower."

As soon as he's gone I take up my vigil by the window. I finally see a car coming up the street. It slows down and stops at our house. Joy emerges, but keeps looking back and waving as she walks up the path. The car has long since sped away.

I open the door to her beaming face. "Where have you been?" I ask through clenched teeth. "Dad's really mad."

"Oh, we had to walk to get to Nick's car." Joy kicks off her shoes. "I'm starving. We had popcorn and ice cream. I wanted to have pizza, but you said I should come straight home so we did."

"Nick? I didn't know you were going with a boy. You said friends from work."

"He is a friend from work."

"Well, I don't have his number. You know we're always supposed to have friends' contact information."

Joy writes his name on a notepad. "I will ask him Monday."

"Do that," I tell Joy, wagging my pointing finger. "I'll warm up some leftover pasta. Tell me everything. How was the movie?"

Joy sits at the counter and in less than two minutes is wolfing down supper. "I loved it. Julia Child is so tall. And she didn't get married until much later. That's why she had no babies. So sad. Every time she saw a baby, she wanted one." Joy leans forward, then whispers. "Nick is very nice. He said that we could do this again. He held my hand when we walked down the hill. There was moonlight." She pats her chest. "It's sooo romantic. Just like in the movies."

"Did he kiss you?"

"Mmmm." Joy toys with a dragonfly pendant I've not seen before.

I'm happy and scared all at once. Happy that Joy might have a chance at love and all the things she hopes and dreams about. Happy that she'll be off my hands. But I'm scared Nick will break her heart, and we'll be right back where we're at before all this. Stuck. Together. Forever.

61

~~~9~~~

A week later, it's Joy's birthday. Joy and I stick our heads together poring over the enormous Julia Child cookbook that I got for her birthday. We decide to make a chocolate raspberry cake, which means another shopping trip. Joy tells everybody she's making her own birthday cake.

I tack the Happy Birthday cat sign at the front entrance, and Joy hangs streamers everywhere. It looks more messy than festive, but she likes all the color. Dad stays in his home office but comes out to see all the food on the kitchen counter.

"Get that cat out of the peanuts and crackers," he says. "Can't you put her in your room, Joy?"

"But Daddy, she wants to be with us." Joy hoists Mel off the counter and kisses her. "Now you eat your cat food, okay? Not people food."

But Mel is spoiled and has a nose for treats. She jumps right back on the counter to sniff the bananas.

Finally, the house is all set, and we wait for our guests. Joy jumps up every time the doorbell rings. The first ones to come are Colleen and her parents. Joy's not one to wait to open presents. She rips Colleen's packet from her hand before she even shuts the door. "Oh, I love it," she says, fingering the felt mice. She hugs Colleen hard.

"Happy birthday," says Colleen.

Diana, Joy's best friend from school days, shuffles in with her parents. Joy immediately displays Colleen's pillowcase.

"Will thu make me fum with fuzzy chicks?" Diana asks Colleen. Diana's speech is slow and slurred because she has

Down Syndrome, but Colleen has no trouble understanding. "I love chickens." It's Diana's job to feed the chickens on her parent's farm. She has named them all and is happiest when she's with them.

"Sure, come by Fabrics and Fashions and we'll pick out all the material together." Colleen is such a sweetie. By the time I was eight, my friends realized that Joy was somehow different and they abandoned me one by one. Only Colleen stayed. I waited for her to quit coming over too, but she didn't. She even played with Joy.

A group of girls knock on the door. They giggle and shout as they bring brightly colored packages to Joy. They are also Joy's school friends from Pullman, but now they live in Spokane in a group home for the developmentally disabled. This is a huge outing for them. We have helium balloons and the girls (they're actually grown women just like Joy) squeal with happiness.

"Let's take one outside," says one of the girls. "We can watch it go up high."

"No," says Joy. "Then it will be gone."

"But I want to!" The girl pouts and I sense the beginning of a temper tantrum.

"Everyone gets to take a balloon home," I say. This creates even more chaos.

"I want the red one."

"Blue!"

I fish for a Sharpie in the kitchen drawer and write names on all the balloons. That makes everybody happy as they crowd around me, munching on chips, dips, and cookies.

Even though we only see them a couple of times a year, they never act shocked around me. They accept the scars as a part of me and hardly notice the changes year to year.

Annika, their caregiver, pays attention though. "Your skin looks great. The lumps are gone!"

"Thanks to modern technology," I say, pulling up my three-quarter sleeve up to show how I can straighten out my left elbow completely.

"They do amazing things nowadays. I'm so impressed how well you're doing."

"Oh, I can be a wreck sometimes." I laugh.

"Yeah, me too," Annika says with a sigh. "It's hard getting all the girls corralled into the van when one cannot find her special white shoes and another is having a fit over a blouse."

"Tough drive?" I can't imagine being stuck in a van with four chattering girls. I pour Annika a mug of rose petal iced tea. She practically sticks her nose into the cup, breathing in the fragrance and relaxing.

"Not really. I'm used to it. But as always, there's some bickering over little things like headphones and ribbons and lipstick." Annika looks around. "It's nice for Joy to be at home, go to work, interact with normal folks." She sips her tea. "It's difficult to get that in a group home. They tend not to interact with others because they have each other. But for the ones who can't work and need constant supervision, it's a great option. Most of their parents find it difficult to care for them at home. They have to work."

"I wish there was a group home for Joy right here in Pullman," I say. "Then I might be able to convince my dad to let me move to Detroit for school." I'm surprised at how easily I can talk to Annika. But she knows the difficulties we face.

"Talk to Tessa. Maybe there's enough interest to have one in Pullman. I'll bet you're not the only one."

"I will." It's such a relief that Annika's first reaction isn't to worry about what will happen to Joy. She takes my wishes in stride. I wish Dad would too.

Tessa arrives the same time as some of the folk dancers. Joy loves the beaded skirt they all got for her. "It's Hungarian," says Hilde.

I can't believe how heavy the skirt is in my arms. It must be very expensive with all the bead-work.

Dad, Mr. Mendoza, and Richard (one of the folk dancers) are the only men at this party and they stick together. Dad laughs and waves his arms about a lot, which means he's happy.

Joy's friends hang out together. They examine all the presents. Joy shares the baby animal book I got for her when we were in Seattle. They exclaim:

"Aw!"

"So cute!"

"I love baby anything!"

What's not to like about baby animals, right? I hit upon the perfect book.

Joy tries on hairclips and rainbow socks with the toes all separated. When she wants to try on tee shirts, I have to remind her to change in her room. She returns with a sparkly red shirt and the Hungarian skirt. She laughs and twirls and makes a bow, then puts on the new CD she got as a gift.

Nobody listens to me when I tell them to turn it down. The girls dance to the hip-hoppy beat. The men get shoved to the side, so join Annika, Mrs. Mendoza, and me in the kitchen.

"You should come folk dancing," Richard says with his charming British accent. No wonder my dad won't leave him alone. He loves the Brits.

"I often go swimming during that time. It's good for the stiffness in my joints."

Richard nods his head like he understands, but he doesn't. Even I didn't know that I'd have so many problems years after I recovered from the burns.

"But you're not swimming now," says Colleen. "Come on, let's dance." She grabs my arm.

I try to twist my arm out of Colleen's grasp, but she has a solid grip. I give in. She snags Richard's arm with her other hand and glides towards the girls in the living room.

A loud cheer goes up. Finally, a man! The girls follow Colleen's lead, raising up their arms and cross-stepping and sashaying across the carpet like it were an aerobic dance class. I don't like the frenetic pace and give up. I dance-hop back to the kitchen.

Richard has fun with the girls. Most people shy away from Joy's friends. Not these folk dancers. Diana also goes folk dancing on a regular basis. Even in the winter, her parents make the long trip from Orofino on a Friday night. Sometimes Joy goes home with Diana to spend the night on their farm.

The doorbell rings. Joy runs to answer it, her blouse askew. She stops to fix it because it keeps coming untucked. She opens the door and says nothing for a little while. Then she screams, "Pizza!"

Dad pays the delivery man, while we dish up steaming slices from the cardboard boxes.

Dad joins us in the kitchen. "Hello, Tessa. It's nice of you to come," he says.

It really is. I suppose if you're a social worker, you don't have to go to the social events of your patients.

"I wouldn't miss it," Tessa says. "Besides I get to check up on Joy. How are things?"

We both know I'm the one that does everything, so it makes me mad to hear Dad say, "Joy's taking the bus now," as if he had anything to do with it. "She cannot handle transfers, but she has taken the C bus by herself all this week."

"That's fantastic," says Tessa.

"It only took her a week," I say. "She's got the route in her head. She pays the exact amount of money and doesn't get confused."

"I've taken all four of my girls to concerts and plays and movies and they've been able to handle exchanging tickets for money." Annika sighs. "But they're not ready to go around Spokane on their own. It's so much easier in a small town like Pullman."

"I doubt Joy could navigate her way around Spokane on her own either," I say.

"See, this is where I disagree," says Dad. "Everybody protects developmentally disabled kids so they don't really give them the opportunity to find out." Suddenly Dad is the expert on how to teach kids with delays.

I face him squarely. "But who's going to have the time to spend?" I ask. "Mom and Meena Auntie taught Joy many things that others said she couldn't do. You and I can't do it."

"Well, yes. That's always the case, isn't it? Not enough resources. I confess I've not had the patience to teach Joy, even when she was a child. It was very frustrating. But thanks to social services, and the dedication of my late wife, Vidya, and now Rebecca, Joy is growing and learning. Just look how far she's come already!" He gazes at Joy with pride. "She's a fantastic cook. She even made her own birthday cake."

I open my mouth to tell him the truth, but the lie gives him so much pleasure, I let him believe it.

"Shall we have cake then?" Mrs. Mendoza gets it from the fridge and places it carefully on the counter. Colleen's mom is a genius, always knowing exactly the most perfect thing to say. I give her a grateful smile.

All the girls crowd in the kitchen. We sing *Happy Birthday*.

"Make a wish," they shout. Joy sucks in a huge lungful of air and blows out the candles. About half go out, and Joy takes a second gulp and blasts the remaining candles with her breath. The whipped cream frosting flies everywhere. Everybody claps. I make a silent wish for Wayne.

Joy turns to Dad and envelops him in a bear hug, burying her head in his neck. "I'm so happy, Daddy."

Dad cups her round face, so much like his own but also resembling Mom's. "I'm happy too, Joy. Every day you surprise me." He switches to his loud classroom voice. "Each year we remember what a miracle Joy Jivanta is. Vidya and I had given up all hope for a baby and were we surprised when Joy arrived. And here she is, twenty-three years later. "Happy birthday, my joy, my life." He raises his glass of wine and drinks deeply from it. His eyes shine wet.

Everyone claps again and the sounds of good wishes fill the air. Colleen's mom dishes out cake and ice cream.

Diana thrusts a plate of cake into my hands. I'm not prepared and almost drop it. Diana laughs as the plate wobbles and I do a dramatic save. I take a small bite, and it's even better than the batter we licked off the spoon this morning.

Music blares from the stereo and there's more dancing.

Mrs. Mendoza and I put things away, clearing the tables of all the remains of the party.

"Colleen tells me you might go away to Detroit," Mrs. Mendoza says.

"I'm applying; that's all. I might not even get in." I wish I could tell her to mind her own business and let me do the dishes by myself.

"Well, if you do, you needn't worry about Joy. We'll be here."

I feel awful about my earlier thought. I give Mrs. Mendoza a hug and swallow a lump.

When the last of the guests leave, Joy goes to the living room window and parts the curtains. It's as though she's been waiting for another guest to arrive. I wonder if she wishes that Mom would just walk through the door and make everything go back to normal. But no other car even drives by.

~~~10~~~

I get applications for the BS/MD programs in Missouri and Louisiana. It's expensive; all these application fees, paying for the transcripts, etc., but I want to have options if I don't get into Wayne. I still haven't mailed in my application because I want everything to be perfect. I can't bear to tell Joy, even though I've talked it over with Tessa. She thinks it'll be great if I get into the program.

"I won't know until next year," I say.

"You're so smart, Rebecca. You'll get in," she says. "Don't look back. You know we'll get something figured out for Joy."

"But Dad…" I don't even know what I'll say about him.

Tessa shushes me. "I'll deal with your father. Believe me; every sibling of a special child goes through this guilt."

She reads me too well.

"If you want to leave, don't let Joy hold you back. She'll be fine. Your dad needs to take more responsibility. I should be having this conversation about Joy's work with him, not you. But we'll get there, bit by bit."

"What if Dad's right and it's too soon after Mom's death for me to leave?"

Tessa pats my hand. "You've got to follow your dreams, kid."

In the meantime, Dad has forgotten about Wayne State, so we've settled into a good routine with work, movies, and surreptitious applications for me. It's work, movies, folk-dancing, and going out with friends for Joy.

My seventeenth birthday comes and goes quietly at the beginning of August. Joy and I study the Julia Child cookbook and settle upon a lemon cheesecake and creamy cucumber soup with sourdough bread. I love cold soups in the middle of a scorching summer. Although gazpacho is my favorite, this would be an interesting change.

Colleen has knitted me a bright red wool hat. "To keep you warm at Wayne," she whispers. I guess it means she's quit worrying about what will happen to Joy. I love her.

Dad splurges on a small Dell notebook for me. It even fits in my batik shopping bag from India. It's a beauty and more powerful than the old desktop we keep in the family room. Joy ooohs and aaahs over it.

"Thought you might want something portable," is all he says.

Maybe it means that he's accepting the fact I might not be here.

~~~

I've been working now at Holland Library for over a month. I shelve books some of the time, but mainly I'm upstairs in acquisitions, entering new books into the library database. I love browsing through them. Hilde is my boss and never yells at me for not being a robot. She knows I read just enough to decide whether I want to put a hold on the book.

Hilde slides a hefty new coffee-table book on folk dance. "This just came in." I flip through the colorful pages that capture motion so well. "You should bring Joy and stay to dance. It'll do you some good."

"I can't."

"Don't worry about what people think or say," Hilde says.

"It isn't that. I'm satisfied with the way my skin is healing. But I'm going to be busy this last year of school and don't want to take on more commitments."

"You study too hard. You should get out more."

"I know, Hilde, but it's nice for Joy and I to have separate interests. Otherwise, we'd always be together and she'd drive me crazy."

Hilde laughs. She understands.

~~~

It's been nice not having lunch with Joy. I call her out of a sense of duty, but she says she's busy having lunch with her friends from work. Once she even said an emphatic "No!" and hung up. She usually loves it when I call to meet her. It must be her growing independence.

This evening, Joy throws up her supper. Stomach bug. Dad thinks so too. "Wash everything thoroughly," he says, but doesn't lift a finger to help me. Typical Indian male. I put Joy to bed after cleaning up.

The next morning, when I have breakfast, Joy barfs her orange juice all over the kitchen floor. Gross. Thank goodness Dad already left for work. I don't need him to give me instructions on hygiene. I call Mrs. Peznokatz and let her know that Joy's got the stomach flu, then clean up her mess.

"You rest, okay? I'll have Mrs. Mendoza check up on you and I'll see whether Dad can come home early from work."

"Okay," says Joy. "I'm pretty sleepy."

I meet Dad for lunch and he agrees to go home for the rest of the day. It's Friday and the lab is quiet anyway, it being summer. I go back to the library and tell Hilde that Joy will miss folk dancing because she's sick.

"Again? Has she been sick all this time?"

"What do you mean ... *again*? She just got sick."

Hilde balances a stack of books on my desk. "She hasn't come folk dancing for a couple of weeks. Didn't you know? This is why I encouraged you to bring her."

Now I'm confused. Joy has been skipping folk dancing? Where does she go?

"I'll talk to her. There's got to be a good explanation," I say, as I arrange and rearrange the stack of books on my desk until the pile topples over.

Hilde helps me to pick up the books. I work straight through so I can leave early.

~~~

I call Joy after work. "Hey, I'm at Dissmores. Do ..." Before I can ask how she's feeling or if she needs anything, she cuts me off.

"You're shopping without me?" Joy loves to shop.

"My period is here. Go check under the bathroom sink and make sure we have enough pads."

I feel the familiar cramps in my lower belly and curse my lot in life. I'm lucky that I didn't start my periods until I was about fourteen. Apparently, getting burned to a crisp has some perks. My development arrested; I had no body fat for a long time.

I hear some banging of cupboards, then Joy says, "No, I don't need pads." She clicks the phone off.

When I come home, Dad is on the phone and Joy is eating a bowl of chicken noodle soup. "I'm all better," she says, beaming.

"Good. What did you do today?" I ask.

"I slept and watched TV. When Dad came home we played Monopoly. He's a sore loser." Joy makes a face.

We spend our Friday night playing another game of Monopoly. It's so rare for all of us to be home like this together, it reminds me of our childhood days. We'd bring out games and Joy always had stuffed animals around the board supervising, participating, with a constant commentary in various voices. Even now, Joy will do that, but not to the same degree. Right now, Buck the wolf goes everywhere. It's funny to see Mel and Buck sitting side by side, with Mel pawing Buck.

Mel takes Mom's spot this time and paws some of the houses as we play our game. Dad is losing as usual, and begs off, saying that he's going in to the lab tomorrow to work on his grant proposal. We divide up his mortgaged property between us and Joy is gleeful about acquiring two more monopolies.

She gets a dreamy look as she puts up a house on St. James. "Somewhere, over the rainbow ..." she starts to croon the song from The Wizard of Oz.

"What dreams do you dream?" I ask.

"I dream of living on a farm. Nick has two old cats and a dog. We'll get new kittens and puppies. And fluffy little chickies. And babies!" Her eyes light up.

"Nick?" This is a surprise. "Is he your boyfriend now?"

"Yeah! We've been seeing each other at lunch and on Friday night."

Mystery solved.

"Why didn't you tell me? What if something bad happens?" And as soon as I ask that, I am terrified that something bad has already happened. I immediately throw the dice for my next move.

I move my wheelbarrow across the board, landing on Reading Railroad, forking over $100 to Joy. She wants my B&O card, but I won't give it to her.

"I'd bet Nick would give you B&O Railroad if he were playing," I say in my most neutral tone.

"Oh, we don't play Monopoly," Joy says with an air of superiority. "We do more grown-up things."

"Like what?" I prod her. "Kissing?"

Joy blushes. "And cooking," she adds. "Nick only had frozen food in his apartment. Last week he went shopping and I made a beef stir-fry. He loved it."

"Wow!" I hope they're just playing house. "You went to his apartment alone?"

"It's like we're almost married," says Joy, ignoring my question. She's forgotten about our game.

"You know that some things have to wait until we're married, right?" I look sternly at her. "Right?"

"Oh, yes, Mommy told me all about getting married and we will get married." Joy begins to sing *Over the Rainbow*.

I can't bear to listen to the song again, so I interrupt her. "Joy, it's okay to have a date and go to a movie and get to know Nick better, but you can't pretend you're married." She is toying with the little houses and not looking at me, so I grab her shoulders. "Look at me. You can't … you can't get naked … and you can't, you can't … go to bed with him, okay?"

Joy drops the houses. "But Rebecca, we're almost married. I love Nick. And it feels so good. I can't say no." She looks right back at me, with not a trace of shame.

Shit. Shit. Shit. She slept with him. She had sex. And loved it. I have an instant headache. I hold my head in my hands to stop the pounding.

"Well, promise me you won't sleep with him again. It's not right. Sex is only for married people. Remember, Mom said the marriage act is for babies and bonding."

Joy is quiet. She rolls the dice and moves her dog along the board, but she's making mistakes counting.

"Promise me?" I ask her again.

"But I love him," she says.

"But does he love you?" I ask.

"Yes! He loves everything about me. If you met him, you would know too."

"I don't know Joy." I'm afraid all he loves is her body. "How do you know he loves you and not just using you?"

"I know!" Joy flings a house at me. "You're just jealous because you've never been in love!" She throws her dog as well. "When you love somebody, you'd do anything for them."

74

"That's what I'm trying to figure out." I pick up the pieces before she decides to pitch the rest of them. "Looks like it's time to put away the Monopoly."

She stomps off to her room.

~~~11~~~

Joy and I both sleep in the next morning. I think about what Joy told me last night. Nick has awakened a lot of feelings inside her. She's no longer the same. I wish Mom were alive. She'd know what to do. She'd invite him over for dinner.

I lie in bed watching the morning breeze ruffle the curtains. I hear Joy up and about, but they're not the usual sounds of her singing and talking to Mel, but barfing sounds in the bathroom, banging the cupboards, letting the lid to the toilet seat slam down. Suddenly I'm wide awake. Could she be pregnant?

She peeks into my room. "Are you up?"

I pull the sheet up over my head. Mel jumps on my full bladder.

Joy crawls into bed with me. "I feel awful. I want Mommy."

My stomach twists in a knot. "I have to pee," I say, getting out of bed. I know what I need to do. Get a home pregnancy test before panicking further.

I pull on jeans and tell Joy to stay in bed. "Listen, I'm going to the drug store and we'll figure out why you're sick, okay? You can rest here with Mel."

I shoot out of the house and for once am glad that Dad's at work. Both the guy at the counter and I are embarrassed at this purchase. I slap a twenty-dollar bill on the counter and run out of the store without collecting my change.

At home, I take the stick out of the sealed foil and tell Joy to pee on it.

"Ewww!" Joy scrunches up her nose. "At the doctor's office they make you pee in a cup and that is so hard. Some pee always goes down my leg and I hate it."

"This will be easier. You just pee like you normally do and hold the stick under the stream." I demonstrate with a toothbrush under a running faucet.

Joy is not one bit embarrassed doing this in front of me. In fact, she is triumphant as she sits on the toilet seat and shows me the stick. One dark line—the control. But there's a faint line coming off the dark one. Just barely there. Oh, please God, let it be a mistake. I feel dizzy and brace myself by pushing against the wall.

My head is pounding. What is going to happen? Dad is going to kill me.

"Don't tell Dad," I say, trying to stay calm. "It kind of looks positive, but the line is very faint. The instructions say it's best to take the test in the morning with the first pee so that the chemicals are all concentrated."

"So we can do it tomorrow morning?" Joy asks.

"We'd better," I say, thankful that I grabbed a 2-pack. We wash up and I finish reading the instructions in my room. Purry little Mel helps me stay calm. Even if it's not a '+' but just a 'T', one has to consider it positive. So she is pregnant. I look at the rate of false positives. Negligible unless the woman is taking fertility drugs. I look for anything that might negate this result, but there's no hope. Unless she takes the test tomorrow and it's negative.

Joy finds me reading all the instructions. I pat the bed. "I think you might be having a baby—that's why you're sick."

"But I'm not married yet." Joy shakes her head. "How can that be?"

"If you have sex, you can get pregnant. That's why you have to be married first."

"Oh!" Joy takes my words in. Then she says, "No!"

"Tomorrow you take the test first thing in the morning. If it's also positive, we can talk to Nick." I don't know whether this will help, but he's got to know. It's his baby too.

"Then we'll get married. It'll be wonderful. I'll go to California with Nick." Joy dreams of the future and tells me more about how they met, in the Animal Care Center down in the basement of Heald Hall. He's a teaching assistant for Biology. Her eyes shine with love for Nick. "Oh, Rebecca. We have so much to do!"

I hold Joy and make her look at me. "You cannot tell Dad until we've talked to Nick, okay?"

She nods her head, but she's so happy she won't be able to keep this a secret. I can tell she's planning a wedding in her head.

I can't concentrate on my application to Wayne State. I can't focus on the books beside my bed. I can't even watch television. Joy bustles about the house as though everything were just fine. I want to shake her. But in the afternoon, she takes a nap.

Colleen calls but I tell her that Joy still has the stomach bug, so it's probably best she not come over. Dad has been invited out to dinner so we barely see him. He just pops in with a bunch of journals and tousles my hair as though I'm a little girl. He smiles at Joy because she is baking cornbread. "My little chef," he says. "I'm going to a faculty dinner. Don't stay up."

"Have fun," I say.

I'm relieved when Dad leaves. Joy and I watch *Mississippi Masala*, one of my favorite romantic movies. But tonight, the love story makes me feel dejected. I can't ever hope for this, and look where it's landed Joy. In a heap of trouble.

I go to bed, but lie awake thinking how selfish I've been by not supervising Joy enough. When Mom was alive, she always knew what Joy would be doing. She spent many hours at the vocational training center. We knew when Joy was going folk dancing or if she was meeting a group of friends downtown.

I was making Joy more independent by letting her make decisions for herself. I was happy she was making new friends and going to movies or to Pizza Hut after work. They would always drop her off and I thought she'd be just fine. I didn't have to think about her constantly. But I failed to account for people like Nick, people who'd take advantage of her.

I never thought a guy would have sex with her. With the way she talks, I never saw her as a sexual person. She's like a kid—in a woman's body.

I do manage to fall asleep because the next thing I know Joy is shaking me awake. "Look! We must go tell Nick!"

I bury my face into the pillow. This is a nightmare and it will go away. But Joy waves the stick near my face and I can smell her morning pee. I turn my head and even without my glasses I can see the 'T' on the stick.

She's pregnant.

~~~12~~~

We drive over to Nick's apartment and Joy knocks on his door. No answer. "Nick?" Joy calls out. She raps the door hard. I stay in the shadows by the stairwell and run my hand along the chrome handlebar of an expensive mountain bike chained to the railing. Probably Nick's.

He finally cracks the door open but when he sees Joy, doesn't invite her in. "Hey Babe." He's only wearing shorts, showing a very hairy chest.

Joy leans her head toward him. "Nick, we're having a baby! Now we can get married and live on a farm and you can bring your dog and cats, and we can even get kittens ..." Joy can hardly contain her excitement.

"Whoa!" Nick spreads his arms out to deflect her. "What? Are you crazy?"

I step forward. "No, she's pregnant!"

"Who are you?" Nick asks.

"I'm her sister, Rebecca." I'm aware of how high and girlish my voice sounds. How ineffective.

Nick shakes his head. "I'm outta here in a couple of months."

"No! Don't leave me." Joy is on the verge of crying with her bottom lip quivering.

That's when it hits me. I also just want to get out. And I love Joy. This guy doesn't. And he sure doesn't want to be stuck with her.

"How do you know it's mine?" Nick asks.

"Joy has only been with you," I say.

"And you said we'd get married." Joy sobs openly.

"That's a lie," Nick says. He looks at me. "Look, I only said we could hang out. She's making all the rest of this marriage stuff up. I'm too busy finishing up my Masters to have time for this."

I believe him. "Then how could you? She's just like a little girl."

Joy smacks my arm. "I'm a woman!"

"See?" Nick folds his arms across his chest and leans against the door. "You're a woman alright."

"And she's pregnant!" I say.

"Then get rid of it. For all you know, it'll have problems too." Nick scratches his chest.

Joy opens her mouth, then closes it again. She looks like a dumb fish.

"I can't see you anymore, Babe. You're really fun but I don't really have time for this."

What a bastard!

"I love you," Joy says in a small voice. "Don't you want to be a daddy?"

"No, I don't."

"You should've thought of that before having sex," I say.

I try to put myself in Nick's shoes, but it's hard. He tricked her into thinking he liked her just to sleep with her. Didn't the possibility ever occur to him that she might get pregnant? How could he just discard her?

Joy takes Nick's hand. "But you're mine. You loved me," she says. It makes me want to puke the way she still wants him.

"I don't think so." Nick withdraws his hand. "Bye," he says as he shuts the door.

Joy crumples on the doorstep. "He loved me," she whispers, fat tears rolling down her cheeks.

I squat down. "No, he never did Joy. He only loves himself." I help her up to her feet. "Let's go."

81

$$\sim\sim\sim\mathbf{13}\sim\sim\sim$$

I'm glad Dad is out of the house this weekend. You'd think summers would be easier for him, but with no classes to teach, he focuses on writing grant proposals. This kind of work takes up more time than regular teaching. It's his personal work, work that he prides himself in.

Mom worked alongside him before Joy came along. They did research on blood disorders. But Dad shifted his focus from finding how people get various kinds of leukemia to what genes are responsible for them. Now he also works as a private consultant for GenTex, testing for genetic diseases. They offer these to pregnant women and to couples who have a history of diseases.

I suppose if I knew that I were going to have a baby with Down's or Tay-Sach's, I would choose to end the pregnancy. Why make a baby suffer like that?

Colleen had a baby brother who lived only a few days. He had a malformed heart that doctors couldn't fix. Colleen and I barely remember him, only that he died. The whole family could've spared themselves the grief if they had gotten rid of it before it was born. But Colleen's mom had the baby, knowing he would die, unless he got a heart transplant right away. And what are the chances of the right infant donor dying at the same time?

Of course, now it's relatively easy to get an abortion. It's safe and legal. I'll take Joy to a family planning clinic and get it over with. Nobody wants this baby. I do some studying and discover that the baby is just the size of a bean. A legume.

Dad can't find out about this. "You can't ever tell anybody, okay?" I tell Joy. I used to think she couldn't keep a secret or lie, but I was dead wrong. Joy might not lie, but she's crafty enough to hide the truth.

Joy is numb from the sudden breakup with Nick and just nods. I'm scared Dad will notice she's not her usual talkative self and ask what's wrong and she'll spill all the beans. Damn beans.

I open the pantry. Joy has already gone through a box of rice crackers. They are mild and one of the few things she's been able to keep down. I'll have to go to the store again. She doesn't even want to walk to the bottom of the hill. "It'll do you good," I tell her.

"I'm just so tired," she says. Depressed is more like it.

So I amble by Colleen's so we can walk together a while. She's my best friend and I want to tell her why Joy is sick, but I can't. Colleen's family is Catholic and doesn't believe in family planning. She's the last of six kids. Seven, if you count her baby brother who barely lived, but they are probably one of the happiest families I know.

So I opt to tell Colleen that Joy is still sick.

Colleen's concern is immediate. "Is she okay?"

"Yeah," I say. "I'll take her to the doctor tomorrow and see if he can help her." I neglect to tell her what kind of doctor.

Sunday afternoon passes by uneventfully, thank God. Dad is busy. Colleen has to work at Fabric and Fashions, so Joy and I keep to ourselves. We are all alone. I look up abortion services in the area. Pullman doesn't have any, but it's not like I'd bring Joy to one in the area anyway. Everybody knows everybody's business. The kid who rang up the pregnancy test probably blabbed to his friends about me. I've never even been kissed. Well, I would've kissed Sheldon that July Fourth if I hadn't burst into flames. A lump forms in my throat as I think of him having the best summer ever down in California. I doubt he's thinking of me or that almost kiss.

Thankfully, I find an abortion clinic in Walla Walla where we can walk in and get help. It's the same in Kennewick. These are farther away than Spokane but you have to have an appointment in Spokane. I don't want anybody calling here to confirm the appointment.

I decide on Kennewick because we'll never have a reason to go there again. Plus they do both the abortion pill and the vacuum method. We might even get an appointment right away since it's out in the middle of nowhere. I can't imagine women lining up there to have an abortion.

I've never seen Joy so sad.

"I've found a clinic, Joy, and you'll be better soon," I tell her.

"Okay," she says in a disinterested voice.

On Monday I call the Animal Care Center and tell Mrs. Peznokatz that Joy needs to go to the doctor. Then I call the library and tell Hilde the same thing. They both say to take care. As soon as Dad leaves for work, I get Joy ready to go. I pack extra underwear, pants, and pads for her. I wear a white cotton shirt, and even though the sleeves ride up, I don't mind. My skin is smoother. I still feel naked without a scarf so wrap a silk one with purple swirls loosely around my neck. I tuck my hair behind my ears for driving but I can shake it loose easily to cover my face if I need to. Not that I am planning on speeding.

I make one last stop at the bank to withdraw $500 of my hard-earned money. Resentment rises to the surface as I enter in my security code at the ATM. It spits out the money, which I stuff in my purse.

Joy perks up in the car. She loves going on drives. We have crackers and ginger ale and Cadbury chocolate bars with us.

It takes a couple of hours. Joy slips on earbuds to listen to music and I concentrate on driving—without cruise control. The black tarmac feels out of place amidst the rolling wheat fields; they're ready for harvest. School will be starting soon and I'm grateful that we can take care of everything now. I want my senior year to be uneventful.

I glance at Joy; she seems content. You'd think we're going for a drive, a joy ride even. I worry though. I don't know how much Joy will bleed, if she'll be okay, but I've done a lot of reading and abortions are routine and safe. They say they're even safer than having a baby! I've just got to trust that these doctors know what they're doing.

I'd printed out directions and it's a good thing because although I can see the plain white clinic from the highway, I can't very well drive across the sage brush. I don't park the car right in front even though there are many spaces available. Instead I pull into the side parking lot. A few people in the corner of another white building hold home-made posters. God damned pro-lifers. What do they know about people like us? What a bunch of self-righteous morons.

We have clear access to the entrance, but I don't like that we have to see pictures of dead babies. It's a freaking bean. That's all. It's not like we're killing a baby after it's born, or throwing out a baby in a box. I don't often dwell on my beginning but it must've been awful, to not be safe and secure in my mother's arms. This is so much better. Don't they know anything?

Joy is scared now. "Thou shalt not kill," she reads aloud. "Every baby, a child of God."

"Don't pay attention to them," I say.

There are even men out there, like they'd know anything about women's problems. If men were good, we wouldn't have to be here.

Another sign reads, "Choose life ... your mother did." I think about this one. Even though my birth mother didn't want me or couldn't take care of me, she didn't abort me. She gave me life. A small chance. And here I am.

"I feel sick." Joy leans on my arm.

"That's because you are sick. The baby is making you sick. You'll get better after you get rid of it. Then you won't be sick any more. You'll just have a heavy period, that's all."

Joy looks back over her shoulder.

The pro-lifers are praying the rosary quietly. There is a girl my age holding a sign saying, "Save your baby. Save yourself."

From what, I wonder.

"I can't do it, Rebecca." Joy clings to me even more. I keep walking forward, pulling her with me. How can a short walk from the parking lot to the clinic go on forever? I want to hurl stones at these judgmental people standing with their judgmental signs. They don't know our situation. Our pain. What Nick did to Joy is rape because no matter what, she cannot really consent to sex. And consenting to sex implicitly involves consenting to have a baby.

"Come on, Joy. You're not killing a baby. First it was a poppy seed, then a peppercorn, and now it's a bean. Nothing more."

Joy gives me a weak smile and lets me lead her through the double doors. Her grip on my arm lessens as we take in the greenery in the lobby. A woman behind the desk greets us. "May I help you?"

"Yes," I say. "Could we talk to a nurse?"

"Sure," she says. "I'll buzz her. In the meantime, fill out some paperwork." She slides a clipboard with papers across the counter.

I take them and we sit down. I make Joy fill out the form, while I direct her. It's all standard stuff. I leaf through several magazines showcasing beautiful women with flawless skin. But I can't focus on anything. The titles are all about getting a boyfriend, becoming more beautiful, or improving your sex life. I doubt I'll ever have to worry about these things.

"I don't know when I had my last period," Joy whispers.

"Guess."

"June?" she mutters.

I take the clipboard from Joy and walk to the receptionist. Before I hand it to her, I check the box for Abortion Service and Emergency Contraception. In the comments section, I add: developmentally delayed.

I go back and flip through another glossy women's fashion magazine. Pretty faces look right back at me. They have articles about following your dreams, getting the man of your dreams, and dreaming big. They don't have a single article about getting through a nightmare.

"Joy?" A nurse holds the clipboard.

We both walk towards the nurse, hand in hand.

"Come on in. I'm Laurie," she says. "And you are?"

"Rebecca."

We walk into a small room, just like at our family doctor's office. I sit in a hard-back chair. Joy climbs upon the examining table. Laurie washes her hands. "What can I do for you today?"

"I'm scared," blurts out Joy, her eyes darting all over the place.

"She's pregnant," I say. Isn't that why people come here? To no longer be pregnant? Why else would we be here all the way from Pullman?

"Nick said to get rid of it," Joy says. "We were going to get married. He said he loved me, but he doesn't." She starts sobbing.

Laurie pats Joy's knee. "There, there. We're here to help you. First of all, are you sure you're pregnant?"

87

Joy nods vigorously.

"She had the home test twice. Both were positive," I say.

Laurie looks at the clipboard again. "So let's try to narrow it down when you had your last period."

Joy mumbles.

"It's okay if you don't remember, because we will do some tests." Laurie pulls out a calendar and scoots her swivel stool even closer to Joy. "Try to answer the questions I ask, so I can help you. Okay?" She looks up at Joy and smiles, placing the calendar on her lap. "Can you show me on the calendar all the times you remember having sex with your boyfriend?"

Joy scrutinizes it carefully. "We went to a movie. He held my hand. And I kissed him." Joy jabs the first Friday of the month in July—her birthday weekend. "Then here and here." The following two Fridays she skipped folk dancing and I didn't know. She also points to a few weekdays and I realize she had sex during her lunch breaks. She puts her hand to her face. "He loved me."

"It's okay, Joy." I get up to rub her back.

"This is good news," says Laurie. "You're in the very early stages. At the most, eight weeks. We'll confirm it, of course, with ultrasound. Now, I have to have to ask the most important question. Look at me."

Joy looks at Laurie.

"What do you want?" Laurie asks.

"I want to have babies with Nick. Not without," Joy says. "I'm scared."

"A baby doesn't fit in our plans," I add. My voice sounds matter-of-fact, like Dad's. What I want to say is: A baby doesn't fit into *my* plans.

Laurie smiles. "I understand. But remember, this is Joy's decision to make. Joy, if you choose, you can end this pregnancy."

"I'm scared," Joy says again.

"Let's do some tests and I'll give you some paperwork to read, then you can come back tomorrow, okay?"

"We can't come back tomorrow," I say. "We've come a long way."

"I understand," Laurie says. "It's a hardship for many of our clients, and we try to do this in the fewest possible appointments. But it's very important that Joy have a chance to look over all the materials so she understands what her choices are, and what's going to happen. Even if she goes for the pill, she'll still have to return for a follow-up appointment two weeks later."

I'm not happy about this.

Laurie is kind and treats Joy as an adult, wants her to understand everything, but it's aggravating because she doesn't realize Joy cannot really make these decisions for herself. She's like a kid. Isn't it enough that we tell her what is going to happen and be done with it?

"In the rare case the pill doesn't work, she must come in for a proper D&C abortion. The medication is toxic to the fetus and will cause birth defects otherwise."

"Can you explain everything today so we can at least get started?" I ask.

"Sure," says Laurie. "But you have to understand that our first concern is Joy's health. You can't just expect to walk in here for the abortion pills. We still have to do the tests to make sure."

"We have to do it today." I try not to grit my teeth and show my annoyance. On the website, it said walk-ins were welcome, that they could take care of everything the same day. But they want to drag it out. I feel the weight of cash—all $20 bills—in my purse. I don't even know what this is going to cost, but I don't care anymore. Anything, just as long as it's all over with.

"Let me bring you some more paperwork and we can go through all of this together." Laurie leaves.

"This place is scary," says Joy, rocking back and forth. "I don't want to be here. I never want to come back."

"Don't you understand, Joy? You get rid of this now and you won't have to deal with anything else. Our lives will be back to normal." Except nothing has been normal since Mom died. I press on. "You can't have a baby. You can't even properly take care of your own self. Let's get this started and in two weeks you'll be all better."

"But…"

"No buts." I have to be firm. "This is a huge problem, and if Dad ever finds out, we'll both be in a lot of trouble."

Joy begins to cry. "Nick loved me. I still love him. Maybe this baby will make him love me again."

I hug her. "I know it's hard, but remember Nick doesn't want the baby. And since you made a mistake, you must now fix it. As much as I hate Nick for doing this to you, he's right. You have to get rid of it."

I give Joy a tissue and she blows her nose and gives a loud sigh. "I need to go pee."

"I saw a bathroom in the hallway. Come right back."

Joy opens and closes the door quietly. I feel terrible. Everything is a horrible mistake. Joy. Me. This.

Laurie bustles in with a sheaf of papers. "After I go through all of this, Joy will need to sign the consent forms before we proceed."

"Joy is developmentally delayed," I tell her. "She's like a ten-year old. She can't make these decisions for herself."

"Yes, I saw that on the form. You can't be her guardian, right?"

"No. I'm seventeen. Dad can't find out about this. He'd kill us both." I knew it. I shouldn't have said anything about Joy's mental status—not on this form, not to this nurse.

"I think it's best if Joy signs the consent form herself. She understands what going on. In Washington, we don't have to notify the parents if our clients are developmentally delayed or even if minors come in for an abortion, so you don't have to worry about your dad." Laurie smiles and I find myself feeling more relieved.

"What happens after?"

"After the abortion, we encourage all sexually active women to be on birth control and take tests to ensure they don't have sexually transmitted diseases. Do you think Joy will comply?"

"I don't know. I never thought she'd even have sex, but now I know that men can take advantage of her. She'll believe anything they say because she is so trusting."

"She's intellectually disabled." Laurie completes the thoughts I had. "I always recommend sterilizing people like her. That way, they can have the benefit of an intimate relationship without the threat of a pregnancy."

Mom always told us to save ourselves for our future husbands. She was right. What's the benefit if you're not going to get married? Oh, yeah, diseases, bastard babies, and boyfriends who disappear. Would Joy be capable of waiting?

"Do you do that here as well?"

"No, I'm sorry. It's more complicated and needs a lot more thought on everybody's part. This is something that needs to be discussed with your parents."

"Of course." I fiddle with my purse, feeling stupid for even asking. "I didn't mean that you should sterilize Joy right now. I just wanted to know if you offered that service. Oh, hell."

"It's okay." Laurie pats my knee as if mental delays run in our family. I want to kick her.

The doorknob rotates and Joy stands there, her shirt spotted with water. I can tell she's feeling better from her smile.

Laurie goes over all the paperwork. She explains how the abortion pill works. Then she talks about the procedure that many women have up to twelve weeks—dilation and curettage. "It only takes five minutes," she says.

The smile on Joy's face disappears. "That's horrible! The baby is sucked up in a vacuum cleaner?"

"It's the best way to clean out the uterus. It's not horrible. I've had one." Laurie gives the papers to Joy. "You just need to sign these and then we'll prepare you for an ultrasound."

"Will it hurt?" asks Joy.

"Not one bit. We put some gel on your stomach and run a probe over it. The probe shows the uterus and any contents and growths in it. It's routine. Nothing to be scared of."

Joy signs the forms.

Laurie takes away the papers and brings a large glass of water. "Here, drink this. You need a full bladder and I know you just emptied. I should've had you wait. I'll come get you in an hour."

Joy gulps her water. I go to the lobby and get Tim's salt and vinegar chips from the vending machine. It's nice of the clinic to have snacks available for purchase, otherwise we'd have to look at the stupid signs the protestors are holding up.

Joy eats the chips while I read through all the literature that Laurie has given me. The pill seems straightforward. I just hope everything works out as it's described. You take the first set of pills to block the hormone that maintains pregnancy. The embryo dies and the body expels it. It's like a normal miscarriage.

I remember reading in my biology book that a quarter of all pregnancies in the first trimesters abort spontaneously. Something is usually wrong with the baby and it's nature's way of culling the ones that can't survive. There's nothing wrong with giving nature a helping hand.

Finally, after hours it seems, Laurie is ready for Joy.

~~~14~~~

After all this dead time, talking and going through the brochure, suddenly there's a burst of activity. Joy and I walk to a different room—it's dim in here and another woman dressed in a white coat asks Joy to lower her bottoms. "That way I won't get the goop all over your clothes."

Joy climbs up on the padded table, the paper sheet rustling beneath her. I help her to push her shorts and underwear low. She lifts up the shirt too. I hold her hand. This is my first time to hold *her* hand through something.

"That's great," says the ultrasound lady. Her metallic name tag shines, with the black letters etched into it: Tammy. "We're just going to have a look to see how far along the pregnancy has progressed. Okay?" She squeezes out gel on Joy's lower belly.

"It's nice and warm," says Joy, relaxing now, as the gel is spread all over her stomach.

"It helps to transmit the picture," says Tammy. She keeps her eyes on the screen, her left hand on the keyboard and her right hand on the probe, gliding it over Joy's stomach.

Tammy clicks on the keyboard, then presses the probe into Joy's lower belly.

"Ow!" Joy digs into my hand and raises her knees. "Stop!" She pants. "Stop!" She whimpers. "Don't hurt me! Don't hurt my baby!" She pushes Tammy's hand away.

"Stop this drama!" I tell Joy. "It's not hurting."

"No, but it's going to hurt," says Joy. "And I have to pee."

Tammy waits a few moments for Joy to recover, probe in hand. "Can you stand it once more? I promise to be quick. Then you can go pee."

"No." Joy shakes her head. Her eyes glisten with tears.

"I suppose I can try to get measurements from this. I'll go give them to Laurie." She gives us some paper towels to wipe off the goopy stuff and closes the door behind her.

Joy doesn't even give me a chance to clean her up before she curls to her side and sobs. "I want to go home."

"Soon," I say. "We're almost done. The nurse will give you the pills and we can go home. Okay?" I try to get as much of the gel off her belly and clothes as I can.

I know how awful it is to have anything done to your body. I remember screaming through all my debridement even with all the painkillers working at full dosage. It was more fear than pain. They soaked me in a warm tub and my dead skin would peel off. What didn't come off had to be scrubbed off. They'd hold me down and rub away the stinking flesh. The nurses always said they knew I didn't have inhalation injuries because of my strong lungs. I wonder how I survived as I scrape the paper towel over Joy's beautiful belly one last time. She doesn't realize how lucky she is the pregnancy is not permanent. She can return to her normal life after this crisis is over. I have not been so fortunate. The massive burns have changed me and my life forever. I'm not even the same person I used to be.

When I go to throw away the goopy towels, I look at the screen. It has the last shot, a grainy one, showing an almost empty cavity shaped like a giant kidney bean with a couple of blobs inside. One looks like a shrimp. The other blob is much tinier and round.

Joy stands beside me. "Is that the baby?"

"Must be." I take a pen on the counter and draw on the paper sheet Joy was lying on. I draw two cells, then four, and how they grow into a hollow sphere. "That's how it begins. It's just a cluster of cells." But even as I say it, I marvel at how the cells know to become a pinky or a big toe.

"It's so neat," says Joy. "I want to take a picture with me."

"You don't want that," I say. "It's like an alien from a movie."

There's a tap on the door. It's Laurie. "Are you feeling better, dear? Tammy got the measurements so we're done." She notices us looking at the screen. "I'm sorry. Tammy was supposed to clear the screen."

"I want a picture," says Joy.

Laurie and I look at each other. I doubt it's a good idea to have a picture of a baby that you're not going to have.

"I don't think it's possible," Laurie says. "We don't have a printer hooked up." It's true. I don't see any printers in the room.

"Can you email it?" Joy is persistent. "I really want that picture."

"I'll see what I can do," says Laurie. "Excuse me."

When Laurie leaves, we look at the screen some more. It's ugly.

To my dismay, Laurie returns with a printout of the screen. Joy is pleased. "Thank you," she says.

We walk to the first exam room. Enroute, Joy stops at the bathroom. She thinks for a minute and then passes the picture to me. "Hold this." I take it and stare at it. I sure hope Joy doesn't plan on storing this as a keepsake.

Laurie looks at the picture too. "Joy is at an early stage—the embryo is no more than seven weeks—so we can give her a pill abortion, if that's what she wants."

I'm relieved to hear this.

Joy joins us in the hallway and we enter the brightly lit room. Laurie is brisk, setting down the papers we need to sign.

The cost is steep. I'll walk away without the bulge in my purse.

Laurie speaks to Joy. "I'm going to explain in detail how to take the medicines, and after you sign the papers, we can get started."

She holds up a bottle. "You'll take the mifepristone here. It stops the pregnancy from going further." She holds up a second bottle. "When you get home, you take the misoprostol. Within four to six hours, you'll start to cramp and bleed. There'll be blood clots and even some tissue. It's nothing to worry about."

Laurie holds up a third bottle. "And just to be safe, you take antibiotics for two weeks to prevent infection."

Joy has a glazed look with all the technical jargon, but I need to know more. "Must the miso –"

"Misoprostol." Laurie completes the name of the drug.

"Does it have to be taken right away?" I ask.

"No," says Laurie. "The mifepristone blocks the hormone progesterone, and without it, the uterine lining begins to break down, and the contents are automatically expelled within a few days."

I learned about these hormones in my biology class. "So you don't really need to take the misoprostol."

"That's correct. Misoprostol is not really a necessity, but we prescribe it to make sure the patient can choose the time of the contractions. For instance, Joy could take the misoprostol over the weekend, so she can be sure the abortion occurs at home."

"Yes, that will be good," I say. "I want to make sure she is comfortable and the cramps are not too bad."

"Will it hurt?" asks Joy.

"Some women say it's like having a normal period and others have bad cramps. You can take some ibuprofen to relieve the pain. No aspirin, okay?"

"How will we know everything is okay?" I ask.

"The bleeding can continue for fourteen days, but most women begin feeling better within just a couple," Laurie explains. "Make sure you bring back Joy for a follow-up exam. We want to make sure she's well."

Damn. But yes, we'll do it. In three weeks tops, everything will be back to normal. There is a light at the end of this tunnel.

"I'll make sure she follows all the instructions," I say. I feel better knowing all the details. "Come on, Joy. Let's get this started."

We wait for Joy to sign the papers and take her first pill— mifepristone—but she's looking at the fuzzy ultrasound picture. "No," she says. "I want to go home."

"Can I take the pills home with me?" I'm hoping that once we are at home, I will be able to convince Joy to take the medication. She's scared here.

"I'm sorry. We cannot do that. We must make sure the patient takes mifepristone."

"Just take this first pill, Joy, and then we can go home. You can take the rest at home." I try to hold her hand and she gives me one reluctantly, the other one hanging on to the grainy ultrasound picture. "Look at me," I say, pulling on her hand. She jerks it back and stares at the picture.

"It's got teensy toes, see?" Joy finally looks up at me. Her eyes are wet with new unshed tears. I look at the picture but can't see any fingers or toes. She's just imagining all kinds of things. "It's my baby."

"You still have some time," says Laurie. "You can make a decision later after you've had time to think about everything. You can come back in a week or even a month."

"I'm never coming back," says Joy.

"Listen to me." I want to slap her. "Take the pills now and it'll be over. Two weeks from now you'll feel much better." I get up and fill a paper cup with water at the little sink. I hold out the two pills to Joy. "Here, just take them."

Joy smacks my hand away. The tablets fly out of my hand and roll on the floor. "No! No! No!" She stamps her foot, opens the door to the exam room, and rushes out.

"Shit," I say. "We're both so dead."

"There's time," says Laurie. I want to slap her as well. There is no time.

"You don't understand," I say.

"I do, honey. I do. I'm sorry. We'll always be here for you."

I run out of the clinic after Joy. It's only when I see her near the car that I realize I've forgotten all the literature about abortion.

For the second time, I see Joy crumpled. This time by my Honda. She rocks back and forth, her head between her knees.

I touch her back. "My baby," she cries, still holding the ultrasound picture.

"Let's go home," I whisper. This is the end of my life.

~~~15~~~

We return home in silence. Joy will not go through the abortion. She has no idea how much worse it will be with Dad. No more folk dancing, going out for pizza after work, or the movies unsupervised. Nothing. As for me? Forget about it. Forget Wayne. Forget having a chance at living. Forget everything.

We make two stops, one to pee and one to eat. Joy has no trouble scarfing down a hamburger. The smell of it makes me sick. You'd think I'm the one who's pregnant.

Dad's already home when I pull into the garage. I don't get out of car right away. I'm petrified. "Don't tell Dad," I tell Joy, glaring at her.

Dad is in the living room, listening to Ravi Shankar. "Where were you?" he asks, looking up from an issue of *Annals of Genetics*.

"Daddy, Daddy," Joy shouts. "Look at my baby! See?" She waves the ultrasound picture in front of his face and plops down right next to him.

Dad's face turns tomato red. "What is the meaning of this?" he thunders. He looks closely at the picture, then tosses it at Joy, barely missing her face. The picture flutters to the floor.

She bends over to pick it up and I can hear her whisper, "My baby."

~~~16~~~

I look down. I never knew that our carpet had so many shades of beige. When I look up, Joy is a splash of color in her red shorts and flower tee shirt beside Dad.

"I'm having a baby, Daddy." Joy's voice is sweet as she smiles at Dad. "You'll be a grandpapa." Then she scowls at me. "I'll never let you hold my baby." She snuggles closer to Dad, as though he's her protector.

"What is the meaning of this?" Dad asks again in a low voice.

My throat is tight, but when I untwist the scarf around my neck, the tightness remains. "Joy is pregnant. I was trying to take care of it, since you're always too busy."

Dad opens his mouth like he's going to say something, but holds his head instead, like we're giving him an aneurysm. I hate that Mom is not here. We'd never be in this mess if Mom were alive and she'd know how to talk to Dad if it did happen. Dad finally closes his mouth. He looks like a dumb fish. I realize Joy inherited this trait from him.

"And how exactly did all this happen?"

He's asking me how? "She had sex," I offer.

Dad jumps off the couch, spilling his tea all over his *Annals of Genetics*. He shouts at me, "How could you let this happen?"

"It's not my fault?" I yell back.

"All this independence. Look where it has led us!" Dad towers over me, his breath hot and gingery.

"Then you take care of it!" I put my hands against his shoulders and push. He merely takes a step back, but I fall into the chair behind me.

"You should've come to me straightaway instead of going on some wild ride to some clinic. Where'd you go?"

"Kennewick."

"Stupid girl. Don't you know anything? I have *connections*! I counsel people about their pregnancies. I know doctors who are good. You don't just go to some clinic in Kennewick, out in the middle of nowhere."

He strides to his little office that's off to the side of the living room. "I'll call Bhattia in Spokane."

"Daddy, please," Joy screams from the couch. "Please Daddy, I'm sorry. Daddy. Daddy! Don't take me to a doctor. Please."

But Dad ignores her cries. He kicks the door closed and through the glass panes, I see he's already on the phone.

Joy rushes to the kitchen; she's opening and slamming cupboard doors. I don't know how she can think about food at a time like this. I should help her put supper on the table, or at least comfort her, but I can't stand to be with her right now.

Melody meows and jumps up on me. I scratch behind her ears and underneath her chin. She stretches her neck to give me better access. She purrs. I try to relax into Mel. It's out of my hands now. Dad is right. I shouldn't have to take care of this. He knows people. I don't know anything. Who knows whether those pills would've worked. It's actually a relief that Dad knows.

Dad calls me to the office. I bring Mel with me. He asks softly, "How far along is Joy?"

"The nurse said six or seven weeks."

"Good, good." Dad turns his attention to the phone. "Yes, it's early. No need to rush; just whenever you can fit her in. You're a lifesaver, Bhattia."

Dad scribbles on a notepad.

"What makes you think she'll go for it?" I ask.

"I have power of attorney."

"But you'll never get her in the car. Believe me."

"Well, you've made it much more difficult but I have my ways." Dad is confident. "I want to spare her the trauma. Bhattia will do an abortion and tubal ligation under general anesthesia. That way, she won't have any memory of the procedure and if she ever gets into a situation with a boy again, at least she can't get pregnant."

"She's going to hate you," I say.

"So? We have to do what's best for her, even if she's going to cry about it right now. Her mental outlook is that of a little child, concerned only with the immediate. She cannot think of the long-term consequences." Dad scratches his balding head. "You know, your mom and I talked about this, but she was against sterilization. She held out hope of marriage and babies for Joy. But now ..." Dad suddenly looks old and tired. "I don't think it's possible."

"Why?"

"Just think, Rebecca. What normal man would want to marry her? Even if she might look and act ordinary, she's mentally retarded. We don't know what the cause is. Your mom never conceived until Joy, and things didn't go right."

Dad has never been so open with me, and I'm curious. "What happened with Mom?"

He sighs. "We'll never know. We were both on sabbatical in India and I've always suspected it was some viral infection she caught during pregnancy. But Joy's condition could be genetic as well."

"How come you're not sure?" I ask.

"Because we only know of a fraction of diseases with markers," Dad replies. "I had Joy tested along with both your mom and me, but nothing known turned up."

"So Joy's baby could have the same problems too?" I begin to understand how little we really know about genetics.

"That's right."

"What's your plan?"

"She's on his schedule for ten o'clock Friday, so we'll leave first thing that morning."

"What about work?" I ask.

"I'll call everybody. Tell them it's a family outing before school starts. And that's what we need to tell Joy."

"You won't tell her the truth?" I am shocked that Dad would do something like this. But then, I did the same thing when I took her to Kennewick.

"We'll tell her later. If you tell her now, she'll just have a tantrum. Look at her already. Slamming cupboards. All that screaming about doctors. What happened at that clinic?" Dad's anger rises to the surface and I can see he's getting ready to blame me.

"Nothing," I say quickly. "She just freaked out during the ultrasound. It's not like it was hurting her or anything, but she got scared." I take a deep breath. "I'm so sorry about all of this, Dad."

"Me too," says Dad sadly. "Poor girl. Well, she'll have nothing to worry about in Spokane. She'll be out completely."

~~~

Thursday night, Joy pops popcorn. Her appetite's been much better and I'm glad for that. Food is one of her great pleasures.

Dad takes away the bowl. "You can't have that, Joy."

"That's mine," says Joy, reaching across Dad. "Give it back."

"Listen to me. Tomorrow we're going to see Bhattia Uncle and he asked me to make sure you hadn't eaten anything in the night. Okay? The rest of the weekend we'll go boating on Coeur D'Alene. That's the deal." I think how clever Dad is, using 'uncle' instead of 'doctor,' but Joy is not fooled.

"I don't want to see a doctor," says Joy.

She doesn't trust anybody now. I can't blame her.

"Then no boating either," says Dad, keeping the popcorn within her reach. "Besides, you know Dr. Bhattia. He's been here and we've been to his cabin at Coeur d'Alene."

Joy considers this. A trip to the lake in the middle of summer is not something we do very often. Even I'm looking forward to it.

"What will he do?" asks Joy.

"He's going to make sure you are okay. He will make sure you are sleeping while he examines you so you don't have to feel a thing. He's like your uncle."

"And my baby?" Joy places a protective hand over her belly.

I don't even want to think about what's going to happen when she finds out there's no baby.

"Don't worry. Everything will be okay. Just think how much fun you'll have this weekend." Dad somehow managed to answer without lying or telling the whole truth.

"Not even a little popcorn?" asks Joy.

Dad's assessment of Joy is so true. She lives in the moment and right now popcorn is highest on her mind.

"It's best if you follow Bhattia Uncle's instructions," says Dad. "After the appointment, you can have ice cream and popcorn and anything else you want. We'll even go out to an Indian restaurant."

Joy is happy at the prospect. She picks out an old Hindi movie from one of my mom's collections—*Zanjeer*—shackled.

"No," Dad groans. "It's too long."

But Joy is adamant. He sits with her until the intermission, then goes off to bed. Even after multiple viewings, I enjoy how the story unfolds on the screen. It's got plenty of twists and turns that Joy likes to shout out. And with all the catchy songs, we're easily lost in the movie for three hours. Joy loves the knife sharpener (the love interest), but my favorite character is the best friend—Sher Khan. He's a man of strength and character. And the best song comes from him, about friendship, about laying down your life for your friend.

~~~

After the movie is finished, I offer to pack. I still can't believe that we're going to trick Joy into getting an abortion and tubal ligation, but I did almost the same thing Monday when I took her to the Kennewick abortion clinic. Dad and I aren't all that different—we're both selfish.

I don't even know whether this is legal. But Dad has power of attorney over her and he's right. He's thought through everything carefully and this is for the best. There are so many things out of our control. Me getting burned, Joy getting to know Nick and getting pregnant. We make mistakes and mess up. Dad knows how to fix things and this is one mess that he can clean up.

But I toss and turn all night long. I wish Mom were here. What would she do?

~~~

Joy is sleepy early next morning as we pile into the Pilot with our duffel bags full of clothes and slippers and bathing suits and towels.

Dad lets me drive and I'm more confident now. Having smoother skin has changed me. Joy dozes in the back. She didn't even take a shower. If I were having surgery, I would've bathed, but Joy doesn't know the truth and is perfectly content. It makes me uneasy. When is Dad planning to tell her? After she wakes up?

My hands tremble as I think of her reaction when she finds out what happened.

"Watch it!" Dad hollers as I cross the yellow lines on the road. I overcorrect and end up near the shoulder.

"Whoa! Slow down, Rebecca. Pull over."

I grip the steering wheel more firmly. What's wrong with me? I must concentrate on the road otherwise we'll all end up dead. I focus on the mechanics of driving and try to stop thinking about Joy and her baby.

"It's okay, Dad. I don't want to pull over every time I make a little mistake." He grunts, but doesn't insist on taking the wheel. The rest of the drive to Spokane is uneventful. I simply follow Dad's directions and we're at Valley Hospital in less than two hours. No wrong turns.

Except now that I've parked the car, I feel a sense of impending doom. Dad said we'll tell Joy later, but when exactly? I am scared for her. How will she feel when she wakes up, bleeding, and no longer pregnant?

I've come back from the dead and it was a living nightmare to discover that I'd been burned. I wanted to die. But they wouldn't let me. Mom wouldn't let me. I'm glad now, but I was mad for a long time because once I was out of immediate danger, I realized that life after burns is nothing like the life I was used to. I had to wear pressure garments to minimize scarring. Reconstructive surgeries were scheduled on a regular basis to accommodate my growing body encased in skin that didn't stretch or grow. I became a Frankenstein, with seams of being put back together visible.

There was also lots of therapy, both physical and psychological, but it was Mom who was able to bring perspective to this tragedy. She always talked about purpose, and things happening for a reason, and God's will. It's hard to believe in a God who allows suffering, but I do anyway. Mom tried to teach me that my worth did not lie in outside beauty. And bit by bit, I began to accept the new normal, and thanked the people who saved me.

Maybe Joy will be grateful five years down the road when she's not having to chase after a rambunctious kid. Joy doesn't dwell much on the past or the future, so she may recover from the abortion far better than I did from my burns. At least her life will be the same.

But what if she became pregnant for a reason? It's not like she's ill. Are we wrong to intervene just because the conditions aren't ideal?

I vacillate between telling Joy so the choice is hers, and not telling her. What if Joy chooses the wrong thing? But what if *we* choose the wrong thing for her? All these thoughts paralyze me.

Dad and Joy are out of the car. "Let's go," says Dad.

We walk together, Dad leading the way. Joy sees a restroom and announces she has to go. I do too.

"We'll meet you in the office," I say, desperate to have a few more moments to think.

I slip into the bathroom with its rows of stalls and take a deep breath. The smell of bleach makes my nose burn.

What would Mom do? She always said, "Truth shall set you free." The entire time I was recovering from my burns, she was honest. She even let me hate her instead of sugar-coating reality. She'd want to make sure Joy knew what was happening.

So I take the first tentative step. "Do ... do ... do you know what's going to happen today?" I ask.

"Yup. Bhattia Uncle will check me out and then we'll go to the lake and I will have ice cream," says Joy.

"There's more," I say, looking at myself in the mirror, seeing the scarred skin—a damaged girl—and hating myself. Hating the subterfuge I am part of. I have to tell the truth. And so I choose to tell the truth. It all comes out in a rush. "Dad wants you to get rid of the baby and he wants you not to be able to have any more—ever."

Joy is dead silent. Even the tinkling stops. She flushes the toilet and comes out of the stall.

"No," says Joy, washing her hands. There's no shouting or screaming, just washing. She surprises me. No drama. "He promised everything would be okay."

"Everything will be okay," I assure her. "I just think he should've told you."

We look at each other in the mirror. Joy with rosy cheeks, so much like Dad when he's upset.

"Do you want to see Dr. Bhattia?" I ask, even though I know what her answer will be.

"I want my baby." Joy's voice quavers. "Help me. Help me to keep my baby."

Although my synapses are frayed, I have a moment of clarity. Baby. This is about Joy's baby. Mom conceived Joy after years and years of infertility. I know in my soul Mom wouldn't drag Joy to an abortion clinic like I did, nor would she agree to Dad's diabolical plan. She would help Joy adjust to the new normal, no matter how hard it'd be.

I know what I must do. It's going to change our lives forever, but I can't let Joy be hurt any more, nor her baby. Thoughts about Wayne and the future I was planning for myself surface but with Joy looking at me in the mirror, I push them down. I cannot see what the future holds but right here, right now, Joy and her baby need saving. I remember the poster at the Kennewick clinic and I understand what it means to save.

"You leave. I'll deal with Dad." I hold her hands. "I'm sorry about everything. I thought Dad was right. I thought I was right. But now that we're here, I know both of us were wrong, wrong, wrong."

"You'll help me?" Joy's eyes are big and round.

"Yes." I am a mixture of dread and relief, because my little yes will have titanic echoes. I embrace Joy, then fish around in my purse. "Look, I have all this money I took with me to Kennewick. Get a taxi and go straight home."

"Come with me." Joy is scared. She's only ridden the bus alone in Pullman.

"I can't. I need to hold off Dad. You can do this."

"What about the trip to the lake?"

Oh, dear Lord.

"Forget about the lake!" I raise my voice. "Don't you understand? If you want your baby, you need to get out of here. Fast." I place $200 in her hands. "Let's go."

Taxis are parked across the emergency entrance and it's not difficult to get the attention of a driver. One comes right up to the loading area. It's an Indian. Figures. Seems they gravitate towards this job. The window opens. "Where to?"

"Pullman," I say. "How much?"

"Two hundred and fifty."

Whoa! That's steep.

"How about an even two hundred?" What a lame attempt at bargaining.

"This isn't the old country," says the driver. "Two fifty is the price." He looks away.

I hand over sixty more dollars to Joy. She climbs in. "Okay. Be safe." At the last minute I remember she's had nothing to eat. I look through my purse to find a granola bar and juice box— apple. I don't know how old they are, but I hand them to her through the window.

"Thanks," she says, smiling. Joy doesn't break eye contact with me until I turn away. Now it's time to face Dad.

~~~

I run up the stairs to Dr. Bhattia's office. "It's about time you two showed up. Where's Joy?" Dad waits expectantly.

"She's gone," I say, breathless.

Dad is stunned. He looks around the room as if Joy is hiding somewhere.

"I told her the truth and she doesn't want to be here. She wants her baby."

"Where is she?" Dad's voice booms.

"In a taxi back to Pullman."

Dad shakes his head, anger rising to his cheeks. He clenches his hands and even though he doesn't knock me dead, I'm sure my life is over. "Stupid, stupid girl! You have no idea what is best for her!"

"And you do?"

I brace myself but Dr. Bhattia intercedes on my behalf.

"Joshi, my friend. You might have the power to do this, being Joy's father and guardian. I believe you have Joy's best interests at heart, but I wouldn't have performed an abortion or sterilization without her *informed* consent." He lets that sink in.

Dad is speechless as Dr. Bhattia continues. "What you propose is legal, but consider whether it is *right*."

Dr. Bhattia gets up, signaling that our meeting is over. "I'm sorry, Joshi. If Joy is ready later, we can schedule the abortion and tubal ligation then. There is still time—until 23 weeks. But it has to be her choice. Go home. I'll take care of cancelling surgery."

Dad brushes past Dr. Bhattia without a single word.

"I'm sorry for all the trouble and worry," Dr. Bhattia says kindly. "I would never do anything against Joy's will."

"Thank you," I say and follow Dad. I try not to think about the money I just wasted. Joy would've been okay. She'd be here. But Dad might have manipulated her. No, the money was spent wisely: protecting Joy and her baby.

Mom used to say that we know what the right thing is because it's stamped onto our hearts. There is peace even if there are difficulties. I remember when I learned to live again with my scars and deformities, when I began to have hope again, how right it felt. And at peace. I feel that same peace now.

I wish I could tell all this to Dad, but he is full of silent rage as he storms through the corridors. Oh, how I wish Mom were alive. He'd listen to her. She had a quiet strength about her.

We both get into the car. Dad adjusts the mirrors.

"Mom would …" I begin.

"Don't." Dad says. "She's not here."

It's a long hour with all my thoughts about Joy tumbling about in my head. If I did the right thing, why do I feel such dread? Am I going to bear the full weight of this decision? Just as I am reinventing myself and preparing for a life away from here, the chains tying me to Joy pull me towards her. Will I never break free?

I don't know how we actually manage to get home. Dad drives like a madman—angry and fast. What if we both die? What will happen to Joy? Who will care for the baby?

~~~17~~~

When we get home, only Mel comes to greet us with her sweet meows. Worry floods my stomach. I call Joy. "Are you okay? Where are you?"

"I'm fine. I'm at Colleen's and she's really mad at you. She…"

"I'll be right over."

Within minutes, I'm knocking on the Mendoza's door.

Colleen opens it, her eyes cold as ice. I never knew amber eyes could shed their warmth. She crosses her arms. "How could you?"

"Please." I touch her arm, but she flinches. "Let me explain."

"Let Rebecca in," comes Mrs. Mendoza's voice.

Colleen lets me pass and I see Joy right next to Mrs. Mendoza, her arm around Joy. I wish I could talk to her alone, but there's nothing to hide any more.

"I'm sorry." I take Joy's hand. "Please forgive me. I'm afraid too."

"I'm scared, Rebecca. But I love my baby." Joy gives a half smile.

"I know. I won't let Dad or any other doctor hurt you. I promise." I wish I could take away this past week and start over again, but what's done is done.

"You took her to an abortion clinic?" Colleen is indignant with her hands on her hips. "You would've let them kill the baby?"

"Colleen!" Mrs. Mendoza's voice is sharp.

"It's okay, Mrs. Mendoza. It's the truth," I say.

"Alright, I'll leave you all to discuss." Mrs. Mendoza gives Joy a squeeze and heads to the kitchen.

"So? What's your answer?" Colleen asks.

"Haven't you ever made any mistakes, Miss Perfect? What if you messed around with Kurt and got pregnant?" I could just throttle her for being so judgmental. Doesn't she know how hard it is for us?

"I wouldn't," says Colleen.

"But what if? What if he raped you? He could've, you know? Oh, he wanted you very much." I pause for a breath. "You wanted him, too."

Colleen is silent for a moment. I think she finally gets it, but then says, "It wouldn't be the baby's fault. Why should it have to die for something bad either of us did?"

I'm stunned.

"You'd live with it the rest of your life?" I whisper.

"Yeah, or give the baby away if I had no help," says Colleen. "God doesn't make mistakes."

I'm so mixed up. What does God have to do with any of this? A truly just God wouldn't let a rape victim get pregnant. A truly just God wouldn't let the rape happen in the first place. But all these terrible things happen anyway. Why did God allow me to be born to a woman who didn't want me? And why did God allow me to be burned eleven years later? Why? I try to think of what Mom always said about purpose. Could Joy's baby have a purpose? Mom would say so.

"Yeah!" says Joy. "My baby is good."

Joy reaches out for my other hand and pulls me to the couch. We sit there and hold each other tight and weep for what could've happened. Thank God it didn't, but we're still shaking from fear. We don't know the first thing about babies.

Colleen's mom bring bowls of ice cream with fresh blackberries. I fill them in on all that's happened in the past two weeks. Joy chokes back a sob when she hears Nick's name. Mrs. Mendoza shakes her head. Colleen's eyes are wide with horror as though she's watching a bad accident but can't bear to not look.

"We are here to help you always," says Mrs. Mendoza. "Don't be afraid. It's fear that causes us to make the wrong choices."

"Thank you," I say.

"The right choice isn't always easy. It's going to be hard on both of you. I should know; I've raised six children." Mrs. Mendoza sets her bowl down. "Have you thought about adoption?"

Joy shakes her head no as she takes another spoonful of ice cream.

"I've heard the story of my adoption, how happy you and Mom and Dad were," I say to Joy. "Maybe you can do the same for another loving couple who longs for a baby."

But Joy continues to shake her head no. "But it's not the same. I *want* my baby."

"Well, there's plenty of time to figure things out. In the meantime, know that I'll be here to help in any way I can," says Mrs. Mendoza.

When we leave the house, Joy walks ahead. Colleen stops me at the threshold. "I'm your best friend; you could've told me."

"I was scared. Still am," I say. "Wouldn't you be too?"

Colleen gives me a hug and I cling to her, heat and tears fogging up my glasses.

"I'm sorry." She chokes on the words because she's crying too. "Poor, poor, baby."

"I'd better go and face Dad," I say, trying to smile.

~~~

I catch up with Joy. "We're in this together," I say.

She squeezes my hand and we enter together. We take up the entire doorway and it makes me feel strong.

"So, you're back." Dad paces. "How dare you both go against my wishes? Is this what I've worked so hard for? I should throw you out of the house. Then you'll think twice about having a baby! And just how in the world are you two going to take care of this baby?"

I don't know what to say. Even Joy is speechless.

"Tessa can help us figure things out," I finally suggest.

"Tessa. What does she know? She's a social worker, half my age." He pours himself a Scotch and drinks it, grimacing. I don't know whether it's us or the drink that is so unpleasant. "Have you forgotten your roots? In India, all important decisions are made by the parents. They have the wisdom of their years. But no, here, the kids know everything. You are smart. Independent. I can guarantee you that this is all going to lead to more heartache."

"Daddy, I want my baby," Joy says, tears in her eyes.

"I know what you want!" Dad roars. "But I am too old to raise more children."

"I'll probably end up raising this kid," I blurt out. That's the truth that's been weighing me down. Dad hasn't exactly been hands-on with us. Mom did all the work. And when I got burned and she needed help, Meena Auntie dropped her life to care for us. I don't want to be another Meena Auntie with no life of her own.

"This will be a lot like India—with grandparents, parents and children all living together," says Joy.

Dad just grunts.

"Joy, you do need to see an Ob/Gyn—a baby doctor," I say.

"No more doctors." Joy stamps her foot for emphasis. I don't blame her for feeling like this. The very people who are meant to take care of her health try to destroy her baby.

"Trust me. You need one," I beg Joy. "Every woman who is going to have a baby goes to baby doctor. They make sure you're eating properly, the baby is developing as it should. We can get started with our own Dr. Heng. He will tell us whom to see."

"You don't have to see Heng," says Dad gruffly. "You can go see Dr. Storck directly."

I erupt into a laugh. Apparently I'm the only one who finds this funny because Dad is droning on about how she's the best OB in Pullman.

"Stop that maniacal laughter," he says, pouring himself another drink. "I hope you girls realize what a tremendous burden you are taking on."

That's what we are—burdens.

~~~18~~~

Dad makes all the arrangements and I take Joy to her first prenatal visit the following week.

Two pregnant women look curiously at me, since the scarring on my arm is still visible with the loose three-quarter-sleeved *kurta* I wear over a long skirt. I don't belong here, but in the burn ward, where people like me are a common sight. Only a little boy pays no attention to me.

I ignore everybody and take the forms from the receptionist. Joy fills them out. They're much like the ones we filled out in Kennewick. I bring a notebook along to work on my essay for my application to Wayne, but I can't focus. I draw square after square instead. I leaf through a parenting magazine and toss it down in frustration. Dad should be here. To think he spends hours and hours counseling other people, but can't be bothered about our worries makes me mad. He's right—we don't know the first thing about babies. This is exactly why we need him. He's been through all this with Mom.

The small boy keeps bringing his mother toys. When she gets up, she asks the other lady to watch over him and then sweetly to her boy, "Mama go potty, okay?"

"Mama." The little boy throws a truck and follows his mother.

"Wait here," says the other woman.

Joy gets on the floor and beckons him. "Look," she says, stacking blocks. He is immediately entertained and toddles over to Joy. The mother smiles gratefully and leaves. He adds more blocks to the tower until it falls. He laughs. Joy laughs too. She's always been good with kids. But the problem is that she's a kid herself. I can imagine Joy with no supper on the table and a mess of toys on the floor because she's busy playing.

When the little boy's mother comes back to the waiting area, Joy continues to play with him.

A cheery black woman comes to get us for the exam. "Joy?" she asks, scanning the room, and settling on Joy, still on the floor. "Come on in. I'm Loretta." When Joy looks at me, the nurse says, "You can bring your friend."

"That's my sister, Rebecca." Joy gets up and follows Loretta. "She looks different from me because we adopted her. Also she was burned."

Loretta looks back at me. "You have healed very nicely. How long ago were you burned?"

I wiggle my fingers to show her my dexterity. "Six years ago, dozens of surgeries, horrible itchy pressure garments, and lots of therapy." I try to be lighthearted, but I still sound like a big whiner.

"A survivor!" I can hear the smile and pride in her voice. "When I first started out, I worked at a trauma center. Most burn patients do recover and go onto lead wonderful and productive lives."

I love nurses. They are the ones who do the hard work of rehabilitating patients, who have to put up with patients like me, angry as a bear caught in a trap.

I follow Loretta as she steers Joy towards a scale.

"One hundred and fifty even. Excellent!" declares Loretta.

We step inside a small room. A mobile hangs from the ceiling. Monkeys go around. There is a small bin overflowing with board books and brightly colored rattles. The wall is covered with large pictures of the baby inside the womb at different times. The detail is astonishing. This is definitely a room where mothers bring babies, where babies are welcomed.

Joy turns to Loretta. "You won't try to get rid of my baby?"

Loretta is startled, but she seems to understand the situation and says, "No, dear. We are here to take care of you *and* your baby. We will help to bring your baby into this world." She has Joy sit on the examining table. I take the chair. Loretta plants herself on the swivel stool. "I'm just going to take your blood pressure and temperature, and weigh you. It will all go in your chart so that we can start keeping track of how your baby is growing. Okay? You want to tell me what's been going on, sweetie?"

Before Loretta can get the blood pressure cuff off, Joy launches into a speech. "Nick—he likes the animals too—and I, we went to a movie together and he promised we'll get married, and we loved each other, but now he doesn't want me and I'm going to have a baby." Joy takes a breath. "Nick doesn't want the baby. Nobody wants it except for me."

I cringe because I know what comes next.

"Rebecca took me to get rid of the baby because Nick said so but I wouldn't let them. I ran away."

Loretta gives her full attention to Joy and doesn't frown at me even once.

"Then Daddy found out and we went to Spokane but Rebecca ..." Here Joy looks at me. "...but Rebecca, at the very last minute, saved me and my baby." She lets her arms drop to her side but they come up the instant she starts talking again. "She put me on a taxi to come home. It cost a lot of money and now we're here to see the baby doctor." Joy whips out the ultrasound picture from her back pocket of her shorts.

Loretta takes the picture. "Whoa! That's a lot of running about."

Joy nods her head and tears drip down her cheeks. Of happiness or sadness, I do not know.

Loretta gives Joy a tissue to wipe her face. "It's going to be all right. Lots of women have rocky starts. Your baby will be alright. You're a mother!" Loretta returns the ultrasound picture to Joy, writes a few notes in her chart and looks at me. "Are you going to be her partner?"

"Um, yeah," I stammer. "I'm here, so I guess I am."

"Great," says Loretta. She tells us about her own children, how she went through her third and last delivery without a husband because he died in a car crash, and although it was difficult being a single mother, her kids have all grown up very nicely. It makes Joy feel better about not having a husband. When she's done checking Joy's vitals she says, "I'll get Dr. Storck."

I suppress a giggle, but Joy laughs out loud.

Dr. Storck arrives a few minutes later and Joy immediately says, "Storks really do bring babies!"

Dr. Storck smiles. "I used to be boring old Susan Smith in medical school. Good thing I married the right guy."

She has Joy lie down. She lifts up her shirt. With just her stethoscope, she traverses Joy's belly and after a few minutes, gives a smile. "You want to listen?" She places the earpieces near Joy's ears. Joy makes a silent O. I reach over to get the earpieces to my own ears. The baby's heart beats so fast, like it's running laps.

"The baby's heart begins beating at just three weeks," Dr. Storck says.

"Why is it so much faster?" I ask.

"Because it's much smaller in size," she says. "The heart of a marathon runner beats much slower than yours or mine because his heart grows during training."

I love learning stuff like this.

"Can you stand to have a pelvic exam?" Dr. Storck asks. "I know you've been through a lot, but I'll make it quick. It won't hurt the baby and we won't have to do it again until much, much later."

"I don't want to," says Joy. "Can I have another picture of my baby instead?"

"I think it's important to establish a baseline about what's normal for you, so I really need to check and see if everything is okay." Dr. Storck smiles at Joy. "And you will have another ultrasound in just two more months."

"But everything is okay," Joy insists, getting ready to scoot off the table.

Dr. Storck stays firmly by the end of the table. "I'm sure it is, sweetie, but I need to know how you're built so when the time comes to have the baby, I don't have any surprises."

Joy agrees. I hold her hand throughout. "We're in this together," I remind her, and she smiles. Dr. Storck is quick and efficient, pronouncing everything normal. There's no drama from Joy like at the abortion clinic.

"You did great, Joy!" Dr. Storck says. "Loretta will get a urine and blood sample, and then you'll be done here until the next visit."

I step outside with Dr. Storck when Joy gets dressed.

Dr. Storck doesn't waste any time in trying to understand the situation better. She wants to know what my plans are, if Dad is planning on being involved, if I can handle all this.

When I tell her that I'm applying to medical schools in the Midwest and the South, she tells me that I need to get in touch with a social worker immediately. "It will take some time to set up care-givers, and this is an unusual situation. You don't want to leave Joy in a lurch just after she's had the baby."

My heart sinks, my stomach rises. They collide. Why is it all left up to me?

121

~~~19~~~

I make a family appointment with Tessa a week later. Dad, Joy, Tessa, and I sit in the cool shade of a walnut tree but we're all stretched like thin rubber bands, ready to snap. We sip lemonade, something that Joy has discovered that she loves more than anything else since she got pregnant. Joy babbles like a five-year old, about the yellow daisies, the salamander she found beneath a rock, and the cutest baby socks with lace.

I use the socks as a cue and say, "Joy has big news to tell you." I already told Tessa about the baby when I arranged this meeting, but want Joy to have the pleasure of telling Tessa herself.

"I'm going to have a baby," Joy says, beaming. "Everybody is mad about it, but not me."

Dad grunts. He doesn't want to be here but I insisted.

Joy moves on. "I'm seeing Dr. Storck. Isn't that a funny name for a baby doctor?"

"You're pulling my leg," Tessa says, grinning.

"Nope." Joy chuckles. "The stork really does bring babies." She giggles uncontrollably.

Dad snaps. He's heard this a thousand times already. "Don't be an idiot!"

But she is. I will never forget that when I was a little kid somebody said Joy was an idiot. I argued that she wasn't, but the boy said to look it up in the dictionary. I did and found the truth: an idiot is a person with subnormal intelligence.

"This is not a matter to laugh over. Have you even thought about how exactly you're going to care for this baby? You'll be up in the middle of the night, changing diapers, washing bottles. And who's going to pay for all this?" I wish Dad wouldn't shout. All the neighbors can hear.

"How can I help?" Tessa asks, but directing her gaze towards Dad. "You have a good doctor. Are you thinking about …"

But Joy yells, "Never! I'll never get rid of my baby."

"I know. But how will you care for the baby once it is born?" Tessa's voice is soft and gentle.

Joy considers the future. "Babies sleep all the time. I can set up a big cage for it at work."

Dad almost chokes on his lemonade. "Joy, I'll have you know …"

"Let her come to the right conclusions, Shiv." Tessa interrupts Dad. She turns her attention to Joy. "But what about after? Babies want to crawl about, explore things, and put everything in their mouths. What then? How will you go to work and take care of the baby?" Tessa lets Joy think through the process, instead of making her feel stupid. Dad and I are not good at this. He's even impatient with Tessa, sighing and shifting in his chair.

"The baby can play with the animals while I do my work," says Joy. "Too bad we don't live on a farm like Diana. The basement at work is not so nice."

"That's right. It's not a good life for a baby to be stuck in a cage like an animal."

"Maybe Daddy can keep it in the office," says Joy.

Dad snorts. "Absolutely not."

"It's very clean," says Joy, as though that's the most important thing.

"But there's nothing there for the baby to play with," says Tessa. "Tell me, how do other mothers take care of their children?"

The process of getting Joy to understand is painfully slow.

"They stay home, like my mom. Or they get a babysitter." Joy takes big gulps from her lemonade and begins to pour another glass. She asks Tessa, "Do you have a babysitter?"

I wonder too. Tessa knows everything about us, but I don't even know if she's married or has children.

"No, I don't need a babysitter because I don't have children, but that's what I would do. You wouldn't like it if I brought along a bunch of kids to all my appointments, would you? I couldn't give proper attention to you." Tessa sips her lemonade.

"Oh, I wouldn't mind," says Joy. That argument backfired, for sure.

"I know *you* wouldn't," says Tessa. "But you still have to think of all the options and do what is best for the baby. You'd want that, right?"

Joy nods vigorously.

"So what are you going to do?" Tessa shifts the focus back onto Joy.

"I don't know," says Joy. "Mrs. Mendoza said we have lots of time to figure it out. The baby will come in April."

"We need to decide now so that you can prepare," says Tessa. "Your choices are to quit working and stay home with the baby, or hire a babysitter while you work. There's a third alternative too."

"What?" Joy leans forward.

"Adoption, and this might be the best …"

But Joy doesn't want to listen to Tessa anymore. "Never, never, never!" shouts Joy. She stomps into the house and slams the screen door, pinching Mel's tail. The cat yowls.

Dad thumps his glass of lemonade down hard, cracking the glass. "Great," he says, tossing the lemonade into the lilac bush. "And this was the conclusion you were going to make her arrive at by herself?"

"She simply has to get used to the idea," says Tessa. "It will take some time. Let's start the paperwork, so we can set up interviews with prospective parents."

Dad clenches his fists and shakes them. "What good is all this power of attorney if I cannot use it? Look, there is a shortage of newborns for adoptions. I know. This is why we went to India to get a sister for Joy," says Dad.

So it was never about me ever. It was all for Joy. And for that I'm supposed to be forever grateful? I am so angry my hand begins to shake. I put my glass down so that I won't drop it.

"Shiv," Tessa begins.

But Dad cuts her off. "Do what you must to convince her. I don't have the mental energy for this." He takes the cracked glass with him inside the house.

"I thought you were going to help us figure out child care," I say.

"Rebecca, I'm just doing what your father asked." Tessa finishes her lemonade.

Now I know that even though I set up this meeting, Dad is the one who calls the shots.

"You could help. You're adopted. You have a wonderful life here that wouldn't have been possible if your birth mother hadn't given you away," Tessa says.

"I wasn't given away," I correct Tessa. "I was abandoned."

"Yes, I know. But ..."

The screen door creaks open. Dad and Joy stand together, looking equally furious.

"Listen to Tessa," Dad says to Joy with gritted teeth.

"I did," says Joy. "I don't want to give away my baby."

"I know, honey." Tessa is so gentle with Joy. "But can you really take good care of a baby? Can you raise a child? Help with homework? Earn enough money? And all the things that go with raising a child?"

"Yes!" shouts Joy, stamping her foot for emphasis.

"Are you being honest with yourself?" Tessa asks.

"Okay. I don't know." Joy's voice is small. "But I have to try." Joy's eyes fill with tears. "I have to because I am the mother." She comes and sits by us.

I didn't realize how big Joy's sense of responsibility is until now.

"You are a good mother, Joy. And good mothers always do what is best for their child." Tessa scoots her chair closer to Joy's and lifts her chin up. "Tell me what is best for your baby?"

"God chose me to be the mother," says Joy.

Dad snorts.

"I love my baby," declares Joy, but in a small voice she adds, "Nobody else."

"It's true," I pipe up. "Dad and I both took her to have an abortion because we thought of the baby as a problem."

"But the baby is a gift from God," says Joy. "All babies are. That's what Mom always said."

Even Dad cannot argue with Joy. He fills the frame of the doorway even more when raising his hands upward. "Will you please ask your God not to send gifts we cannot care for?"

Tears roll down Joy's cheeks. "I want to keep my baby," says Joy. "Help me! Help me to care for my baby. Don't take away my baby."

I can't take this anymore. "Damnit! Joy is the mother, whether you like it or not. Who are we to rip her baby away from her? Adoption should only be considered if the mother gives up her child, but you shouldn't force a mother to do that. It's … it's …unnatural."

"Rebecca, you are adopted," Tessa reminds me again.

"Yes, but only because my birth mother thought she couldn't take care of me. Maybe she was too poor. Maybe she was unwed. But had she had support, she would've kept me. I know this. It isn't right to sever a family bond unless it's necessary."

"After all we've done for you, you're going to pine for your birth mother?" Dad asks.

"I'm not *pining* after her." I feel my ears growing hot with anger. "In fact, I never gave her much thought until now. I just think that for every family that adopts a child, there's a mother who is grieving the loss. Joy shouldn't have to go through that."

"So what do you propose?" Dad asks.

"Carry on. We get help. That's what Tessa is here for—to figure out childcare. Joy is the mother; you are the grandpa." I drain the last of my lemonade.

"And you are the auntie!" Joy squeals.

"Yes." But I hadn't quite thought it all through. What is the role of an auntie?

~~~20~~~

I am unprepared for classes even though I've had two weeks to get ready. All my time has gone into getting my applications to Detroit, Missouri, and Florida in order. That in itself feels like an accomplishment; however, it's not like I'll be telling Dad about the long essays to get a pat on my back. Thankfully, he has forgotten about it all with Joy's pregnancy eclipsing everything. He's been dealing with Tessa and it's about time he's shouldering some of the responsibility of Joy's care.

Instead of walking with Colleen, I drive to school. I have too many notebooks and binders to carry. Besides, I'm in no mood to discuss how Joy is doing. What about me and my plans? I don't like that almost overnight, she has become Joy's best friend. If Colleen had fur, she'd be Joy's BFFF.

Just last week, Colleen came over with a pretty little knitted hat and booties for the baby, handmade. "Yellow," she told Joy, "since you don't know whether it's a boy or a girl." Joy oohed and aahed over it, tying and untying the little green ribbons, and even testing them out on Buck, her stuffed wolf. Of course, it made me look bad because I have yet to get a baby-gift for Joy. And I'm the auntie! I don't feel like one though.

So instead of laughing and talking about all the classes we're taking, how we'll cut school when senioritis hits, and gossiping about cute boys, I'm all alone, thinking it's been the worst summer ever, and not knowing what the future holds.

Once I reach the hill to the high school, I see a few kids walking. Some are arm in arm. Best friends. Others are lovers, sharing a kiss.

I'm grateful to be able to drive and get to school early, to have some time to get organized before my first class—Advanced Chemistry.

I try the lab door and walk in. It's comforting to be in this familiar space, with its characteristic smell of acid and bleach. I rest my binder on the bench closest to the chemical room, facing the front door. It's my favorite spot, right up front, where I can see everything—the demos, the clock, the instructions on the white board.

Mr. Johnson comes out through the small room where he stores all the chemicals. "Rebecca, my girl! You look great!"

"Thanks," I say, showing him my arms. "The fractional laser got rid of the keloids."

He examines my arms and nods approvingly.

"Some of the seams of the old skin grafts are less visible. Of course, they can't do anything about the loss of pigment in areas, but I can always use some concealer."

"That's the right attitude. Listen, you're just in time to get me a maple bar from the cafeteria." He hands me a five.

I take the five and run to the cafeteria before it gets crowded. The students are milling about everywhere, shouting, screaming. There are so many hugs exchanged, it hurts to watch. Friends. Colleen is chatting with Kurt. I wonder if they'll be a couple this year. I'd walk over and say "Hi," except there are just too many people jostling about. I get the maple bar and head back to the science wing.

It's ten till eight and soon this lab will be full. I place Mr. Johnson's breakfast and three dollars in change on his desk and sit on my stool.

"So how was your summer?" Mr. Johnson asks, taking a bite of the maple bar.

The worst.

"Okay," I say. "I had the laser treatment first. After I recovered, I started working at the library and filling out applications for the BS/MD programs. You're supposed to send them a letter of recommendation."

"Done," he says. "Wayne State in Detroit, St. Louis in Missouri, Florida, right?"

"Thanks. I don't really know why I applied to Florida, though. Probably because it's farthest away."

He pauses eating and looks up. "Do you really want to be on the opposite corner of the country? It gets expensive flying back and forth for vacations."

"Maybe I don't want to visit."

"Ah yes. I forget teenagers want to be independent and away from parents." Mr. Johnson thinks I'm a normal teenager.

"It's more about not having to take on responsibilities," I say. "My dad doesn't want me to go and I haven't told Joy."

"What responsibilities? Why?"

I think about evading the whole issue, but he's the best mentor ever. He's the one who told me to look into the BS/MD programs. I can't keep secrets from him. "Joy is pregnant."

Of course, Dad forbade me to leave before Joy got pregnant, but now he'll chain me.

Mr. Johnson is quiet. I wonder what is going through his head. Finally he says, "That's got to be tough, kid. I can see why you want to get away from all this. How are you holding up?"

"Okay. Some days I don't even think about it, but when I do, I'm scared. I don't even know what kind of help to ask for."

Mr. Johnson looks at the door and the clock above it. "I wish we had time to talk, but it's almost time for class to begin. Remember that I'm here to help, okay?" He swallows the last of his maple bar, wipes his face with a tissue and asks, "Speaking of help, can you help me with General Chem.?"

"Depends if I can drop an elective," I say.

"What's fourth period?"

"Creative Writing."

Mr. Johnson shakes his head. "That's the one class you should not drop, Rebecca. Whether or not you realize it now, a writing class can only help your career. I'll ask someone else."

The door swings open and Sheldon walks in with tinted glasses. I've not seen him all summer and he doesn't look like he's been stuck in a lab at all. His skin is browned, and his hair bleached.

Mr. Johnson claps his shoulder. "So what's your fourth period looking like?"

"Mr. Berry's Creative Writing."

"You too?" Mr. Johnson laughs. "Well, whaddya know?"

Sheldon looks at me, confused. "I'm taking it too," I tell him. A thrill of excitement runs through me to be taking another class with him.

He puts his backpack across from me. I like this arrangement. We can look at each other over the tubes running across the shared vacuum and air spigots if we want. We might even share a meaningful conversation instead of just math or chem. notes.

Maybe this will be the year Sheldon and I will get to know each other again. There is a strangeness between us even though he knows I don't blame him for my burns. I've never forgotten the almost-kiss.

His friends—Kurt, Rocco, and Tom—walk in.

"Hey Sheldon." They only give me a nod.

"Hay is for horses," I whisper.

Sheldon smiles at me and joins them in talking about summer, surfing, and general silliness. They toss their backpacks in a row next to Sheldon.

"Spread out, guys." Mr. Johnson's voice booms in the lab. "Leave every other spot free so that each person will have more space for equipment. This isn't baby chemistry."

The guys groan. "Hey Sheldon, move over here," says Tom. They've staked out a square at the end of my bench.

"Nah," says Sheldon. "I like this spot."

I smile to myself. He's choosing me over them. He also cannot see Dana walk in wearing her low cut shirt and low slung jeans. She doesn't carry a backpack but like me, presses a three-ring binder to her chest. Except she has mountains where I have pebbles. When her pens clatter to the floor, she slaps the binder on the bench and bends over to retrieve the errant pens, showing us the tops of her large white breasts. The boys look and I watch them salivating over her. They palpate her breasts with their eyes. Kurt's whisper to Tom carries over to my ears. "I could go for that."

I hope Colleen doesn't go for Kurt. He might cheat on her.

I'm sure Dana heard Kurt but she acts unfazed. She wants to be looked at. She sits on a stool and faces the front of the lab. She chews her gum and tucks her very short and very black hair (blacker than mine) behind her ear.

Two more boys walk in and sit across from Dana, no doubt for the view. Another girl saunters in.

"Looks like you're all here," says Mr. Johnson, handing out goggles and black aprons to all. "Wear these at all times in the lab." He looks pointedly at Dana. "Cover yourselves. I don't want any burns and accidents in my lab."

All eyes automatically rivet to me.

Mr. Johnson goes over the safety features that we all know, then hands each of us a thin spiral-bound notebook, only it's not a blank book but one with protocols, a lab manual. He moves to the front and begins a lesson on making soap through a process called saponification. I hardly expected something like this to be our first class, since there's so much I've forgotten from last year, but I'm glad he's jumping into something interesting instead of making us do boring titrations.

I'm completely immersed in figuring out how soap-making works when Sheldon whispers, "Is it true?"

"What?" I'm confused. I look at the board and say, "Yes, you add a strong base to the fat."

"No." Sheldon shakes his head. "I heard your sister got … ahem …" He leans forward, pressing his elbows on the bench, causing his notebook to slide off the bench and to the floor. He's always dropping things.

"Pregnant?" I rasp back. "Yes, she's pregnant. What's it to you?" I swallow my bitterness. It's not like he's going to come and help.

"Whoa! Don't bite my head off. I just thought I'd check and make sure. I don't like rumors." Sheldon picks his notebook up off the floor.

"Well, now you know and it's true." I look straight at him. "Who told you?"

"Colleen."

Holier than thou Colleen! Just wait until I see her in class. I don't know why she's so nice to Joy if all she's going to do is gossip. My face becomes instantly hot.

I turn to my notebook and copy the remaining equations off the board. Sheldon and I don't exchange a single glance. It bugs me that he's not said a word about how much better I look. It's all about Joy. Always.

When the bell rings at nine o'clock, I gather my notes and wait for Mr. Johnson to dismiss us. "Tomorrow we'll talk about how salt precipitates the soap," he says. We hang our aprons on pegs and begin filing out of the lab. "Rebecca, wait a minute."

Now what? Some private chewing out? Mr. Johnson should have Sheldon stay back too, since he started it.

"Look. Kids are going to talk. You can't let it get to you. It'll die down, okay?"

Tears fill my eyes. He doesn't realize I cry not for Joy, but for how trapped I feel.

"What's your next class?"

"Calculus," I say.

Mr. Johnson steers me to the emergency eye wash. I remove my glasses and wash my face in the cold water. He hands me a towel. "Keep your cool, kid."

I manage to smile and race to Calculus. I'm not late since math and science are in the same wing, but the wiry teacher paces like a nervous tiger. I slip into the first seat next to the door. I want to bolt the way he's going back and forth, back and forth.

The teacher keeps looking at his watch. At exactly ten minutes after nine, he faces us, grins and begins speaking rapidly. "I am Dr. Rothschild and I come from the university to teach because this is a college level course. However, since you are in high school, I have decided that we'll have the typical four days of regular coursework Monday through Thursdays, but on Fridays we'll do fun applications."

Does this man ever take a breath? I'm tired just listening to him.

He walks to the board and says. "We begin. If you have questions, ask right away. Do not wait until the end of the class to tell me you understood nothing." He begins scribbling on the board as quickly as he talks and I write everything down furiously. I don't want to miss a single step.

A couple of kids laugh loudly in the hallway.

"What I wouldn't do for a shotgun some days," Rothschild mutters audibly enough. He smiles and winks to us, pretending to shoot a gun, "Ps-shoo!" just like a little kid.

Without breaking stride he walks to the door and slams it shut. Our first class goes quickly. No one interrupts because it's all pretty straightforward. I sure hope it makes sense when I go home.

At the end of forty-five minutes, Dr. Rothschild turns around. We are all still copying everything. "Can you make handouts?" Rocco asks. "I didn't catch everything."

"Handouts? There are no handouts in my class. I have no notes. Do you see any notes?" Dr. Rothschild waves his arms. "You will copy them from the board or from one of your classmates. Any other questions?"

I struggle to copy the last panel on the board. After I finish, I raise my hand. "Could you go just a little bit slower? It's hard to listen and write and understand at the same time."

"Miss?"

"Joshi. Rebecca Joshi," I say.

"In another year you'll be in college. At least I think so, if you're taking this class. What do you plan to major in?"

"Biology, microbiology, or chemistry." I gulp. "I'm applying to BS/MD programs." I have no idea why I'm blurting this out. I feel the heat rising to my cheeks.

"Well, then, Miss Joshi. You'd best learn to write fast because things will move a heckuva lot faster in college, particularly in medical school. This is a college course and I am here to show you what you can really accomplish in fifty minutes."

I slide down in my seat, and since I've already made a fool of myself, I decide to ask another question. "Can you give us an example of fun things we'll do on Friday?"

Dr. Rothschild smiles. "If you last the first four days, you will find out."

The class snickers. I walk out the door, confidence shaken.

135

~~~21~~~

The more I think about Rothschild, the madder I get. I'll show him. I'll show him what I can do in fifty minutes! I slam the gigantic calculus book into my locker and head towards Spanish. Colleen is already in the back, chatting—probably tattling—nonstop with a couple of girls. I glare at her but she's too busy to notice. I sit up front and thumb through the textbook, not seeing a single word. I'd like to sit next to her so that we could be paired up for the conversational part of the course, but there's only one thing I want to say to her and it will have to wait until after class.

Mrs. Rodriguez interrupts all conversation with a babble of Spanish. Class has begun. She talks about her summer, and I find it difficult to follow, but get the gist of it: she took a whirlwind trip to Europe in which she covered seven countries in fourteen days. She invites us to share something memorable about our summer in Spanish. The students speak haltingly about vacations, though some who live on farms talk about their animals. I think how much Joy would love to live on a farm with chickens and ducks, a couple of dogs, and a barn full of cats. But when it's my turn I don't mention Joy. I only talk about my job at the library, the smell of dusty old books, and buying new books. I neglect to tell them they're about burn recoveries or that I went to Seattle for my laser treatment. I'm not ready to roll up my sleeves yet and show them how nicely my skin is healing. Not that anybody cares; some are even yawning.

The hour goes by fast and as soon as the bell rings, students begin to leave the classroom. When Colleen passes me, I stop her.

"What's up?" she asks, as though she's innocent. "I saw you in the cafeteria this morning but you disappeared so quickly."

I come right to the point. "Stop talking about Joy."

"I ..." Colleen is surprised.

"Don't you deny it because Sheldon told me."

Colleen rolls her eyes at me. "He asked," she says, and starts walking away to her locker.

I scramble after her. "Why would he?"

Colleen whirls around. "Look, don't get all snotty with me. Sheldon cares, so he asked. Why should I lie? Everybody's going to know eventually. You can't keep it a secret forever."

"It's not your news to tell," I say. I don't care that she's right; I don't want her talking about Joy.

"What's the news?" asks Madison. Man, she has radar.

"News?" says Colleen, picking up her brown bag lunch. "Do you have news, Rebecca?"

"Oh, shut up," I say, wanting to slam both of them against their lockers.

I weave through the throng in the hallway towards my own locker. This time Colleen follows me. I grab my lunch and make my way outside. Colleen, though she has a Mexican dad, takes more after her Irish mother with perfect white skin and she wants to keep it like that so she won't be venturing outdoors.

She surprises me.

"Look," she says, grabbing my arm. "I'm on your side, you idiot. Don't you know that?"

"It sure doesn't feel like it," I say.

"You've got to quit being so sensitive." She steers me towards a shady spot. "We can't go through our last year thinking the worst of each other."

"But you blathered on about Joy."

"Did not."

"Did too." We start laughing. "You made me look bad," I say thinking about the booties and hat.

"You look bad without needing any help."

I hit her shoulder and we both crack up. "Yeah, you're right."

And just like that, school is so much nicer. I can deal with anything with a good friend like Colleen beside me. For the first time, we talk about Joy, my fears, and my dreams, and finally I feel my burden lightening.

We share our lunch and walk to our next class, Creative Writing. I turn toward Colleen. "You'll never guess who's taking this class." I don't wait for an answer. "Sheldon! Maybe I'll sit next to him. He's already across from me in Advanced Chem., so it'll be nice. I've never felt so fluttery before. Oh, shit, I'm babbling, aren't I?"

"He likes you, you know? This summer at the pool party, he asked about you before you got there."

"You never told me."

"I was a little …busy… you know, with Kurt. But I'm telling you now so you can catch up with him." Colleen smiles. "Why don't I disappear for a minute?" She dashes out the door as Sheldon approaches.

I take a seat near the middle, with both adjacent seats free.

But when Sheldon comes into the classroom, he scrapes a chair behind me. Drat! I won't be able to sneak peeks at him.

I turn around. "I never would've guessed you'd take this class."

He grins. "I wouldn't have guessed you'd be here either."

We both speak at once. "I took …"

"You first," says Sheldon.

"Colleen talked me into it."

He gazes at me, and I stay perfectly still. I wonder if he sees the girl beneath the scars. I watch him fiddle with his pencil absently until the tip breaks on the desk and the pencil falls to the floor.

"So what about you? Why are you here?" I wish I didn't sound so stilted, making small talk.

"I like to write," he says simply. "I've written songs and thought this might be fun."

"That's cool," I say. "So you're a poet or a songwriter or both or what?"

Sheldon laughs. "Or what. I just write dumb stuff. Nothing special."

I'm impressed. I didn't know Sheldon was a closet writer. I'm curious about the songs he's written. Has he ever written about us? Does he miss the girl I used to be? I wonder whether he'll ever invite me over to listen. He used to play clarinet, but I don't know if he's kept up with it.

I feel bold enough to say, "I'd like to hear you."

Sheldon opens his mouth to answer but Mr. Berry thumps his desk. I turn to see a stack of composition notebooks tremble. "Pick one. I expect all of you to write in this daily. Creative writing doesn't just happen in this classroom." He goes on and on about ideas being everywhere and how we're to write stuff in here all the time.

Someone asks, "Even in the bathroom?"

Mr. Berry doesn't admonish the student. Instead he scratches his beard and says, "Sometimes that's the only quiet space you'll get, so why not?"

Everyone laughs.

I pick out a sunshine yellow notebook even though red is my favorite color. I want something different. I want to be a different Rebecca. A Rebecca who talks to boys. A Rebecca who dares to write something scandalous in her notebook. I feel wild. This is what it must feel like to be intoxicated. You don't feel like yourself. You feel giddy. Is it Sheldon or the yellow notebook? I suppress the laughter building in my gut.

We are instructed to write for ten minutes without stopping. Mr. Berry whips out a black composition notebook and begins writing himself.

But I don't know what to write. Damage that beautiful yellow notebook with my thoughts? I open my binder and stare at the loose leaf blank papers. I decide to write there. This way I can crumple up anything bad. I'll save the notebook for good stuff.

Mr. Berry yells at us. "No stopping, people. If you have nothing to say, write: *I have nothing to write I have nothing to write*. Eventually something will come."

He walks over to my desk, opens my notebook, points to it and says, "Write in here."

"But ..." I want to explain, but he closes my binder.

"Everything goes in here."

And so I write in the yellow notebook. I write about feeling weird with Sheldon behind me. I'm so glad he can't see the scars on my back. I wonder whether he can smell the sandalwood oil I dabbed at the base of my neck. As the words flow across the page, I replay the scene of our near-kiss but make the ending perfect, with fireworks in the sky as the lovers seal their fate with a kiss. When Mr. Berry asks us to stop, I don't want to. I have so much more to say about everything—my burns, my future, Joy, Dad, and even Sheldon—I could write a saga. I think I'm going to like this class very much until Mr. Berry gives us our first writing assignment—My Summer.

Groan.

He couldn't come up with anything more creative?

~~~22~~~

I somehow get through the first few weeks of school even though there's some talk about Joy, especially from radar-girl Madison. I suppose word gets around in a small town like Pullman that Dad is interested in having Joy's baby adopted, and Madison takes great joy in saying, "Who'd want to adopt that retard?"

I try to let it go and not think about it, but it eats me up inside. Of course, it's only a rumor because there's no way to have an adoption unless Joy consents and she hasn't. Dad's plan is dead. It occurs to me how odd this is—a parent can make a mentally incompetent woman have an abortion against her will, but the state will not allow an adoption against her will. I'm glad for Joy's sake because I can't imagine the heartache of having to give up a baby you want.

~~~

I can hardly stand to be with Joy right now. It's baby, baby, baby all the time. We try to have meals together, but today I beg off, saying I have too much to study.

"You study too much," says Joy. "Come and eat."

"I'm not hungry," I say.

But Joy is persistent to a fault, bringing me a bowl of canned tomato soup. "*You* should bring *me* plates of food to eat. I'm having the baby. I need my rest and relaxation. But haven't I always watched over you? You eat this. It'll help you study. Can I stay here?" And without waiting for my answer she plops down on my bed and thumbs through my books, spread out all over.

I eat. The soup is too sweet, and I wonder if this is what Joy ate earlier. She's going to have to learn to care for herself and the baby soon enough, so I don't ask.

"You're so smart." Joy is looking at the calculus book and it must seem like a whole other language to her. "You'll be Dr. Joshi." She giggles.

"So?"

"So you won't have to listen to Daddy when you're a doctor."

"Wrong." I know better. I'll be under his thumb forever unless I get out of here.

~~~

I'm actually looking forward to calculus. I've been recopying my notes so that I understand everything and so far I've not run into any glitches. Rothschild assigns homework on Friday that has to be turned in on Monday. We're getting used to his fast-paced lectures. They're almost always peppered with laughter and he walks with a spring in his step. I've never met such a happy professor. He must eat, drink, and sleep this stuff the way he goes through all the theorems. Somehow I doubt he sleeps. He's like the Energizer bunny.

I stay up late both Friday and Saturday night doing my homework and wake up to Joy shaking me. I'm in a deep, deep sleep, dreaming of being a college student at Wayne. "What?" I ask.

"You promised me you'd take me to church today."

"I did?" I roll over and press my head into the pillow. I can't remember whether I did the last limit problem correctly. I stopped last night because I couldn't think.

"You promised." Joy's voice threatens to wail.

"Why don't you ask Dad?"

"He's already gone to work."

I lift my head to see what the time is and groan. It's past nine in the morning and the later service starts at ten. "Okay,

okay." I drop my head down into the pillow for a quick snooze. "Give me ten more minutes."

I wake up with a start and it's already quarter to ten. Oh, shoot. I hope Joy hasn't gone to Colleen's. Then it's one more thing I'm not doing right—taking Joy to church. How difficult can it be?

I grab my glasses and pad through the house in my chemise. Mel follows me, meowing. It's just as I thought. Joy's gone. Thank goodness Dad doesn't know what a great job I'm doing keeping track of her.

"Meow." I see that Joy has fed her already, but Mel always wants more. I reach down and Mel jumps to my shoulder, her back claws digging.

"Ouch!" I let her go and rub the places she's punctured my skin. It's not as puckered as it used to be, but my fingers know it could be a lot smoother.

I give Mel a teaspoon of canned food. She only nibbles a little bit, then leaps to the counter to lick the crumbs of toast. I let her have a bit of my banana as well. Her raspy tongue licks my finger clean. I pour a glass of orange juice and leaf through yesterday's newspaper.

There's news about the high school open house for people new to the area. I could tell them stories—most kids have known each other since kindergarten and if you're different, you'll be a target for all sorts of teasing. Prerequisite: thick skin. I wonder what brings people here, to the middle of nowhere, even if there's a university. I don't even know why Mom and Dad settled upon this place. They were at John Hopkins before. I wonder what they were trying to get away from. All our relatives are far away in India. But maybe they wanted a different life after Joy was born. I'll have to ask Dad someday.

I take a cool shower and put on my faded red-flowered skirt that Meena Auntie made for me years ago. She made a matching blouse, but instead of having short sleeves, she sewed long flowing sleeves with cuffs that keep them in place. I'm in a habit of being covered, and I don't know whether I'll ever be comfortable showing any skin. I'd make a good orthodox Muslim, as I imagine myself shrouded in black, with only my eyes visible through a black veil.

I do twenty sit ups, then hug my knees and rock back and forth, stretching my back. I can feel it getting stiffer and stiffer. I've not been religious about doing my exercises since school started, but I need to. It's what keeps me mobile.

I lug all my books from my bedroom to the dining table because it's so much nicer to work here, where it's light and airy, than my bedroom. Physics is a piece of cake. But the calculus is a challenge. I call Sheldon and we talk about how fun Friday's class was. Rothschild showed us how $e^{-\pi i} = 1$.

"I want to get a tee-shirt that says: I am # $e^{-\pi i}$," I tell Sheldon. Not that I'm number one at anything really, except being a freak.

Sheldon laughs. "Don't, you geek."

"You're right. I don't want to be labeled freak on one side, and geek on the other."

"Hey, you want to come over to Kurt's? We're going to do our homework sets together. Swim later."

"I can't. I need to be here when Joy comes home."

"Oh."

I can't tell whether he's disappointed or not. "I can try later. Maybe with Colleen."

"Sounds good. Hey?"

"Hay is for horses," I say before hanging up.

~~~

I finish all my limit problems by the time Joy comes home. She is humming the Gloria and looking cheerful. I'm immediately sorry and guilty for sleeping in. She loves going to church and singing and having doughnuts afterwards. Powdered sugar outlines her lips.

Joy complains that they don't have good tea there, only bitter coffee that tastes like medicine. She rummages in the cupboard, finally selecting a tea bag. I can smell the bergamot as she tears into the packet of Earl Grey.

"Are you sure you should be drinking so much tea? We don't want the baby to get all caffeinated." Suddenly I am conscious our need to watch what Joy puts in her mouth. There are so many things stacked up against this baby; I want to minimize any risks.

"It's just one cup." Joy pours the boiling water into her large Cougar mug. She leans over it, savoring the aroma, then adds a glob of honey. She takes a sip and sighs with pleasure. "I saw a mom with the best little carrier that looked like a spider. The baby bounced in it. Let's go shopping!"

"The baby doesn't need anything yet. Besides I still have a ton of homework to do."

"You never want to do anything with me!" Joy shoves my books off the table and they crash to the floor.

"And you wonder why," I say.

"Sorry," says Joy. "I just want to have fun. But you're no fun!"

I wish I'd gone to Kurt's after all now. But when I call Sheldon to see if I can bring Joy and Colleen over, he hesitates. He asks Kurt and I can hear his answer, "Not the weird sister."

I hang up.

I hate Joy sometimes, but right now I hate Sheldon even more.

~~~23~~~

I know that Joy gets lonely. I make a special effort to take her to St. James, the Episcopal Church Mom used to attend, on Sundays. I know she feels excluded not being able to have Communion in the Catholic Church when she goes with Colleen, even though she has explained very clearly that it's not a matter of excluding her, rather one of belief. "You have to believe everything the Catholic Church teaches and become Catholic before you can have His Body and Blood," Collen said. Joy pouted and said it's not fair, but obeys her. She doesn't listen to Dad though, about buying too many baby things.

I begin to notice baby stuff everywhere I go—strollers, sippy cups, slings and even diapers—and find myself making mental lists of what styles are the most practical or cute. Joy's baby-fever has infected me, just a bit.

It's hard to believe that two months have gone by so quickly. I've settled into a routine of being invisible and that's how I like it. Mr. Johnson was right. The students move onto talking about other things—football, homecoming, and who's going steady with whom. Colleen and Kurt are going together.

She goes home with him sometimes, so I walk home those days. I could take the bus, but I dislike the chatter. Walking alone gives me plenty of time to think. Even though she's my best friend, I cannot express all the conflicting emotions I hold in my heart. Colleen is too idealistic for me. She's had an easy life and so it's natural for her to think the world is rosy. And now especially so, since she's seeing so much of Kurt. I'm not pessimistic, but I've been pricked far too many times to enjoy the blossoms.

But Friday, when I expect Colleen to go with Kurt, she hollers at me as I wind my way around the tennis courts. "Rebecca, wait up!" She's breathless when she reaches me. "Kurt's busy. I'll walk home with you."

I look at my watch. "I'm not going home," I tell her. "Joy has an appointment, so I'll take the A bus."

"Is she okay?" Colleen is always so concerned about Joy, but she never stops to think that it's burdensome for me to make all these appointments and accompany Joy to them.

"Yeah, just routine stuff." I know that if I tell her that Joy is getting an ultrasound, she'd want to come, but this is the one appointment that I'm both anxious and excited about and I don't want Colleen to brush off my worries. They are legitimate. What if there's something wrong with the baby? I don't want to hear anything about God's plans. I'm the one who's going to have to deal with them.

"Come by later?" Colleen doesn't press me about the appointment as she waits with me at the bus stop.

"Sure." A half-guilty wave washes over me. I should be more open with Colleen; she's been nothing but a solid rock, but I have a difficult time dealing with her sparkle and sunshine attitude.

I pull my jacket closed. Winter will be here soon and with a heavy coat, Joy will be able to hide her pregnancy even longer. But how will she keep warm with a big stomach and a coat that doesn't go around her?

I watch the other kids waiting to go to the university. Friday evenings many go out to eat and catch a cheap old movie at the Cub. The last one I remember playing was Julie and Julia way back in the summer when Joy was seeing Nick. He's long gone now, with a new job and a new girlfriend too, I suppose. It irks me that he will not pay any child support.

147

Finally the A-bus arrives. I flash my bus pass and the lady driving asks, "How are you? I haven't seen your sister in a while. Is she okay?"

"She's fine, thank you." I wish people wouldn't worry so much. Joy hasn't been taking the bus since school started because it's so much easier to catch a ride with Dad. But his words echo in my head: *look where all this independence has gotten us.*

I get off at the hospital and walk up the hill. I told Joy to meet me here at quarter to four but there are still twenty minutes to go. I sit in a sunny spot and watch the people walk by. Most are young, but there are older people too—some are clearly faculty with their nicer clothes, but others are students carrying heavy packs. The air is filled with the happiness of a weekend and I wish I could be one of these college kids. I dare to imagine that next year I'll walk with a new best friend to the dorm, in a new place, free from Dad's rules and Joy's demands.

Joy interrupts my reverie, her handbag swinging. "Hurry! I have to pee." Poor Joy. I go directly to Imaging Services.

Stephanie, the technician, escorts us to a room. It's dim but not dark. The room is cramped like in Kennewick, but it doesn't feel ominous. Joy keeps shifting her weight in a classic I-need-to-pee dance.

"Hop up here, dear," says Stephanie. "I'll be quick and we'll have the best pictures of the baby; then you can go pee." I wonder how many times women have peed on that table.

Joy lies down and Stephanie asks her to lower the waistband of her pants and underwear. Joy willingly pulls them down past her hips; even her pubic hair peeks out. Stephanie adjusts the monitor so Joy can also see the screen. She rubs the gel onto Joy's stomach. Underneath the fat, I can see that there's a certain firmness that she didn't have before.

Stephanie presses the wand over Joy's gelled belly and soon a very human picture emerges on the screen.

It no longer looks like a shrimpy alien. The baby has skinny little arms and legs and fingers that open and close. The head is enormous compared to the rest of the body. It has features— a pug little nose, huge eyes, a pointy chin. I swear I see teeth! The baby's spine is perfectly defined. Joy is riveted to the screen just as I am. We both say, "Look, how cute!" when the baby gives us a thumbs up. Then the thumb goes into the mouth. Out again.

Stephanie points out the heart. "It's fully formed," she says, taking a closer look. "Everything looks good here," she declares. I can clearly see all four chambers and how they squeeze and pump in synchrony. It's truly a marvel how from a collection of unspecialized cells, you get cells that organize themselves into a beating heart. Dr. Storck told us that the heart starts beating at three weeks! Some women don't even know they're pregnant yet. Maybe they think their period is late but the baby's heart is already beating. And to think I told Joy in Kennewick that her baby was just a bunch of cells. I don't realize I'm crying until Joy wipes the tears from my cheeks.

"Isn't she beautiful?" whispers Joy in awe.

I nod and smile through my tears. Yes, the baby is beautiful as it moves around freely in Joy's womb. I'm surprised at how fat the umbilical cord is—as big as or bigger than the leg. The baby is tethered to the cord but never gets tangled. It somehow knows how to move in this space. But how does Joy know it's a girl?

Stephanie seems to anticipate my question as she concentrates on the private parts. "No penis in sight."

"It's a girl!" Joy shouts. "I've always wanted a girl baby."

Stephanie smiles. "I have the best job ever." She focuses on the baby's abdomen and shows us the stomach and liver and the teensy kidneys. She scans up and makes more measurements on the head.

Stephanie zooms out so we can watch the baby swim around a bit more. She tells us this ultrasound session is recorded on DVD as she wipes Joy's stomach clean.

"Really?" Joy has the biggest smile ever. The baby isn't even born yet, but already starring in a movie.

Joy rushes to the ladies' room to relieve herself. I watch Stephanie as she works efficiently to get some prints of memorable moments and file a report to the doctor.

"Is everything okay?" I ask.

"Oh, yes. The baby is growing just as she should be." Stephanie smiles.

"What happens if everything isn't perfect?"

"It's devastating. But early detection means we can have a neonatal team ready to operate when the baby is born. Specialists can also perform fetal surgery if it's necessary for its survival."

"Wow!" I am amazed at how ultrasound technology can save lives. Of course, in India and China, this same technology is used to abort girl-babies. I'm not sure how that's any different from infanticide now. Where do you demarcate the line when it's okay to kill a human being? I realize how much we've slipped down the slippery slope of devaluing life.

Stephanie must realize I'm anxious because she allays my fears. "Don't worry; everything is perfectly fine with the baby."

Joy bursts into the room and Stephanie hands her a DVD along with some still shots and reminds us to go see Dr. Storck right away.

"Thank you, thank you so much!" Joy is ready to kiss Stephanie.

I'm relieved there's nothing horribly wrong with the baby, but I worry that if the baby has developmental delays, we won't know until she starts growing up, just like Mom and Dad discovered with Joy.

We go to Dr. Storck's office, Joy exuberant.

The doctor is happy with the results and tells Joy to keep taking good care of herself. When she asks if we have questions, I jump at the chance to make a suggestion. "Shouldn't we do some genetic testing to make sure absolutely everything is okay?"

"No more tests," says Joy. "I want to go show Daddy."

"You go ahead," I tell her. "I'll meet you there."

Joy walks out with a jaunt.

Dr. Storck puts her arm around me. "Relax, Rebecca. There is no history of any intellectual disability in your family— Joy's condition is truly an anomaly. Your father told me about the results when they discovered Joy's delayed development," Dr. Storck says. "The baby's fine."

"But what if ..."

"You worry about what ifs when the time comes," says Dr. Storck. "There are no guarantees with babies. Perfectly healthy babies can develop terrible diseases later in life or have accidents. You can't go through life worrying about everything that can go wrong."

I burst into tears without warning. I was perfect too!

Dr. Storck gathers me to herself and rubs my back. "I know you've endured a lot of pain and it's natural for you to want everything to be just right. It's hard not to worry when the situation isn't ideal. But the baby is growing beautifully. Everything is going to be okay."

"Thank you."

"Will you be alright?" Dr. Storck asks.

"Yes, please don't let me bother you anymore."

"It's no trouble, Rebecca. We'll make sure social services is right on top of this case. Okay?" Dr. Storck pats my shoulder.

I wash my face, focusing not on my beginnings, but those of Joy's baby. She's fine. She's beautiful.

I run to catch up with Joy.

She is heading straight down the hallway into Dad's lab, waving the pictures around. "Look! Look!" she shouts. "Where's my daddy?"

A student says he's in the dark room before going to his own work-bench.

Joy plants herself on the nearest stool and lays out the pictures on the bench. When Dad comes in, she gives a large smile. "There's Grandpa!"

"Joy, how many times have I told you to wait in my office?" Dad is annoyed seeing the sonogram pictures spread out.

"I also have a movie!"

"Later, Joy, later." Dad makes her gather the pictures and steers her out of the lab and into the office, across the hall. "Rebecca, you know better."

"Everything's normal. Why can't you at least look?" I ask. That man drives me crazy with all his devotion to his students, poring over their every stupid X-ray, but not caring to see the first pictures of his own granddaughter.

That's when it hits me. Dad cannot think of himself as a grandfather until the door to adoption is closed completely. He still must be thinking up ways to put the baby up for adoption, even though Joy has made it clear she will not give up her baby.

"Can I play the movie, Daddy? Please?"

"Fine. I just need to wrap up some stuff and I'll be in the office." Dad leaves and Joy pops the DVD in the computer. We watch Joy's baby tumble around in her womb several times, but Dad does not return except to lock up.

Joy is extremely chatty on the way home and Dad's unusually quiet. He doesn't even say "uh-huh" or "mmm" or nod in understanding. When Dad parks the car, Joy takes my backpack and orders me to go get Colleen. "Let's all watch my movie."

Dad groans.

~~~

I knock on the Mendoza's door and let myself in. "It's me, Rebecca," I sing, my nose directing me to the kitchen, not from the delicious smells of churros or flan baking, but from the characteristic smell of paint and turpentine. Colleen must be in the middle of an art project; she's making cards. Some have a painting, others have a collage. There are a couple with papers folded intricately.

"Is this one for Joy?" I point to a card with the silhouette of a very pregnant woman with a paper baby folded in the circle of her belly.

"Do you think she'll like it? It's a practice card for when she's due."

"Oh, yes. She loves everything you've made for her—the booties, the cap, the mittens— and she'll love this card." I accept a glass of pink lemonade from Mrs. Mendoza. "When you're done, come and watch the movie Joy brought home."

"Don't tell me. It's about some pregnant teen keeping her baby." Colleen rolls her eyes.

"It's better." I grin like an idiot. "You should come too, Mrs. Mendoza." I know exactly how Joy feels—joyous at this miracle made visible inside her. Mrs. Mendoza has always been here for us and she'll be the constant when I leave. I want to include her in all the significant moments of Joy's life.

Colleen looks up from her work, confused. I know she can sense somehow that I'm different. I cannot explain it either, but I do feel more relaxed about Joy's baby.

So I sit and wait for Colleen to finish up her painting while Mrs. Mendoza shreds some carrots for a cake. I admire Colleen's cards. She's got a cute one with a dog and a hole cut out for its tail. I slip my finger through the hole and wag it; something so ridiculously simple makes me laugh. Colleen laughs too.

Before we know it, Joy is knocking on the door, barging in with her hands on her hips. "You are taking forever," she complains. "I'm waiting and waiting and Daddy only wants to read the paper. He keeps saying 'in a minute, in a minute.'" She hands me the DVD. "I brought the movie here."

I take the DVD and hug her to myself. "Daddy doesn't know what he's missing."

Colleen and her mom wash up, the cards and carrots forgotten temporarily. We sit in the living room and Colleen's eyes grow round with surprise when she pops the DVD into the player and looks at the label: *Joshi baby 18 wks*. "Oh," she whispers.

We settle down to watch the clip of Joy's baby. I find myself comparing the images now to the one burned in my memory forever, that of the baby at 6-7 weeks. And it hits me again that shrimp-like creature was—*is* human—not just a potential human.

People use the word 'awesome' without really understanding it. Joy's baby is awesome! Joy is awesome. I don't understand how someone who is so "simple" can have such wisdom. Why did I not recognize it was a baby in there? Or I knew, but decided to call it a bunch of cells so that I wouldn't feel bad about getting rid of her. Never again. I will never again think that a fetus is disposable. My heart overflows with gratefulness knowing Joy's baby is alive and I had a part in keeping her safe.

Joy gives the commentary about the heart and liver and stomach. And how the baby's eyes are closed shut right now but they can sense light and dark through her stomach. "She's no longer a bean baby," says Joy, "but a pickle."

Everyone laughs. "You are so lucky," says Mrs. Mendoza. "I've had six babies and I never knew a thing until the baby was born. It was always a surprise."

"You never had an ultrasound?" asks Joy.

"Oh I did, but I told the technician not to tell me whether it was a boy or girl. Only for the last baby, I knew, but that's because they also found he'd need a transplant right away." Mrs. Mendoza becomes quiet as she remembers. This is the baby that died; he had heart problems that couldn't be fixed.

But she pores over the printed pictures of Joy's baby. My favorite is what Joy has dubbed: thumbs up!

"C'mon," I tell Joy. "Let's go show *Grandpa*." We erupt into giggles.

~~~24~~~

We almost always have our first snow by Thanksgiving so it feels right on schedule when big, beautiful snowflakes drift to the ground on my way home from the school the second week of November. I raise my palms to catch them and watch them slowly melt and I can't help but stick my tongue out to feel them landing ever so softly like butterflies. By nightfall, a thin blanket of white covers everything. I can barely see the blades of grass poking through.

I love walking in fresh snow. Even though we only got a couple of inches, I already see snowmen in some of the yards and the path the snowball took as it came to its final resting place.

~~~

"Aaaaiiiiieeeeee!" Joy screams as she slips on the ice and lands on her bum. The little bag of fruit she insisted on holding slips from her hand and apples and oranges roll away in the parking lot of Dissmores.

"Are you okay?" I ask, holding out my hand. She gets up, but her feet are beginning to slip, so I let go of the cart and support her. She regains her balance and I leave her momentarily as I run after my cart that is headed for a car.

I grab the cart moments before it makes contact with the back end of a Neon and steer it to my Civic. Whew!

Joy is trying to gather her errant apples. She suddenly doubles over, dropping the apples and supporting her protruding stomach.

"What's wrong?" I walk her to the car slowly. Joy has tears in her eyes, but it's the look of pain in her frown that scares me.

"I think I just peed," says Joy.

"That's okay." I don't say how gross it is. "We're going home, so you can clean up soon."

I leave her in the car and put away the grocery bags, then examine the dropped fruit. The apples are too bruised. Let some crow eat them. I collect as many oranges as I can.

I'm not gone more than five minutes, but when I get ready to drive, Joy rocks back and forth. "Buckle up," I say, but she ignores me. I do it for her and notice she's lost the color in her cheeks.

"We're going to the hospital," I announce, a sick feeling developing in my own stomach.

Joy doesn't respond. I'm afraid she's losing the baby, and probably bleeding. I cannot believe a fall can be so dangerous. Maybe they can stop it—plug her up or something.

I drive as though I'm in a race on Stadium Way. Thank goodness I don't get pulled over for speeding. I park illegally and half carry, half support Joy into Emergency. I place her in a chair and go to the front desk. "Quick, please. She fell. She might lose the baby."

The triage nurse is efficient and before I can even sit with Joy, she has orderlies place Joy on a gurney and whisk her away. I stay to fill out paperwork. It doesn't take long. I park my Civic in the parking lot. I call Dad. I'm betting he'll be overjoyed that the problem is solved. No more baby.

"What's up?" Dad asks.

"Joy fell. Come to the hospital. She might lose the baby."

Dad is quiet. "I'd only get in the way," he says. "There's no sense in pacing at the hospital when I have a mountain of work to do. Call me when you get a firm opinion from the doctor."

"Don't you care?" I yell into the phone.

"Of course I do. Call me if Joy wants me to come over, okay?"

I shut the phone off. I can't decide if I'm over-reacting to Dad's complete nonchalance, or if this is the way he deals with trouble. When I ask to go be with Joy, the nurse says I'm not allowed yet.

I browse through the magazines on the corner table. *Family Fun* catches my eye because it has a young pregnant model reveling in her very pregnant state as a toddler presses a chubby finger into her rotund stomach. Everybody is so happy. Why can't our family be happy? Why can't Joy show off her growing baby belly? I bet that model has a husband and a supportive family. But when I read the article, it's about single parenting—how single mothers juggle the world of work and home and sitters. I don't know how Joy is going to cope. Would it be better for her to lose the baby and suffer grief for a short time or have a burden for caring for a child? Maybe I am more like Dad than I care to admit.

A nurse comes out into the waiting area. She smiles at me. "You can go see Joy now. She's resting and baby is fine."

I immediately feel guilty for even having a thought otherwise.

"She's bleeding a little and we'll be transferring her to maternity for a day or two, until it's under control, but don't worry. A week or two of bed rest is all she'll need."

Tears well in my eyes and when I see Joy, I'm flooded with relief.

~~~25~~~

December brings an ache with it because Christmas just isn't the same without Mom. Last year, we did all the things we used to do—bake cookies, hang up lights, set up the crèche—and even more, hoping the emptiness would disappear, but the pit in my heart grew bigger. Halfway through stringing lights on the gutter, I gave up. Joy cried. I cried. We held each other. Dad said he wished he'd bought tickets to go back to India but he didn't want everybody to feel sorry for us. Besides it was too late to buy reasonably priced tickets. You'd think he'd have bought some for this Christmas, but no. Mom used to arrange our trips to India.

So when Meena Auntie calls, we know there's either a wedding or a funeral scheduled. I'm unprepared when she tells me that their mom—our Aji—has had a series of small strokes. "Tell that big brother of mine to get here pronto, not in his next life. And make sure he brings you two as well."

Orders are orders, so I tell Dad. He listens. He calls Meena Auntie to confirm what we've told him. His mom may not be around much longer. She may die instantly like Mom, or she will deteriorate with time. We've got to go now.

But he balks. "Are you crazy? We can't take Joy in this state. She's showing."

"So we're never going back then? It's not like the baby is going to disappear."

"Of course not. Once everybody gets used to the idea we can go back. Can you imagine all the criticism, the name calling, the gossip?" Dad voices my own fears, but they are small compared to the sorrow of never seeing Aji alive. She may not be here much longer.

"And Aji?" I ask Dad. "You don't want to see your mother one last time? I would." Unshed tears prick my eyes. I miss Mom. I think of the first time Aji saw me after the burns, nearly two years later, and how she taught me to be grateful for my life. I learned about the practice of sati, where widows were burned upon their husbands' funeral pyres. She made me aware of women and children who suffered much more—the children maimed by pimps, the brides burned for perceived slights against their husbands, the immense poverty. My emotional recovery began with Mom, but Aji helped me to step outside myself. I was able to press coins into the hands of a begging child, or give away bowls of food to the poor who had just a cardboard box to call home.

Aji's patience outmatched Mom's. She taught Joy so many things, like knitting, sewing buttons, and cooking, that even Mom couldn't. Aji gave us all hope.

"I want to see Aji before she dies." Joy is clear as can be. "Meanie Auntie is right."

"Don't call your auntie mean," says Dad.

But Joy and I glance at each other with laughing eyes. Meena Auntie isn't soft like our mom. Meena Auntie doesn't know the meaning of the word soft. She's hard and unyielding, and always gets her way.

~~~

So here we are! I couldn't have done all the organizing and packing without Mrs. Mendoza and Colleen. Poor Colleen, she's never been out of the country and wishes she could take a trip anywhere. "Even Canada would do, since it's closer," she said. I know she longs to visit Mexico, but she no longer has family there. All her living relatives are in California, Oregon, and Washington.

160

I take this ease of being in places completely different than Pullman for granted. I've been to Mexico and Belgium and Italy with my family. Dad had to go to scientific conferences and would take us all along. Mom, Joy, and I always had a blast experiencing new foods and customs.

Outside the airport terminal, the warm, humid air of Mumbai is a shock to my system after the dry and ice of Pullman. My skin literally begins soaking in the moisture, and the smell of earth rekindles ancient memories within me—of being in a stroller, stepping in cow dung, of being with hundreds of children.

Some poor and frightened woman gave birth to me on this soil. I'll never know who she is, whether she's alive and happy now or if she's still in a miserable situation. I like to imagine her with a good husband and healthy children. I wonder if she still aches for the infant girl she gave away. How I wish I could tell her someone rescued me, that I live in America, the land everybody dreams of. What would she think about the burns and me now though? I swallow a lump.

Skinny brown men jostle each other, trying to get attention to carry luggage. A girl, younger than me, carries a basket of fruit on her head. Had no one adopted me, I would probably share her fate. I go forward and press a dollar bill into her hand. She smiles widely at me as I choose two sugar apples—*sitafal*—from her basket. The lumpy green skin is blackened in places and the fruit has just the right squishiness. I feel so comfortable here, like I belong. My facial features more closely resemble the darker Indians, like those of the fruit-girl. I am thin and angular, not fair and soft like Joy, and the richer Indians.

Joy is delighted with my purchase and ready to eat the sitafal right away. I have to remind her how messy it is, that we should wait until we get home.

We find Meena Auntie in the crowds. The first thing she says is, "I don't know why you always come in the middle of the night." She gives us a big hug and tells me I need to eat more. She tells Joy not to be a piggy.

Joy is getting ready to open her mouth to tell Meena Auntie the truth, but must've remembered Dad's instructions to keep quiet and closes her mouth. Another dumb fish moment. Since she's chubby, people can mistake her baby bump for fat.

The first thing we do after we arrive in Meena Auntie's apartment is wash up and tear the sitafals open. We sit at the Formica table and make a mess scooping out the sweet white pulp, spitting out black seeds.

"How much did you pay for those?" Meena Auntie asks.

"A dollar," I say.

"For that, you should've gotten the whole basket of fruit! Do you realize what the exchange rate is?" Meena Auntie is so practical.

"Thirty rupees to the dollar," I answer. "And the smile on the fruit-girl's face was priceless." I dig into the pulp. I could eat an entire basket of these.

We finally crawl into bed at five in the morning. It feels so good to stretch out. Joy and I sleep together and for the first time I feel her baby kick. Oh! I wonder how Joy can sleep through this because if I press my hand into Joy's side, the baby kicks again. I remember the ultrasound movie, how the baby waved and sucked her thumb, but I couldn't have believed it was such a vigorous kick.

I inch closer to Joy and she places her hand over mine and moves it in a circular motion where I'd touched her just moments before. The baby quiets down. Joy instinctively knows how to take care of her.

It's noon when Meena Auntie shakes us awake. "Enough sleeping for now. You can sleep tonight."

162

I take a warm shower. The spray isn't as strong as at home, but still it revives my groggy brain. I check out all the cool stuff in the bathroom. I like the lotion that smells of roses. I dust my armpits with the talcum powder even though I cannot sweat, at least my left armpit, since all those glands were burned off. I notice how contracted the skin is there, and in need of repair, but I'll wait until after school ends. I'm still growing. Good thing I always cover my shoulders. I love Indian clothing because it hides my scars so well. All people see are my face, hands and feet. And although the skin grafts on my hands are creepy (my palms have pigment), I'm grateful Mom made me wear those compression gloves all those months to prevent contractures from developing in my hands. The wispy *chunni* that Indian women drape around their necks doesn't cover mine completely, but people don't look at necks that closely. I wish I'd feel more comfortable wearing these in Pullman, but I don't. They draw attention to me, given their costume-y nature.

The front room is full of chattering relatives from my Dad's side of the family. I wish Aji were home. I wish we could take her back with us, though she probably prefers being here, with all her kids and grandkids visiting her daily. She'd said she likes the sound of Indian chaos over American orderliness.

The moment I step into the living room, I am crushed with hugs and kisses. They are not freaked out by my scars even though they look at me with great curiosity because there's always some reconstructive surgery I've gone through since the previous visit. The youngest cousins who don't remember me stay close to their mothers. But the older ones hold my hand. They know I have presents for them—windup toys, Mt. St. Helen's ash, tee-shirts and bouncy balls that hit the ceiling. But when Joy enters the living room, the kids all run to her, my presents forgotten. She'll play with them all day.

"Where's Dad?" I ask.

"He went to the hospital first thing," says Meena Auntie.

"Without us? When will we get to see Aji?"

"Don't worry," says Meena Auntie. "Here, eat some *jilebee*." She thrusts a bowl full of the saffron-colored fritters dripping with syrup. I don't ordinarily have a sweet tooth, but a whiff of cardamom makes my mouth water.

So in typical Indian fashion we get sugared up with tea and sweets from the street vendor. I have two jilebees to the approving looks of my aunties. They probably want to feed me the whole bowl given how skinny I am. I lick my sticky fingers whilst everybody talks nonstop at the same time.

I escape to the kitchen and wash dishes but Meena Auntie follows me soon after, telling me it's not polite of me since I am a guest for just a few days. Besides, they have a *bai*, an old woman, who comes to do the wash. And what will she do if there are no dishes to wash? I'm led out into the cacophony.

Everybody wants to know the details of how we manage our life without Mom. It's hard to explain. We do all the same things, but there is an emptiness nothing can fill. I concentrate on the future and my plans to go to medical school someday. I don't mention the BS/MD program.

"Good, good." They bobble their heads and declare what a joy it must be for Mom and Dad to have a smart girl like me, and lament how hard it's been for them to have a child with special needs like Joy. Their voices blend together:

"Aiii, how will they marry her off?"

"They couldn't tell she was going to be dim before the birth?"

"Here they do lot of screening. Heart disease, water on the brain, all kinds of things."

"Even sex selection."

Of course, I know all about how every family wants to have a boy first. In the villages, girl babies are often left to die. But my birth mother loved me enough to put me in a cardboard box and leave me where I'd be found. I wonder whether it was something simple as my mother not wanting a girl or whether the situation was more dire—perhaps I was the tenth child and everybody was going hungry. They couldn't afford another mouth to feed. Or maybe my mother was a beautiful young woman raped by a ruthless bandit. Whatever the cause, she didn't want me. But at least she didn't deny me my life.

Everyone marvels at my good fortune. I remember Mom telling me how all the relatives advised against adopting. "You don't know what you're getting." Well, they were right. I could've been as insensitive as any of them here.

The talk switches to what kind of doctor I should be. For women, they feel gynecology and pediatrics are the best specialties. "No woman likes to go to a male doctor."

"Actually, I want to specialize in trauma and burns," I say. "I can give hope to others."

"Wah! Wah!" they say.

I soak in the applause.

Bam! The front door slams against the wall as Anjali, my littlest cousin, comes running through. She shouts, "Mummy! Guess what? Joy is going to have a baby and I'm going to be an auntie!"

~~~26~~~

Meena Auntie grabs Anjali's skinny arm. "Don't make up stories." But she glances at me, daring me to deny it. Perhaps it occurs to her that Joy isn't just plump.

"Actually, Anjali is right," I say, squeezing my eyes shut. "I'm going to be an auntie, too."

A silence never heard before comes upon this room. I can hear the air passing through nostrils.

Anjali breaks the silence with: "I told you! I'm going to be an auntie!" She is so pleased with herself as though she had something to do with it. "When will the baby come?"

"Soon. In April," I say.

"Hai Ram!" One of the aunties gasps for air. "The scandal! If your mother were alive this would never have happened. Isn't anybody watching over that poor child?" She pats her chest like she's having a heart attack. Good God. Whatever made us think that Joy could keep this a secret? For two weeks at that. Our vacation is ruined. And as always, Dad is away from the heat. I'm the one who's in the middle of the fire. Well. I. Am. Done.

I slam that same door shut behind me as I race down five flights of steps to confront Joy. "You were not supposed to tell," I say with gritted teeth, "but since you did, you can go answer all the aunties. I am not doing it."

"But the baby was kicking." Joy is all innocence. "See?" She takes my hand and places it over the side of her bulge and I can feel the kick. "I'm so happy!"

I know she is. I'm the one who's miserable. "Good! Now go talk to the aunties!"

We plod upstairs and the chattering stops immediately. Joy has all the aunties feel her stomach and they marvel at the kicking baby as though it's the first one ever. Then the questions and comments come rapid-fire, leaving Joy confused.

"How did this happen?"

"What will you do with the baby?"

"The scandal!"

"Too late for abortion."

"Will you give it up for adoption?"

Finally, Joy shouts over them all. "She's my baby! I'm keeping my baby!" Her eyes glitter with angry unshed tears. She stands feet apart, ready to fight. I've never seen her like this before and I am proud of her. Suddenly, huge tears make a path down her face, splashing her pretty top.

"This baby did not get the most auspicious start," I begin before I am interrupted again.

"Who is the father?"

"Why he's not marrying her?"

"No father and a retarded mother. Hai Ram!"

"Stop right there!" I shout.

The aunties stop. They shoo the little kids out of the room.

"We are only concerned, *beti*," Ritu Auntie says. "There is no need to shout at your elders."

"You have a funny way of showing it," I say. "Now you know why we didn't want to tell you. You're so, so ...." I don't have words.

"Mean." Joy has the perfect word.

"We worry," says Meena Auntie. "Even though I have a good job, I would not want to raise a baby on my own."

"That was my thinking too," I say. "I took Joy for an abortion," I confess. "But Joy has loved this baby from the moment she knew of her. She has never, ever wavered, or thought about her own self. Granted, this baby did not begin her life under ideal circumstances, but that doesn't mean she's going to have a rotten life. She has a great future." And as I say it, my own fears about how we are going to care for the baby begin to dissolve. "I think perhaps we worry too much, instead of taking joy."

"You have a youthful optimism," Meena Auntie says. "We worry because we've experienced the hard life."

"And you can't think of a single good thing?" I ask.

"Well, it's not going to be easy, that's for sure," Meena Auntie says, her eyes full of incomprehensible sadness, her shoulders sagging as if she were bearing the entire weight of raising Joy's baby.

I take Joy's hand. "Come on."

We leave as we came in, the door slamming behind us. The aunties' shrill tones indoors create an air of disharmony. No doubt they are discussing how rude I am and how foolish we are. I can see where Dad gets his bad temper from. It runs in the family. We hurry down the steps and into the warmth of the winter sunshine.

"We are in big trouble," says Joy.

"So what? It's not like they are going to take care of the baby, so I don't know why they can't just say something nice. If you were married ..."

"...and not retarded," Joy adds.

I wince. "Yeah, they'd be excited and happy. I guess we shouldn't be too hard on our aunties. Remember how mad I was when I first found out? And Dad? He exploded!"

Joy laughs. "Just like Mt. St. Helens."

People stare at us. We are laughing till our bellies hurt. There is nothing funny about any of this, of course, so I have no idea why we're acting so crazy.

"Let's go to Juhu beach," I say. I'm not often spontaneous, but this seems like a great afternoon to feel the sand beneath our toes and eat some spicy snacks from the vendors. "I'll go get my purse."

I am no longer angry and I know the aunties will come around to Joy's way of thinking just like I did. Time. That's all it takes. And a bit of wisdom.

Joy follows me and is immediately engulfed by the aunties. I go to the bedroom to escape the noise. The chattering in the apartment is awful. Everybody is eager to place blame. Something is wrong and it shall be made right. At what cost? Who will pay the price? Obviously not the aunties. They criticize but have no intention of taking care of Joy and her baby. No. I'm to be the sacrificial lamb. My name pops up far too many times.

Thank goodness I didn't tell them specifically about Wayne. All I would've heard is how selfish I am to even consider going so far away when Joy needs me. I know I was adopted so that Joy would have a caregiver for the rest of her life. No, they wouldn't actually call me a caregiver. But a "sister." I am to be my sister's keeper. It's the only explanation. Did it ever occur to them that I might want to do something else with *my* life?

I don't want to go the beach with Joy and pretend that everything is okay. Instead I call Dad. He doesn't answer, so I leave him a text: *Cat out of bag.*

I lie down on the bed, and watch the ceiling fan turn the stale air. I hear snippets of Joy recounting her failed romance with Nick. The aunties cluck, alternately scolding and babying her. Joy does have a way of invoking sympathy, and she does it without a fight.

It strikes me that Meena Auntie sacrificed her own life when I got burned. With me in Harborview long term, Dad needed someone to be with Joy in Pullman. Meena Auntie came. I don't know what she gave up. Her job, for sure, but also her friends and family. She didn't just come for a month

169

or two, but an entire year. She was cheerful and competent, never once acted resentful towards me for doing such a stupid thing as getting burned.

I wake up feeling hot and stiff. Joy is next to me and there's a lot of shouting from the front room. Dad is doing a fair amount of it. I guess this is the way Indians are—always talking over each other. The loudest one gets his or her way.

I stretch. "I guess we won't be going to the beach today after all," I say.

"You promised!" whines Joy.

"Did not! It was just an idea, but you were babbling nonstop to the aunties."

"Daddy said we can't go either, because he's going to take us to the hospital to see Aji." Joy pouts.

"Well, isn't that a good thing?" I ask. "We can go to the beach another time."

But all I get are black looks from Joy.

~~~27~~~

Dad hails the ubiquitous yellow and black Tempo—a three wheeler with open sides— outside the apartment to take us to the hospital. The driver has a small statue of the goddess Lakshmi with a garland of fresh flowers on the dashboard. He flips the lever on the meter and soon is part of the throng of buses, cars, cyclists, cows, scooters, and bullock carts, everybody honking and hollering. There are no prescribed lanes. Our driver weaves through the multitudes and any anxieties of what Aji might have to say about Joy's baby are replaced by anxieties of getting to the hospital in one piece. I have to hold on to the sides of the Tempo for fear of falling out and getting maimed.

Joy has packed snacks the aunties prepared—sweet *laddoos*, *kaju burfi*, spicy *sev*. It's funny how I think those terms instead of lentil balls, cashew pastry, and I can't even think of an English equivalent for sev—skinny noodles?

Dad says, "Aji can only have a bit of plain soup, so what's the point of bringing all this?"

"She can smell it," replies Joy. Yup, I can smell it through the stackable steel containers—*tiffins*.

Many people are visiting at this hour (8 pm), carrying tiffin boxes that smell of curries and fragrant spices. Nobody wants to eat at the cafeteria. I don't blame them. I doubt hospital cafeteria food anywhere ever tastes good.

Aji is on a quiet wing. I'm apprehensive before I walk through the door, wondering how bad the brain damage is, but the moment we lock eyes, my fear dissolves into love.

"Shiv?" she asks.

171

"I brought the girls, Ma."

We sit on either side of her and squeeze her. She's so bony now. The right side of her face is slack and she doesn't hug me back. I rub her arm, straighten out her crooked fingers and massage them. Aji smiles. "I knew I was waiting for you. See all my beautiful grandchildren." She closes her eyes and gives a deep sigh. "Now I can go in peace."

"No Aji!" Joy bursts out. "You have to see my baby." She grabs Aji's good arm and places it on her bulge.

"What baby?" Aji frowns in confusion.

"Mine!" Joy is giddy. "It's a girl. Feel her kick!"

Aji smiles. "She'll be sweet."

"You're not mad at me?"

"No."

"But I'm not married." For the first time Joy looks down, ashamed.

"Well, it's better to have a husband first, but you'll be all right. Both of you." Aji's eyes are more alert now as she focuses intently on Joy.

Aji's hand is still on Joy's stomach and she whispers in *Marathi*. I recognize the names of the Indian gods—Vishnu, Lakshmi, Ganesh—she is blessing the baby. Joy bows her head low as Aji prays over her.

Even this short visit tires Aji. Her eyes flicker open to focus on Joy but she is almost asleep with her arm in Joy's lap. The hand I hold is unresponsive. She can't drift off now. She might die! And I have so many things to tell her.

"*Challo,*" Dad says. "It's time to go. Let her sleep. We'll come back tomorrow."

"Can I stay here?" I ask.

Dad considers. "I don't see why not. You can catch a ride with Meena Auntie."

"I'll leave you the tiffin box," says Joy.

Aji breathes easily and I wish she were at home. I've spent enough time in a hospital to know that nurses cannot come to your aid right away. They have too many patients to care for. Worst of all is the boredom the patients go through.

I realize that Aji doesn't really need to be in a hospital. She needs care for sure, but at home. I should bring this up with the aunties. I prop my feet up on the bed and feel my eyes getting heavier and heavier as I ponder what is best for Aji.

The next thing I know a nurse is jerking me awake. I glance at my watch—it's nearly 10 pm. I have no idea what she's saying, but I think she wants me to leave. Visiting hours must be over.

"I'll be back, Aji," I whisper. I use the toilet. I don't know how other Indian women manage so much loose clothing. By the time my salwar is tied, my kameez smoothed over, and my chunni rearranged the nurse has Aji in a sitting position for feeding. At this hour?

"May I feed my grandmother," I ask.

"You from Amrika?" the nurse asks, placing the tray on a side table.

My American accent gives me away. I might blend in with the traditional salwar-kameez here, but the moment I open my mouth, it's obvious I'm a foreigner.

"Yes," I say, "but I was born here."

She smiles. "So how did you go there? Tell me."

United States is the land where dreams come true, so everyone loves to hear of the journey, especially in an American accent. When I was little, all the relatives tittered when Joy and I spoke. It must sound funny to see this accent coming from a dark brown person like me. And so I recap my life, from the doorstep of a church in India to small-town America.

The nurse would like to chat more but seeing that Aji is being fed by my capable hands, she leaves. "If you need anything, press button. Okay?" She does the typical circular bobbing motion of the head that never fails to make me smile. I've tried it a thousand times, but I cannot do it.

"Okay," Aji and I both say in unison. We laugh.

The bowl is filled with a watery lentil soup with some rice. When I bring the next spoonful, Aji says, "They never give me chutneys or pickles."

I bring the tiffin box over and set it on the hospital tray. "Do you want some spicy sev instead?" Aji lights up at this suggestion and I put the crunchy threads made from chickpea flour into the bowl. I take a taste. The sev definitely adds a bite and flavor to the plain soup. It's not a mango pickle, but it sure perks up Aji. "I'll ask the nurse to give you some pickle."

Aji waves her good arm feebly. "I asked, but it's bad for me. So what? I'm going to die anyway."

"I don't understand their logic either." I smile at Aji. She's had a stroke, for crying out loud. She's not dead. Why give her tasteless food?

"*Bus*," she says. Enough. I wipe her mouth, since some of the soup dribbled out. "You eat." But the soup has cooled off and isn't very tasty. I snack on the sev instead and take a bite out of the sweet laddoo. The sweetened and buttery lentil ball melts in my mouth. Yum. I spoon bits of laddoo into Aji's mouth. She swallows and sighs in pleasure. "Nothing like good home-cooked food."

"Joy loves to cook," I say.

"Your Ma taught that darling girl," Aji says proudly, and I'm happy to let her believe that Joy does it all. "And you? You will become a doctor? A good one?"

"Yes."

I tell her everything—applying to the BS/MD program and how far away the schools are from Pullman, my hope about coming back here to practice. My dreams. I didn't even know I wanted to be married and have a family until I say the words. I don't know how it's even possible to think about it looking the way I do, but talking to Aji makes me feel it's no longer impossible.

She nods and says "uh-huh" many times, agreeing with me. But I can see that she's feeling sleepy again. Her eyes give her away.

I have her lie down, but before I can turn out the lights, she is out. She mumbles. A slight half-smile lingers on her lined face. Just like my scars tell a story, her lines—laugh lines, worry lines—tell a story. Suddenly I'm sorry that I don't know much about her childhood, and what she dreamed of as a young girl.

I sit on the bed and massage her feet to improve circulation. I do the same with her hands. She squeezes her good hand and smiles.

"Goodnight, sleep tight, don't let the bed bugs bite," I whisper softly. Her half-smile deepens as I finish the rhyme: "But if they do, grab a shoe and crack 'em in two."

~~~

I hear Meena Auntie come before she even steps into the room. Her bangles jangle and her shoes make a click-click sound. She doesn't wear rubber-soled shoes but prefers western pumps. She enters the room and switches the light on. "Aiii, why do you sit in the dark? *Pagal hai?*" Are you crazy?

"Shhh. Aji's sleeping. Don't wake her up."

"Don't shush me. Your grandmother sleeps a lot. After a stroke, people feel sleepy. And you want to be a doctor?" I don't know how she always manages to make me feel like I am stupid. "Your father, he is terrible. Goes to bed and asks me to come and get you. Like I have nothing to do."

"I'm sorry," I say. "Dad thought you came here every night."

Meena Auntie waves my sorries aside. She scans the room. "Get the tiffin box. I hope you were not feeding Aji this stuff.

175

Doctor wants her on a simple diet." I say nothing as I put together the canisters with a satisfying snap.

I take a look at Aji, sleeping peacefully and switch the light off before leaving the room. I follow Meena Auntie's clicking feet down the hall.

There's not much traffic. The cows must be sleeping somewhere as well.

I get into bed with Joy, making sure no mosquitoes come inside the *muccherdani*. Mosquito net. Already I'm picking up the Indian words, whether Hindi or Marathi I don't know, as if they're already in my blood.

Joy mumbles in her sleep about babies and sparklers and fires. She says sorry over and over again. I fall back asleep, her dreams invading mine.

Sheld and Becca sitting on a tree. K-I-S-S-I-N-G... Sheldon and I make hearts with the sparklers. *The hills are alive with the sound of music ...* there's Joy running up the hill waving a sparkler. *Somewhere, over the rainbow ...* Joy and I play Monopoly. *Nick and Joy sitting on a tree. K-I-S-S-I-N-G. First comes love, then comes marriage, then comes a baby in the baby carriage! Sucking her thumb, peeing her pants, doing the hokey-pokey dance!!!* Me on fire, flailing my arms.

I scream from the smell of my burning flesh, the searing pain, the sheer terror of being burned alive.

Joy tries to shake me awake. "Rebecca, it's just a nightmare." But I can't stop screaming.

The bright lights remind me of surgery.

Meena Auntie is standing near. "Shhhh. Shhhh. Go back to sleep." I am confused by all this. But I allow my stiff body to relax as Joy rubs my back. But my mind won't be calm. It is frantic trying to separate dreams from reality. Why did Joy have a sparkler in my dream? That just doesn't make sense. But I'm exhausted and have no energy to figure things out.

~~~

176

There's a lot of noise first thing in the morning. I can tell it's early by the way the light slants into the room and from the coolness in the air. At first I think all the aunties are here but no, it's only Meena Auntie and Dad. Arguing. I can't tell what she's saying because she sounds like a tin can full of pebbles, but it must be about Aji because she keeps saying "Ai"—mother.

I join Dad and Meena Auntie on the porch. "Did something happen?"

"Hai Ram! In the middle of the night your grandmother had another stroke. This time it's very bad." Meena Auntie waves her arms about and spills her tea. She promptly slurps it from the saucer.

I know Aji is dying, but I'm not ready to say goodbye yet. We have so much to talk about still. I do what Aji has taught me so well—stop navel-gazing and concentrate on others. I watch the scene unfolding on the street. People living in the shacks are getting ready for the day. Children squat anywhere to do their dirty business. Women walk two-by-two and carry small jugs of water off into the distance for some privacy. Men stretch and go the other way.

Strange how insulated one can feel from the lives of these people right outside the building when you're up on the fifth floor. Our lives are completely different. Privileged.

"Ai cannot do anything. She cannot talk or eat or anything." This is the first time I've seen Meena Auntie so flustered. "She's a ticking time bomb." Meena Auntie gets up from her rattan chair, and takes the aluminum teapot off the coaster. "I'll make more tea. Then I must call the others."

Joy joins us. "She blessed me and the baby yesterday."

"Does this mean Aji is going to die?" I ask Dad, even though I know the answer.

"I think so." Dad pats my hand and looks off into the distance. I do too. Here we are in a little enclave of peace and

177

quiet, when I notice that Joy is sobbing. I hold her close and our tears mingle on our cheeks. Dad kisses the tops of our heads and leaves the porch, probably to cry or compose himself. It bothers me that he cannot share his pain with us. We're in the same boat, but you'd never know it. He distances himself. It must've been hard for my mom to deal with all the things that have happened. No wonder she ate so much. Food was her comfort, filling the void. Dad is probably not even aware of it.

Within the hour, most of Dad's family assembles. And the biggest question is what to do with Aji if she stabilizes. I feel compelled to speak for her. I don't know why, given that I'm hardly even compelled to speak for myself. But try as I may, I can't get a word in. I cough, but nobody pays attention.

I do the only thing I know how to do. I raise my hand. Meena Auntie slaps it down. "*Arré*, what are you doing? This is not a school."

"I want to say something," I shout. "Aji should be home." I suddenly find that I'm the only one talking, and very loudly. "It's so nice here. Aji will like watching the little kids and when it's time for her to die, she can be surrounded by family, instead of being in the hospital."

Everybody jumps on me saying why they can't do it.

"And who is going to watch over her?"

"Meena, Ritu, and all the men will have to go back to work after Christmas holidays."

"The rest of us have our own work and households to manage."

"Are you staying here? No, you will leave."

I raise my voice again. "I'm just saying that I've spent months and months in a hospital and I wouldn't have wanted to die there." The family listens. "If there's no hope, why not bring Aji home? Everybody could take turns visiting her." I know that the convenient thing is for Aji to be in a hospital because it's disruptive to have an invalid at home, but what comfort is there for the sick and dying person in a cold and impersonal place? But the family is right—I am leaving. So I add, "I promise to stay by her side for the time I'm here."

The aunts titter. I am ridiculous. They don't speak to me directly but amongst themselves.

"Yah, she comes from America with all the answers."

"Once every two years."

"Oh, yah. She will send her patients home with two aspirin."

"Still, Rebecca makes a good point." Dad's lone male voice is suddenly welcome. He supports me. "I agree that work makes it difficult to have Ai at home, but I will be happy to pay for an ayah to stay with her."

"Not an ayah, Shiv!" Meena Auntie says. "A nurse— someone who can give her injections and take care of her properly."

"An ayah can be taught to give pain medicines." Dad is on my side; he'll convince Meena Auntie.

"And what if she makes a mistake? It's not like Ai can correct her, or instruct her."

"Nurses make mistakes too," says Joy, putting her hands on her hips. "I was always watching everybody. Big sign says: Wash Hands with Soap. But people went to see Rebecca without washing. I sent them back to the washing station, even some nurses."

"Good point. I'll try to find a good ayah," Meena Auntie says with a smile. "Ai has always lived with me and Rebecca is right. She should be at home."

I'm elated. Nurse or ayah, it doesn't matter. Meena Auntie wants Aji home! I look at her in a new light. It's not been easy for her being a single woman. She has to take care of everything herself. Maybe this is why she's so hard.

Finally, I feel like I've done something useful and good here, my desire to be a doctor meshing with taking care of people. I ask Dad if we can go to the hospital for a little while to visit and he's glad to do so.

Aji is ashen, her skin a sallow brown. There's no tinge of pink anywhere. Her chest rises and falls steadily. A tube snakes out of her mouth. It probably hurts, but at least she's sleeping.

This is the end, then. You live, you die. The dash on the headstone encompasses your life. But Aji will remain in my heart forever.

Dad talks to the doctor briefly and it looks they might be willing to send Aji home in a couple of days. We have a lot to set up at home.

~~~28~~~

Since Aji has to be in the hospital for a couple more days, Dad says we should go to Pune to visit Mom's relatives. We ride in the first-class compartment on the train. The seats are clean and cushioned and there are no mobs. The third-class cars have people crammed in without regard to numbers. Men hang out from open doorways. Some even sit atop the train. I guess they're hitching a free ride. Nobody can do anything about them because, like the squatters, they just claim their space and jump off and go where they will. I don't know how people survive this nomadic lifestyle, with no home, no knowledge of where the next meal is going to come from, and no prospects for the future. Yet they smile and shout and sing with delight.

The whole time, Joy is smiling, as she takes in the vivid sights and sounds of India. She's bought three mechanical toys already—a little ballerina that whirls around when you push a lever, clucking and pecking chickens, and a windup bunny that hops. They are cute, but noisy. I hope she doesn't break them before we get back to Pullman. I know her friend Diana will love the pecking chickens. I still haven't bought anything, but the aunties will be taking us shopping when we get back. I will get a silk sari and salwar-kameez for Colleen.

We are dusty when we arrive in Pune. Dad hails a taxi and negotiates the price effortlessly. I am surprised at how easily he moves in this world. It's the only place other than the academic setting that Dad really fits. Even at the grocery store, he's out of place.

Beggar children come—they can smell we're made of money. I instinctively take a step back but they are bold and come close enough for me to distinguish each strand of unwashed hair. Some have awful deformities. I know some were deliberately blinded or maimed so that we'd take more pity on them. It makes me ill to think how these children are pimped.

I am covered so they cannot see I'm one of them— damaged. My revulsion turns into compassion when I imagine the hope I can bring to these kids. These are my brothers and sisters. I am meant to come here and take care of them when my education is complete. This is why my life has been spared over and over. This realization comes quietly, without any fanfare. The mystery of why I was burned begins to fade in my mind. It no longer matters.

I wish Mom were here so I could tell her she was right—all my suffering was for a greater purpose. I know Colleen will understand; she says everything happens for a reason.

I look over to Joy and wonder how I can abandon her. She wasn't even able to take care of Mohan, the littlest cousin when he scraped his knee. Mohan was screaming and Joy screamed right along with him until Mohan's mother showed up and snatched him away from Joy. How will she react to a colicky baby that won't stop crying? Or a naughty toddler who refuses to listen? Who is going to step in if she's not taking proper care of the baby?

Do the needs of the many outweigh the needs of one or two? I don't know. If I devote myself to taking care of Joy and her baby, won't it be at the expense of the others I can help? I must go to medical school. That's what makes me feel the most alive. It's what I'm meant to do. But Joy, how does she fit into the picture?

Joy pulls me into the taxi; all our baggage is loaded in the trunk. We are whisked away from the chaos of the railway station to the serenity of Bhagat Marg and St. Mary's Church.

"Opposite, opposite," Dad says. The driver makes a U-turn and parks in front of a small but freshly painted yellow house with a peach trim.

My aunts and uncles from my mom's side of the family have gathered. Mom's youngest brother, my Chottu Uncle, is the pastor here. I flash back to the photo album Mom shared with us countless times. Chottu Uncle, a ring-bearer at Mom's wedding, celebrated twice, once in the Christian manner, with Mom in a white sari, for purity, roses draped diagonally across her body in this church, and once under a tent in Mumbai in the traditional Hindu manner, wearing red, for fertility, with garlands of orange and yellow marigolds. But Mom and Dad only celebrated the court wedding date—that actually makes three wedding ceremonies for one couple. Everything in India is done to the extreme.

The moment we step out of the taxi, we are engulfed by the family and kissed, sometimes both cheeks at once. The smell of coconut oil on their hair reminds me of Mom and without any warning, my eyes turn into faucets, unleashing all the longing, the missing, the frustration of not having Mom here to take care of everything, leaving me free to do what I need to do.

They usher us into the house and I don't know how thirty people can fit into such a small space but the entire clan is here. None of them were able to come to Mom's funeral last year, so this Sunday we'll have a special memorial service for her. Chottu Uncle had asked for a copy of my eulogy I wrote last year. It's strange my grief is so raw right now, even though just days after Mom died, I was not only doing my schoolwork, but comforting Joy and writing a eulogy, while Dad made all the funeral arrangements. I wish I could return to that autopilot mode.

I could use it right now as the commotion begins with Joy confirming to yet another little cousin that she does have a baby in her tummy. Tea spills into saucers, sweets fall out of open mouths, and an eventual silence descends into the room as Joy is invited to tell what happened.

The mothers quickly send the little children out to play so as not to contaminate their innocent ears as Joy recounts her love story with Nick. She doesn't mention that Dad and I tried to get her to have an abortion, so I am surprised when they ask whether we considered it. Joy glosses over it, and I am grateful.

It's strange that regardless of the beliefs of the two sets of families, one Hindu, the other Christian, that their reactions to the baby are nearly identical—horror tinged with pity. Instead of exclamations of "Hai Ram!" we have "Lord have mercy."

Joy is unfazed by all the negativity and beams when Chottu Uncle prays over Joy and the baby to keep them healthy and safe.

The conversation shifts to God's will in general and how "thanks be to God, cousin Jeet has gotten a job at Heavy Electricals." They forget that Jeet had to put in effort to get the job. I'm a little bit irritated that they take the same approach when I talk about my plans for medical school. "God willing," they say. I nod my assent. Far be it for me to sing about my own efforts and studies. God willing I'll get an A in Calculus.

~~~

We return to Mumbai after the weekend. On the train ride, I carry in my heart the lovely memorial service Chottu Uncle gave at St. Mary's. It was full with the usual parishioners, many of them who knew Mom as a child. I revised my eulogy to reflect that she was not just a wife and mother, but also a daughter, sister, friend, and nurse extraordinaire. Without Mom I wouldn't be here, integrated into society. Mom would be proud of me, even though I delivered my speech with tears streaming down my face.

Aji is still in the hospital. Meena Auntie already has a hospital style bed with railings in the living room, though there's no danger of Aji falling off, considering that she can't move anything but her eyelids.

This gives me an idea. We should have twenty questions and just like they show in the movies, one blink can mean yes, and two rapid blinks, no. I write down a bunch of questions like: *Do you want another blanket? Would you like music? Is it too loud?* Meena Auntie nods her approval. She's busy interviewing women for the position. The older women are intimidated by the idea of having to give a morphine shot. Of those who are eager, it is difficult to tell who is trustworthy. I realize I will have to go through this process when I have to find a babysitter for Joy's baby. Or Joy. It's scary to wonder if strangers could love your grandmother or sister enough to take proper care of them. It's not like family always does a great job. Better a willing stranger than a reluctant family member.

The ayah Meena Auntie chooses is the same age as Joy and has a toddler of her own. She's a married nursing student at the nearby Women's College who stopped going to school because she got pregnant. Meena Auntie likes that she is educated but the best part is that she has interest in taking care of people. She was a nursing student after all.

"Just call me Sue," she says when I stumble over her real name: Sushila.

I try out my twenty-question grid and refine it with Sue. Her little boy, Deepak, is a handful, but I have a feeling he will provide much entertainment to Aji when the grandkids aren't around.

Joy is in love with Deepak and I can't help imagining the future as I watch Joy and Deepak playing together. God willing. Oh, India and the relatives have gotten into my soul like never before.

~~~

I get to spend five whole days with Aji. The aunties want me to take advantage of our time in India to go shopping, but I beg off. However, Joy is only too happy to accompany them and returns home with bundles of clothes and wooden toys for herself and the baby. I adore the little kitchen set with tiny stainless-steel pots and pans, plates, cups, glasses, and even the teensiest tiffin-box.

"How are we going to carry all this stuff?" Dad grumbles. "We'll have to buy another suitcase, which means another baggage fee."

"Oh, Shiv! Don't be spoiling our fun. When will she get another chance?" Meena Auntie asks. "Soon she'll be busy with the new baby. Besides things are much cheaper here."

Dad is no match for the aunties and has to give in. Even I do. The aunties take me to a fabric store and I pick out material for salwar-kameez.

The fitting session doesn't go well. I like loose clothing, but the aunties insist that I need to have several pairs of salwar-kameez that are fitted to show off my figure. What figure, I wonder. I have no curves like Joy, just bones jutting out at awkward angles. I feel horrid standing there in front of them in just a tank-top and shorts as they measure me and look at my scars. I feel naked. Although they are never unkind, I hate the pitiful look in their eyes because my body is so ugly.

My cell phone rings. It hardly ever does. Colleen is always busy at Christmastime with her large family, and there's really nobody else. I check to see who's calling, and feel self-conscious.

"Hello, Sheldon," I answer. "What's up?"

"Merry Christmas."

I smile and the aunties chuckle. "She has a boyfriend," they say.

It's embarrassing to talk in front of the others, but even more so in my underclothes.

"Thanks, but I can't talk now. There's ... um ... no privacy."

"That's okay. I hope you're having a good time."

I want so badly to talk to him about all my ideas about getting a mobile clinic set up here, but they're all so nebulous and this isn't the right time to talk. "Hey? Let's talk when I get back."

"Hay is for horses," says Sheldon.

I laugh and bid him a Christmas goodbye.

Meena Auntie pulls up my tank to bare my midriff, checking for the proper length of the blouses I will wear with the saris I've bought.

"Don't be shy," Meena Auntie says. "Nobody will notice the scars. The sari will cover them. You must have some pretty clothes to wear for parties and formal occasions. Especially now that you have a boyfriend. You'll be glad you did. Trust me. You don't want to end up like me, with no husband."

I take in a quick breath.

"Sheldon is *not* a boyfriend," I say. "Besides, who will want a girl like me?" I ask.

"Lots of men would like a smart, beautiful girl like you," she says with a smile. "These scars ..." She lifts my chin so that I'm eye to eye and continues, "... will not matter. You'll see. But first you must have some attractive clothes, not those drab things you wear all the time."

"How come you never married?" I ask. She's smart and good looking. Maybe it's her prickly personality.

"Oh, boys wanted me alright. And I would've loved to get married and have a family. But I never met my ideal man, one who would love and cherish me," says Meena Auntie, without a trace of bitterness. "But it all worked out. See, because I was unmarried and independent, I was able to come and help your mother and father at a time they desperately needed it. It was fate. Everybody said I was too picky, but something good came from it."

This surprises me. *She* rejected the boys. But she's right about being able to come and care for us.

Meena Auntie continues, "You deserve the best, too. Just look at your parents—they were so good to each other. True partners. Sharing all their joys and hardships."

It's hard to see Dad in that light, but it's true. I don't remember Mom and Dad fighting. If anything they argued because Dad wanted to pamper Mom, but she didn't want to leave us to go on a holiday by herself. She'd always say, "I don't need that. Just be home for supper." Mom and Dad shared hugs and kisses freely. She was queen of the house and Dad's sounding board. And Dad took care of us all with his work. He would bring small unexpected gifts for Mom—pins, scarves, funny tee-shirts, sweets. And if he traveled away, he always brought something for all of us. Usually clothing. He'd wrap a shawl or a kimono around us.

Meena Auntie drapes different colors over my shoulder to see what looks good and continues to give me advice. "You try too hard to be invisible, but you're always going to draw attention, so it's better to give people something good to look at. Wear your scars with pride." She smiles at me. "You are a not a victim, but a survivor. You lived!"

Meena Auntie has the guts I don't have. But why not? Why shouldn't I reinvent myself when I go to college? What harm will come if I wear clothes that are not only comfortable but far more beautiful than the pants and long-sleeved shirts I wear? Would I be deceiving anyone? Not if I told a man beforehand. I imagine though, the look of horror as he unwraps my sari. Would he still want me then? I endure standing there, being fussed over until all the measuring and deciding of the materials is done. I slip on my old cotton salwar kameez over my underclothes and turn my thoughts to working in India someday.

I ask Ritu Auntie to help me choose some basic books on learning and writing the Hindi alphabet. She's a school teacher and is delighted that I'm taking an interest in my Indian heritage.

I like the curly alphabet so much that I begin practicing while I spend time with Aji. She's home now and looks much happier. Meena Auntie helps me to talk Hindi and Marathi and I provide great entertainment for all the relatives.

"I didn't realize you have a gift for language," says Dad. "You've picked up a lot during this vacation."

I feel a warm glow basking in his praise. "It might come in handy if I come here to practice medicine."

He doesn't say anything about me leaving Joy, but smiles as if he is accepting that I have my own dreams as well. A breakthrough.

~~~30~~~

When we return from India, there's a huge pile of mail to go through. We sit together, drinking gallons of hot tea, fighting jetlag, and missing the warmth of Mumbai. Joy nabs all the Christmas and holiday cards. She tapes them to the doors and it's so much better than having them on the kitchen counter. "They're so pretty," says Joy.

"Good idea," I say. "That will give us time to reply to everybody and tell them about our trip to India."

"And my baby too," adds Joy.

"Nonsense," says Dad. "Best not to talk about the baby yet."

"Why?" asks Joy.

"Yeah, Dad. Why?" I goad him.

"Oh, do whatever. Your mother always wrote all the letters." Dad is grumpy.

"We'll write one letter and mail it to everybody." I get Joy a yellow pad. "Make a list of the people we need to write to."

Joy begins copying names from the return-address labels, but gets frustrated quickly. "There are so many cards!"

"Here's an easier way." I cut away the address labels from a couple of envelopes and paste them on a different sheet of paper. "See, now we will have them all in one place." It would be nice to have them alphabetized but that's a difficult task for Joy. She knows her ABCs but she cannot put names or books in order.

Joy is happy to cut out the pretty labels and tape them to a blank sheet of paper.

Dad turns a business envelope a couple of times in his hand before tossing it to me. "From Florida?"

"Yeah, BS/MD program." I avoid eye contact.

"Really? I thought I'd made it clear you're staying here."

I take a deep breath. "I applied to Detroit, Missouri, and Florida." I open the envelope and scan it quickly. "Looks like I made the first cut."

"You applied even though I told you not to?" Dad's quiet tone belies his anger. He knows I'm defying him openly.

I gather all my courage and stare at him. "It's my future, and you can't stop me."

He throws another envelope at me. This one's from Detroit. My first choice. I tear into it as well. Another interview. I want to shout for joy, but keep it all inside.

Dad takes the letter from Florida. "Absolutely not!" he says, thumping the table and making all the letters and cards vibrate.

I snatch the letter back from Dad. "It's MY life!"

"You are not going anywhere, you selfish little brat."

"You're calling *me* selfish?" I shoot back at him. "You're clinging to me, when this country offers so many resources for taking care of Joy. You're denying me my dreams that would help poor children in India, who have so little."

Dad is taken aback. Maybe it's the first time he's thought about how he's stealing me away from the poor and neglected.

"You're leaving?" Joy asks.

"Not yet. I'm just going to check out some schools, that's all."

"Not on my dime," says Dad. It's obvious it's all about what's convenient for him.

"I'm not asking you," I tell him. "I've earned enough money through my summer jobs."

"You can't leave!" shouts Joy. "What about the baby?"

"What about it? You're having it. It's yours. Not mine. And if you don't want it, give it away." I jab the air. "I shouldn't have to stay here because of you and your baby!"

I grab my mail and go to my room, slamming the door shut. I could scream right now because this is exactly why I did not want to talk about the BS/MD program until it was final. I hate all this drama. My hands shake as I read the letters again. This should be a cause for celebration, instead Dad is mad and Joy is sad. Most people don't even get an interview. I've been invited. Doesn't that count for something? It makes my resolve to leave this trap of a family even stronger.

So why do I feel so crummy? Is it because I'm becoming an auntie?

~~~31~~~

As Colleen and I trudge through the snow to school, I tell her everything. I can't even think about preparing for the interviews what with all the dumb things I have to take care of here, like figuring out where to put the crib and hiring a sitter to help Joy.

"Why don't you go during spring break?" Colleen suggests. "That will give you three months at least to take care of things." I think it over as we enter the warmth of the school. My glasses immediately fog up and I stumble on the central staircase. Colleen steadies me.

I shake my head. "No, it's too close to Joy's delivery. What if the baby comes early?"

A shrill voice adds, "Like we need another retard."

I can take just about anything but that hateful word. I whip around to see Madison with a new nose ring of all things leaning against Jake, enjoying my misery. She giggles in her characteristic way, like a bird being strangled.

I make a fist and swing hard, making contact with her face. "Like we need you!" My knuckles throb in pain. I massage them with my other hand as I look upon an astounded Madison and a slack-jawed Jake.

A semi-circle forms on the landing, but I walk up the stairs with Colleen, my head upright, not looking at the steps but focusing on the gun-metal lockers lining the wall. My face feels like it's on fire, as I try to swallow a lump in my throat. Shit. I cannot, will not cry.

The kids automatically open a path to let me pass.

I shove my backpack into the locker.

"You okay?" asks Colleen.

I nod. I grab my all-purpose notebook and binder and walk-run to Advanced Chemistry. I take my place and instead of asking Mr. Johnson if I can get him anything, I look over my rough notes from the first day of class. Soap, soap, soap. Mom used to scrape it over our teeth when we were rude. I wish I could wash out the mouths with soap of all the kids who've ever made fun of Joy.

I run my right hand under cold water. Madison's jaw must be made of steel. The last time I did something like this was way back when I was a kid, before I got burned. Colleen slapped my face for something I'd said, and I slapped her back. I was surprised to see the imprint of my fingers on her cheek. We ran into the house to look in the mirror and laughed like crazy girls. Joy came to see why we were laughing. She had her hands on her hips just like Mom. And she was mad. Mad because she thought we were laughing about her.

My cell phone vibrates in my pocket. I am tempted to answer it, but it's nearly class time. It'll be Joy asking about some stupid thing and I don't want to get into trouble.

Sheldon and Kurt walk in to the classroom together. "I heard you decked Madison," says Kurt.

"Sorry to have missed it," says Sheldon, slapping his notebook on the bench.

I rub my fist.

Sheldon laughs. "Your fist still hurts? Man, I need to teach you how to hit."

Mr. Johnson comes into the lab, brushing sugar and crumbs from his moustache. His green-gray eyes are not sparkling with laughter like they usually do. He leans against my bench. "You're wanted at the vice-principal's office." When I get up, he adds, "You'd better take all your things."

Sheldon glances at me as I gather my pencils, notebook and binder. "Will you let me borrow your notes?" I ask.

"Sure." His smile vanishes.

Madison is already there holding an ice pack to her left jaw. She glowers at me.

The secretary motions me to sit down. Ten minutes pass. Then fifteen. I hate missing class.

"Excuse me," I tell the secretary, "but I don't really want to miss my next class too."

Vice-principal Mooney opens his door inviting me in. "I'm afraid you'll be missing all of your classes if what I've heard is true."

"It's true," I say. "I hit Madison." I look at her. "Wouldn't you if someone called your sister's baby a retard?"

Madison rolls her eyes.

"Let's take this inside," says Mooney.

I step past him into the office. It's luxurious with leather chairs and a large desk. It's so tidy; I wonder whether he actually does any work in here at all.

"Sit down, Rebecca. What's going on?"

"From the first day of school, Madison and her friends have taunted me about my sister's pregnancy. I ignored them. But it's gone on too long. When someone calls my sister a retard, and the baby she's carrying a retard too, well, I can't let that stand. Not anymore." I could explode but I push the boiling lava back into my body.

"That's not a reason to hit," says Mooney, as though I'm in kindergarten.

"I'm sorry. It won't happen again."

"I'm sorry, too, Rebecca." Mooney reaches for the phone. "You are a bright student and I can imagine you've had to deal with a great deal of unpleasantness from your classmates, but I cannot make exceptions. It's never acceptable to hit a fellow student. If you cannot handle a situation, you need to ask a teacher to help you." He punches in my dad's number and while he waits to be connected, says, "I am going to suspend you for three days effective immediately. I will release you to your father."

This is not happening. But Mooney's voice is awfully real.

"Yes, Dr. Joshi. Rebecca is in serious trouble and I'd like you to come over as soon as you can." He pauses. "Fifteen minutes? Great."

When I open the door, Madison's mother is in the waiting area with Madison. Her mouth takes an ugly downturn as eyes settle upon me.

"I cannot believe this! How can you stand there? Look at what you've done! You ... you ... monster!" Madison's mother removes the ice pack to show a redness that won't go away. "I have to take her to the dentist. If her jaw is broken, you'll have hell to pay."

"I'm sorry, but I've already been to hell and back," I say. "My sister is pregnant. She's intellectually disabled. But she's wiser and has a bigger heart than your Madison."

I cannot believe I'm talking back to these adults, but something seems to have snapped in my brain and I can't stop myself.

"Rebecca! That's enough! You are out of control. You may stay home for the rest of the week," Mooney hollers. "Gather all your things. I will notify your teachers."

"What about Madison? Is she going to get a suspension too? What she said is worse. Where's the justice?" I don't wait for a response but walk out of the office. "I'm gone." I don't even care about Madison. Her types get away with murder. At least I spoke the truth.

I grab everything from my locker. The heavy calculus book thuds to the floor. I don't know why I'm being so reckless. Maybe I should go apologize, but honestly, the thought of saying another 'I'm sorry' makes me want to puke. I am not sorry.

Tears sting my eyes. I'm so angry. Angry at Joy. Angry at Dad. Angry at myself. Dad is going to make everything horrible.

I wait for Dad in the office. Thank goodness Madison and her mother are gone. I chew gum and crack the joints in my fingers.

Dad is breathless as he enters the office as though he ran all the way to the high school. He takes a clump of hair that's on his forehead and brushes it back. "What? What happened?" he asks.

The secretary quietly calls Mooney on her telephone. "Mr. Joshi is here."

I smile because I can hear him think, *it's Dr. Joshi, you moron.*

"I lost my temper and hit a girl." I show him my bruised knuckles. "And then I mouthed off to the girl's mother." I chew my gum noisily and blow the tiniest bubble.

"That's correct, Dr. Joshi," says Mooney, striding out of his office. "I cannot tolerate any physical violence. It's an automatic suspension for three days. But we're giving Rebecca a week because she'll need to see a counselor before returning. We need to make sure this never happens again. Rebecca must learn to control her temper."

Oh great! Counseling! I've been to many, too many to count. Why shouldn't I feel rotten when life is throwing rotten tomatoes at me?

I still remember one counselor asking me about the silver lining behind my burns. I didn't find it until my latest trip to India. What about when Mom died? There is no silver lining. Nothing good has come from her death. Our family is tearing apart.

Dad is all ears and contrite as can be. "You must be aware that our family situation is very delicate right now, Mr.

Mooney. I didn't realize Rebecca was under so much strain. This is precisely why we took a vacation to India."

This is news to me. I had nooooo idea that Dad could peek into the future. I got the damn stress after we returned from India, when I made it through the first round of medical school applications.

"Ummm, excuse me. I wasn't stressed until we got back from our vacation." I decide to be a stickler for the truth, like Joy. Why should Dad be allowed to lie so smoothly? He should take some heat.

Dad glares at me, but addresses Mooney. "This would be her first offense. Won't you reconsider?"

"I'm sorry, Dr. Joshi," Mooney says, cocking his head at Dad. "The rules are in place for a reason. Rebecca will have some time to cool off at home and not be exposed to the gossip that triggered this behavior."

Mr. Mooney is one cool cucumber.

Dad agrees. "Well, then, we'll be going." Dad and Mooney shake hands. I swing my heavy backpack over my good shoulder and follow Dad. I know I'm going to get a lecture as soon as we're out of earshot, so I brace myself.

"What is the matter with you?" Dad whispers into my ear before we're even out of the school. "Have you lost your mind?"

I cover my ears and hurry outside.

Cold air stings my cheeks as I open the main doors. Dad teeters on the ice and lunges for my arm. "Look at me!"

I see rage. I shake him off.

"I haven't lost my mind, Dad, just my temper," I say, walking even faster. "You don't know what it's like going to school. That Madison has had nothing nice to say about Joy and now she's going after the baby."

"Don't you think I know that? I tried to stop all this heartache."

"But you couldn't," I remind him.

"That's not the point, Rebecca. You need to develop some self-control. You have brought all this upon yourself through your actions. If you don't get admission into any university, let alone a medical school program, remember that it's your own fault." Dad gets into the Pilot.

I toss my backpack to the floor of the car and strap myself in. "Great. Blame me for everything. You're completely innocent."

"I didn't hit that girl."

He's right. I did, and for what? To put Madison in her place? To let off steam? I am so stupid. It finally sinks into my thick skull that I probably sacrificed my future and trapped myself here. What school would want a thug?

Dad pulls into our driveway after a couple of close calls ramming into the poles that line the street. I open my door to get out, with Dad calling after me. "I have to go teach a class now, but we are not finished. You are completely grounded. No going anywhere with anybody, unless I say so. Stay put and do your work. Do I make myself clear?"

"Yes, Dad. I'm sorry." I mean it. "Please."

"Please what?"

Please don't be mad. Please be the adult. Please take care of Joy. Please take care of me. Please let me go. Instead I say, "Nothing, just please. I'm sorry. I'm sorry about everything."

"You should be sorry, the way my blood pressure is going up."

I take a deep breath and let it out. It's all about Dad. It's all about how things make him look and right now he looks like a father of a future felon. I take my backpack and kick the car door shut.

I'm under house arrest. It's not like I have anywhere to run to. Being a juvenile delinquent is not on the path to becoming a doctor.

I check my email, but there's nothing. I log onto the school website but there aren't any assignment to download. I spread out my books as though it were a Friday night, and get ready to study. Mel sits on them. I scratch her chin and she purrs. I decide to take a day off.

~~~

I get another lecture from Dad when he comes home from work, Joy in tow.

"Let's see the work you've done," he says.

"I don't have any assignments so I just read my books." It's a lie, but what am I supposed to tell him? That I fell asleep with Mel and spent the afternoon on the couch watching General Hospital? Good thing I left my books on the dining table, because at least they look like they've been thumbed through.

"This isn't a vacation from school, Rebecca. I need to see some real work. What math problems have you done? What essays have you written? None!"

He confiscates both my cell phone and laptop and checks on his parent portal. He doesn't say anything except to remind me I won't be allowed to get together with either Colleen or Sheldon to share notes and study. "You will work alone and use your books. Once I take away all the privileges that come from going to school, you will finally appreciate it." He stomps across the room to his office.

"Why are you two always fighting?" Joy asks. "I hate it."

"I hate it too," I admit. "We disagree on so many things and it doesn't help that now I'm in real trouble."

Joy's eyes grow big and round. "What did you do?"

I don't want to tell her. What if her feelings are hurt? But she needs to be strong to defend herself when people make fun of her. It's a good thing she doesn't always realize that people are being callous. There've been so many times when kids told her they're playing hide-and-seek and she'd go hide, but nobody would try to find her. Once I found her squatting behind some cattails by the detention pond after all the other kids had gone home. I don't know how long she'd been there. God, I hate kids sometimes.

"I hit a girl," I say, "because she called your baby a retard."

"Did you have to go to the principal's office?"

"Uh-huh."

"Oh, boy. You are in big trouble."

"Yup."

"For me?" Joy is serious. "Never do that again."

I can't promise anything.

~~~

The next morning, Dad wakes me up and tells me to pack all my books because I'm to study in his office.

"At least let me sleep in," I say. "I can study in my pajamas."

Dad reminds me again that it's not a vacation and flings the down comforter off me. The cold air bites.

I do exactly as he says—toe the line, dot the i, and cross the t. All the while I'm falling behind in calculus. And I cannot take calls from the two people I rely on at school, Sheldon and Colleen.

I was supposed to be the phoenix rising from the ashes but I feel as though my newly sprouted wings are being clipped.

Dad hurries me on Wednesday morning because I have an appointment with the psychologist, Dr. Sellick. Mooney must think I'm going to buy a gun next. But I've already come to the conclusion that Madison and her types aren't worthy of anything, even my anger. In fact, I'm genuinely ashamed that I lost my temper, and with it, the privilege to go to school. I'm annoyed Dad was right. I suppose I can save all this for Sellick; he'll be happy that he's helped another juvenile delinquent turn things around.

"Come straight to the lab after your appointment," Dad commands.

"Yessir." I salute him. Joy giggles. Dad doesn't know this, but it's been comfortable studying in his office. Although his desk is messy, it's large and I have a corner of it for my books. When I get tired, I can run down to the third floor common area where the graduate students have their mailboxes. There are candy and Coke machines, ratty old couches, and even an ancient boom box where people occasionally pop in a CD to listen. The atmosphere is friendly and I've gotten some help on my physics homework sets. Many of the pre-med students are fascinated by my burn scars and interested in the treatments.

Dad drops me off at Sellick's office. It's very quiet. Not even the secretary has arrived. I'm his first victim.

"Oh, hi! I haven't seen you in ages. How are you?" Sellick is full of fake sunshine. As if he doesn't know. This is the kind of chit-chat I cannot stand. Dad already gave him a report of what happened at school and I'm sure he's gotten some official thing he has to sign telling the school I'm not a total basket case who'll go shoot somebody.

"I'm fine, but the vice principal doesn't think so."

"Why don't you start by telling me what happened at school? I have the official school version and another that your father told me. I'd like to know what you think."

The way he asks me implies that there are several different realities, when in fact, there's only one. It's only the point of view that differs.

So I tell him what happened. When I come to the end, I let him know that I'm not some half-crazed person who is going to hurt someone.

"Being out from school has definitely helped me see how stupid it was to hit Madison. She's not worth it. I promise you I've learned my lesson and will never lose my temper … to this extent again." I am completely sincere, but Sellick scratches his chin.

He finally answers, "So what's going to happen when other kids taunt you about Joy as she gets even bigger, or when you're about town with the baby?"

"I'll ignore them, just like I've been doing for the past few months," I say. "This is my last year here and I'm getting the hell out. I've applied to BS/MD programs in the Midwest and Florida." There. I've laid bare my plans.

"So, if everything is set, why is it that you're still so angry?"

"You think a punching bag would help?" I laugh. "You don't understand. I'm mad at Dad. He's the problem. Not Madison or those dumb jocks at school. Dad. Ever since Mom died, he hasn't had much to do with Joy. I'm the one who talks to Tessa—she's the social worker— because Dad doesn't seem to take any interest. He's not even like a father anymore. He's Dr. Joshi. It's work, work, work with him. That's what he cares about. He wants me to stay here and take care of Joy. I want to go to medical school. Away from all this drama." Everything pours out of me. The frustration. The unfairness of it all.

"I'm very glad you told me how you are feeling, Rebecca." Sellick taps his pen on the table. "I can see the home situation is difficult. All of you are still grieving your mother, and your father unfortunately has retreated into his work. He is not present to comfort or care for you or Joy. And he's not taking responsibility for Joy."

Duh, I could've told him that. I know Dad is not a heartless monster. But don't the immediate needs of our family take precedence over any unresolved grief? I'll be missing Mom for the rest of my life. I don't bother to tell any of this to Sellick.

"We must have a family conference because you and your dad need to work out a lot of things, the most important being Joy. How about if you both come back to see me Friday morning? Let's see if we can open up the channels of communication," Sellick, ever optimistic, says.

I don't flinch from his gaze. "I'm leaving one way or the other."

"You still need to get along for the remainder of your time here." Sellick punches in Dad's number on his desktop phone. "And you don't want to leave on a bad note."

I look at the walls decorated with pastel paintings that are meant to be soothing, but look lifeless, devoid of any character. This could be a dentist's office.

"Dr. Joshi?" He pauses. "Oh, no, Rebecca is being very cooperative. But I think we should have a family conference soon." He moves the handset away from his ear. Dad's shouting. Good. He doesn't want a conference either. I could've told that to Sellick.

"Do you think we can all meet on Friday? You can be my last appointment at 4:30 pm." But he doesn't pencil us in. Instead he says, "Well, soon, then."

I get up, swing my backpack over my shoulders. "Are you going to approve me for school? I promise you I will not lash out in anger at anybody. I know I was wrong."

"Yes." Sellick looks defeated. He's had a taste of Dad.

I glance at the clock behind him and see that I have fifteen more minutes. "Can I go now?"

"Yes, you may Rebecca. But please come back. I can't make you, but I can help you."

Yeah, right. It really bugs me that some people have therapists for years and years. If therapists are doing their job right, they shouldn't have long-term clients. I've been to burn camps and have had lots of counseling, but really it's the other kids, Mom, Auntie, and Aji who've made the most difference in my outlook. I can live without Sellick.

"Thanks." It's all I say to make him feel better. Hopefully the next miserable person will be more grateful.

~~~33~~~

Dad invites me to eat at the Cub with him and Joy on Friday. For good behavior? I don't know, but it's a treat for me, so I'm happy about it. He gets a hamburger and I get two slices of pepperoni pizza. We both get tall glasses of Coke.

I finally see Joy, swinging a red plastic bag from the Bookie. She scans the cafeteria for us and I stand and wave. People around me stare and I sit down quickly. Meena Auntie was right—I draw attention.

Joy walks towards us with a big smile, shaking the bag, and I notice how much her stomach sticks out. She cannot button her winter jacket. Yet, she hasn't once complained about being cold.

"Look, I got the cutest onesie! It says: *I wanna be a Cougar!*" Joy removes the contents of the bag, one by one, with great flourish, as though she's a magician. She has three pairs of Cougar socks, two onesies, and a soft fleece blanket with the Cougar logo.

"Mel will love to sit on this," I tell Joy, as I stroke the blanket against my cheek.

Joy frowns at first, then smiles. "Mel will be the guardian kitty."

"Go get something to eat before the lines get too long." Dad is halfway through his hamburger already. "Do you need money?"

"Nope!" Joy removes her wallet. "I have lots. I went to the ATM."

Mom set up a bank account for her to teach her how to manage money, but she'd only put in enough of her earnings for fun things. With the way Joy is shopping, I don't know how quickly she'll run out. How will Joy ever manage money for the household?

"The whole house is filling up with baby stuff," says Dad.

"I guess it's time for you to teach her how to shop properly for the baby." I fold all the cute little clothes into the blanket and shove it all into the bag. "You'll be a grandpa."

Dad is speechless. I enjoy this moment.

Joy returns to our table with a hamburger and an extra-large portion of fries. I nab a few.

"I'm starving," she says, sticking two fries into her mouth.

"Are you sure you can eat such rich food?" Dad is worried she'll barf. But what he doesn't realize is that Joy hasn't been sick for a long time. Once in a while, something will trigger it, but she can pack away food like a football player.

Joy ignores Dad and concentrates on spreading ketchup evenly on her hamburger. She takes a bite. "I love juicy hamburgers," she says with her mouth full.

I gobble up my pizza before it gets cold. Dad is already done. He sips on his Coke and tells Joy not to eat like a *junglee* because she is stuffing her face with fries.

Someone taps me on the shoulder. I turn around to the smiling face of my calculus teacher, Dr. Rothschild. He greets Dad. "Hello, Shiv."

"Sit down, sit down, David," Dad says. "Joy, move your bag."

She grabs her Bookie baby bag and gives it to me.

"You know each other?" I ask.

"We've sat on a few committees together," says Rothschild, removing the pickles from his burger. "Are you ditching school?" His wrinkles deepen as he smiles at me.

"I got suspended," I say, looking at the red bag in my lap.

"Suspended? I can't believe it! What did you do?" Rothschild's surprise takes me aback. He doesn't know? Didn't Mooney tell all my teachers?

Joy pipes up. "Rebecca hit a girl because she said a bad word."

Rothschild laughs loudly.

This is funny?

"You shouldn't be so sensitive. Do you know how many people call me 'weirdo' and worse?" Rothschild laughs again. "If I reacted to them, I wouldn't have time to do my work. But it helps to have a few repartees ready to go. Perhaps you need lessons in that as well."

Dad clears his throat. "I'd appreciate if you don't get Rebecca into more trouble."

"Don't worry, Shiv. You know I'd never teach her anything bad." Rothschild grins and his green eyes crinkle with mischief.

I think I have an ally.

"If you want, we can get started right away. You're not busy, are you?" Rothschild offers.

"I can't." I look at Dad, then at Rothschild. "I'm grounded."

Rothschild gives another hearty laugh. "Monday, then."

"It's okay." Dad is so magnanimous. "Just make sure you come back to the lab when you're finished."

"Thanks, Dad. I've had a bear of a time trying to teach myself this stuff. It's not intuitive."

"Wait till you get to quantum mechanics," Rothschild says. "That's not intuitive either. But mathematics will show you the answer. It's never wrong. It can tell you what is theoretically possible." This could be the beginning of one of Rothschild's Friday fun features. "Mathematics tells us that it is possible to travel in time, that there are other dimensions than the ones we perceive."

"You mean *'Back to the Future'* is possible?" I loved that movie.

"That's right."

We sit there for a while, talking about the movie, with Joy adding completely irrelevant bits about other movies she has seen. But Rothschild is never condescending. He speaks to her with respect and explains time travel for the umpteenth time.

In the end, Joy gets it. "If I went back in time, I'd have nothing to do with Nick. He was a bad boy." Her eyes shine wet. "But then there would be no baby." She holds her belly protectively.

A hush settles upon our little table. Dad turns pink. Rothschild watches us all. I am thankful for my dark skin because it doesn't betray me like Dad's light brown skin.

Rothschild is never at a loss for words or ideas. "There is a theory that every time you make a decision the universe splits into two. So there is an alternate reality out there where there is no baby. It's interesting to think about, isn't it?"

Joy is perplexed. "There's another me with no baby?"

"And another Rebecca who doesn't get suspended." Rothschild smiles. "Mathematics and physics say it's possible."

I think about a universe in which I never get burned, a universe where there's a Fourth of July kiss. There might even be another universe where Joy and I are both perfect and another where I die before being discovered by a kindly priest. I doodle the little splits on a napkin, but the only branch I know is the one I'm living.

Joy looks at her watch and declares lunch is over. We all get up, clear the table and say goodbye. Dad goes alone to his lab in Fulmer Hall while Joy, Rothschild, and I walk towards Heald Hall. We leave Joy to do her work in the basement and walk down the hill to the math department.

I spend an afternoon getting a private tutorial on everything I missed this week. What luck to run into Rothschild. He only teaches the one calculus class at school; the rest of the time he's here at the university. Rothschild is wonderfully patient, slowing down when I have trouble keeping up. He doesn't think any question is stupid, but some of his explanations end up going way over my head. He laughs and back tracks saying that we'll be covering various techniques to solve the different problems in a couple more weeks.

"We don't want you to get ahead of everybody, now, do we?" he says.

"I wouldn't mind. I'm struggling like everyone else, so I'm really, really thankful for this extra help."

"You're welcome. It's been a pleasure. You'll do great in medical school." Rothschild smiles as I gather my notes. "I have another sheet for you. Read any Shakespeare?"

I'm confused. Shakespeare? "Yes, of course, for school. *Hamlet, Midsummer Night's Dream.*" I don't mention that I didn't care for it, but he knows already from my unenthusiastic reply.

"Well, then. You'll be familiar with some of these insults," says Rothschild. He hands me a paper titled *Shakespeare Insults*.

I scan the paper and laugh. "This is great! Thou beslubbering beef-witted barnacle!"

"Study and use these wisely, and perhaps you'll enjoy Shakespeare better next time."

"Thank you, and I will." I could give this man a hug, but he hardly ever stands still.

I walk uphill to Fulmer Hall with my stash of notes collecting teensy snowflakes. I must recopy them as soon as I get to Dad's office. I think of how jealous Sheldon will be when he finds out I received help from the calculus god himself. And the Shakespeare insults are pure genius. I try some out, but I know I'm going to need a lot of practice before I can say, "You surly beetle-headed foot-licker" without cracking up. I think of what would suit Madison best: vain idle-headed miscreant. That's what I'll call her the next time she says "freak" or "retard."

I poke my head in the office and see Dad's not there. I find him in the lab holding a dripping wet film that's just been developed. He gives a half-smile. He loves working with his students, helping them decipher the marks on films and discussing all their results. It's strange how much attention he bestows upon them. And the students flock to him as though he were dispensing pearls of wisdom. He's generous with his time, and doesn't get annoyed when he's interrupted, or has to explain things. I guess Sellick was right; work is a balm. Dad throws himself into it because it's the only thing that brings him joy. Without Mom, there is nothing to keep him at home; Joy and I are a burden.

I recopy the calculus notes and marvel at how clear everything is when Rothschild explains it and how muddy it is when I try to do the same. But I know enough that I'll make progress on my homework problems tonight.

Joy comes to Dad's office when her work is finished. "It was fun to run into your teacher. He's so nice."

When I think of Rothschild, I think of multiple universes, of the choices we make, and where they lead us. If I hadn't decked Madison, I'd never have had that discussion with Rothschild. I guess I'm no longer grounded because I take Joy folk-dancing and stay to dance.

34

I am good as gold at school, thinking Dad will be happy, but he's pissed off about me not dropping the BS/MD program. When he sees me making the travel arrangements he says, "We've just spent five grand on the trip to India, along with shopping excursions your aunties took you on. I refuse to pay for this."

I don't even look up from the computer. "I've got it covered. It would be nice to have your blessing, though."

Actually, I don't need his blessing and he knows it. It gives me a small sense of victory to see him powerless.

I make sure Joy isn't around when I prepare for the interview. She lives so much in the moment, she's forgotten about me going away until Colleen shows up on an icy February morning to take me to the airport. But unlike Dad, Joy is all smiles. She's coming along to send me off because it's Sunday and she'll go to church with Colleen afterwards.

Colleen has been a real rock through all this. She's made me model all the clothes and arranged them so only the least bit of my scarred skin shows. She made me practice answering random questions clearly. I'm learning to not open my mouth right away, but absorb the question and formulate what I want to say. The silence feels like it's going on forever, but Colleen pointed out that it's only a minute at the most. As I walk onto the tarmac of our little regional airport, she shouts, "You'll do great! Be yourself."

"Come back soon!" yells Joy. "Have fun."

It's not easy being me when I'm still reinventing myself. Here I am in a long-sleeved embroidered red *kurta* that makes me stand out against the gray of the Palouse and the muted colors that everyone else wears. I am comfortable, but the clothes make me feel like a foreigner. People stare at me. I don't know whether it's better to be thought of as a potential terrorist than looking as though I might have a contagious disease and have people recoil when they glimpse a scarred neck or arm.

I cannot lift my left arm up over my head to put my small suitcase up in the overhead bin. I ask a man for help, and he does. I know what this means. Surgery. This should be my last one to release the contractures that have developed in my armpit. People don't realize that after you are out of danger from the burns, the scars remain with you forever. The grafted skin is not stretchy, and so has to be released as the long bones and muscles grow. So many people in poor countries are crippled for life because they cannot afford to have follow-up surgery.

As we take off, I peer out the small window to see the little houses dotting the undulating farmlands. Even though the wheat and lentils are snow covered, I know they're growing beneath, ready to burst forth in spring, just like Joy's baby, who started out life just like a little seed. I think of Joy, forgiving me for trying to get away from here and wishing me "good luck" and "come back soon" without any thought for herself and wish I could have more charitable feelings.

I change planes in Seattle and doze on the long flight to Detroit. I dream of dazzling everyone at the interviews.

~~~

The next day I look like a proper little Indian immigrant in my orange-red *salwar-kurta*. Who knows, maybe this will give me an advantage—being brown *and* female. My short ski jacket looks ridiculous on top, but it's too cold to just wear a sweater, even though I don't expect to be taking any strolls. I walk carefully in my rubber-soled flats on the short strip of sidewalk where the hotel shuttle drops me off. The chill creeps up my legs but I know I'll warm up soon enough.

Two boys, one white and one black, dressed in sharp black suits, are already waiting in the reception area. I feel out of place in my Indian "costume." It doesn't look professional at all. Oh, what was I thinking? That I could reinvent myself as a traditional Indian in the time it takes to take a flight to Detroit? I should've splurged on a fitted suit even if it were just for the interviews. This is America!

I swallow my nervousness as I enter the room with the sign: Dean of Admissions. Everything about this room feels imposing, from the large mahogany desk to the perfectly clean beige carpeting. Could I ever belong here?

I introduce myself to the secretary. She has me wait with the boys, Brandon and Race. The nervous energy in the room is so high, I want to throw all the doors and windows open to let it escape. I've never been good at small talk so I stay silent. The boys are so much more at ease, talking about sports. Race lives here so he's a fan of the Tigers.

Finally we're ushered into a room with a long walnut table and several chairs. The secretary gives us paper and pens and tells us we have thirty minutes to write an essay.

My topic: Who would you choose to speak to right now, dead or alive, and what would you say?

I steal glances at the boys. Brandon stares off into space as he formulates what he wants to say. He looks cool and collected. In contrast, Race twiddles with a pen, gets a white handkerchief from his pocket and dabs imaginary drops of sweat on his ebony skin. He opens and closes his fists, as though he's getting ready for a fight. Then he begins to write.

I think about Mom and write as though I were free writing in Mr. Berry's class. Absolutely everything tumbles out of me as I write a letter to Mom. How Joy wouldn't have gotten pregnant in the first place, how I'd be free to go, how I wouldn't be in trouble if she were still alive. I write about my views changing, how much more I value my life because of all that's happened. Oh, Mom, I miss you so much. I hold back the tears that threaten to spill. I write and write all my hopes and dreams for the future. I'll make you proud, Mom. I miss you. Love, Rebecca.

Until I hand in the essay, it doesn't occur to me that the faculty members, waiting to judge me, will be reading this.

The boys and I are all quiet, immersed in our own thoughts as we wait for our personal interviews.

~~~

The secretary escorts the boys to separate rooms for their interviews. She tells me to stay and a few minutes later, a tall and broad-shouldered African American man and a tiny Asian woman walk in. She's dressed in a short pin-striped suit, not some Asian kimono-style outfit.

"I'm Dr. Northup." The man extends his hand and I shake it. "And this is Nancy Ichiro, a fourth-year medical student." I shake her hand as well. "We've both gone over your file and have just read your essay."

I want to crawl into a hole, but manage to say, "Thank you."

"Ms. Joshi," says Dr. Northup. "We are very sorry about your mother."

I'm flooded with emotion. Not now, I tell myself. "Thank you," I say. I tell myself to say something else. Anything. I swallow. "Perhaps I shouldn't have written about her. It's not like I dwell on her absence all the time. I focus on school work." Oh God. Shut up. I'm babbling. I can't stop. "But given the topic, she's the first one who popped into my head."

"We love to read essays from the heart, so don't worry," Dr. Northup says, smiling. "You have a very interesting and unusual background, and I was hoping you would tell us more about why you want to become a doctor."

215

This is easy so I launch into the why right away. "It wasn't until I was almost fully recovered from my burns that my goals of becoming a doctor solidified in my mind. Until then, I was more wrapped up in my sister's dream of being a vet. Once I became the recipient of extensive medical care, I realized what a gift I'd been given. It made me realize human medicine was more important to me. Of course, that's after I got over wanting to be dead myself." Uh-oh. I shouldn't have said that last part. What is wrong with me?

"That's interesting. What are your views on euthanasia? Michigan's citizens will be voting on legalizing it this fall."

"Washington State went through this a few years ago and we had many debates." I remember that I was for euthanasia at the time it was passed, but my views about life have been shifting over the past few months. I remember it's okay to outline my arguments in my head before speaking.

I continue. "There is too much potential for abusing this law. What if an old person feels like a burden to his family? He might be coerced into committing suicide. It smacks of a world where the chronically ill will be threatened."

"And what about the high cost of medical care?" asks Dr. Northup.

"Sometimes I feel guilty thinking what I've cost my parents. But I would do the same for my child. I would fight to keep my child alive." I realize how fierce Joy's love is for her unborn baby. She will go to any length to protect her. But I am getting distracted. We're discussing euthanasia.

"I spent Christmas vacation with my grandmother who recently suffered a series of strokes. She needs a full time caregiver. She is not thrilled with having a feeding tube or being in diapers. No matter how inconvenient it is for family members, we could never assist her in committing suicide. Giving her basic nutrition is not only humane, but the right thing to do." I twiddle the ends of my *chunni*, thinking what more I can add. "We aren't making my grandmother go through treatment after treatment to extend her life. She deserves to live the rest of her days in peace and die a natural death. And if she's suffering, we can offer palliative care, not hasten her death."

I sit back in my chair.

"But euthanasia is about having the right to die," says Nancy. "After all, it is my body and my life; therefore shouldn't I be free to end it? How would you advise a patient whose suffering is unbearable?"

I loosen the *chunni* around my neck and roll my sleeves up a bit so that they can see my scars. "I'll tell the patient that once upon a time, I wanted to die too, but I'm glad nobody listened to me. Instead they managed my pain better. I received mental health care as well. Emotional pain is just as important to treat as physical pain. I'll tell the patient that sometimes it takes greater courage to live, and to hold on, that it's not really up to us to decide who should live and who should die, not even the patient." These are all things my mom spoke to me about and how right she was.

Dr. Northup leans forward and studies my scars. "So Nancy couldn't convince you to pull the plug."

"No sir. I would take the original Hippocratic oath, where the physician does not play God, nor cause the willful death of another human being."

"Interesting." Dr. Northup. "So you wouldn't assist in an abortion either, I assume."

"That's correct," I say, taking a deep breath. Am I ready to say out loud what I think I believe? "Euthanasia and abortion are two sides of the same coin. It's not up to me, or you, or even the mother herself to decide whether or not she should terminate the life of the baby."

Dr. Northup and Nancy Ichiro both look at me, expectantly.

"You've read my essay. Let me elaborate on it. My sister is unmarried, intellectually disabled, and pregnant. You'd think all these would be causes to get an abortion, and when I first discovered she was pregnant, I took her to an abortion clinic. It's legal and I was thinking of what a burden this baby would be, and how neither of us were prepared to care for it. I encouraged my sister, tried to tell her it was only a clump of cells, but my sister instinctively knew this clump of cells was on the way to becoming a baby, one that is going to grow up into a little child and then an adult. She would not consider getting an abortion."

"But is she competent to make that decision?" Dr. Northup asks.

"Legally, no. My father is her guardian even though she's twenty-three years old. But my point, and it's the same one with euthanasia, is that it isn't *anybody's* decision to make. Nobody should have the right to take the life of another. The baby is clearly a distinct and separate person from the mother, with its own unique DNA. It's not like ..." I fumble for the right words. "It's not a tumor or like an appendix."

Nancy smiles.

"You do realize this will lead to many unwanted babies," Dr. Northup says.

"And what about all those babies who are conceived from rape or incest?" Nancy asks. "You would ask the woman to carry that baby to term?"

"I was unwanted," I say quietly. "I was left at the doorstep of a church. I have no idea why. Maybe my mother was raped. Maybe not. Even though the woman who gave birth to me felt that she couldn't care for me, she hoped someone else would. Being unwanted shouldn't give anybody a right to kill me. I am thankful someone rescued me, even though eleven years later, I was severely burned." I try hard to keep my voice even, to not betray my emotions. This is an interview, not a therapist session. "Unwanted babies are born here too. I know that. But I don't believe snuffing out the life of a baby before it even has a chance to breathe the air is the answer. Adoption is a noble alternative."

I grope for some clarity. "I don't know what the solutions to these social problems are, but killing off the people you don't want—old or young—because they are inconvenient, is not how a society should treat its most vulnerable."

Nancy leans forward. "What if a patient came to you, pleading for an abortion because she's a victim of incest? How would you advise her?"

"Or if the baby is known to be anencephalic?" Dr. Northup interjects.

"These are both terrible situations to be in," I say. I don't remind them that Joy's case is technically statutory rape, given her mental status. Still to be forced to have sex and then have a baby from that horrible union would be unimaginably difficult. I remember what Colleen said all those months ago. The baby did not ask for any of this. Why should it have to die for the mistakes made by others? I ponder all this and finally say, "A year ago, I would've agreed to help with an abortion out of kindness for the woman. But seeing my sister pregnant, I have begun to appreciate that the unborn baby, who has no voice, who is completely at our mercy, deserves a chance to live. Death can never be a cure. Pregnancy, even if unwanted, is not a disease. I can no longer take the life of another human being. I would ask the patient to consider that the baby is an innocent little human being, no matter how it came to be, no matter how deficient it is, and no matter how we feel about it. The baby doesn't deserve to die at our hands. I would refer the patient to a crisis pregnancy center."

"These are strong opinions, Ms. Joshi. You do know that abortion is legal in this country," Dr. Northup reminds me of the law.

"Well, slavery was legal once too, but that didn't make it right," I shoot right back. Dr. Northup should understand given how his people were treated and how wrong it was.

The room is silent. I know the position I've taken is considered extreme. I wonder if these strong opinions of mine have cost me a place in medical school.

"I'll let you have the last word on this," says Dr. Northup. He doesn't smile and I can't tell whether he's for or against me. "I'd like to discuss your activities, or rather, your lack of activities. Although you are strong academically, we are looking for students who are well-rounded."

Ouch.

"Pullman is a small community," I begin, "and doesn't offer a lot of volunteer opportunities." This is so lame. And it's not even true. Colleen is always busy with some volunteer activity or the other through her church, and there are all sorts of programs offered through school.

"Actually, my scars have made me not want to be with people," I confess. "But my mother encouraged me to help at hospice and with developmentally disabled children. After she died, though, Joy became a huge responsibility for me." This is going so badly. All I'm doing is making excuses. But then I remember something else Mom used to say: Charity begins at home.

I think of the future I envision and say, "As I grow older and less ashamed of my scars, I realize that I can use them to give people hope. This Christmas vacation in India, I kept thinking of how much I would enjoy practicing medicine there, or setting up a clinic to provide basic medical care to the poor communities. It is within our collective reach."

"Given the recent death of your mother and the responsibilities with your sister, I'm wondering if being here in Detroit is the right choice for you," Dr. Northup says.

Joy! Why does everybody want ME to take care of her? How come my dreams of opening a clinic in India are ignored? I feel anger rising to my cheeks. I do not want to blow this interview so I take a deep breath and say, "Washington State doesn't have a BS/MD program and my father will take care of Joy's needs. A social worker helps us as well."

We talk about my visit to India again, how I feel called to serve. But the point about charity beginning at home pricks my conscience. I circle around to the question of whether the needs of the one at home outweigh the needs of many who are far away, both in time and distance.

The conversation nears its end when Dr. Northup drops a bomb. "There's just one more thing. You were suspended for physically attacking a classmate?"

Nancy's eyebrows shoot up.

"I have no excuses," I say quickly. "I lost my temper when a girl kept insulting my sister. I cannot stand the word 'retard'. I should've just walked away, but I didn't."

"Why?" asks Nancy. "There are always people who will call you names. I've been called 'chink' too many times to count."

"I'm sorry," I say, thinking how terrible words can make you feel. "I'm no stranger to being called names: ugly, freak, and much worse. I have thick skin—only metaphorically." I fake a laugh. "But when it comes to my sister, I try to protect her. She doesn't even know she's being made fun of sometimes. It's awfully hard to bear at times."

"Do you have a problem managing your anger?" Dr. Northup asks. "Medical school is high pressure."

"Until that moment, I've never lashed out at anybody," I say. "I even met with a therapist and we talked about ways of managing the negative feelings. I understand there is no justification for what I did, and I am deeply sorry." I neglect to point out that if I'm away from Joy, I wouldn't really have to deal with these issues.

"Good, then I think we're done. Oh, one more thing," Dr. Northup says.

I didn't know there was more bad stuff to cover.

"I have a seven-year old niece. She wants to be a doctor. What advice would you give her?"

This throws me completely off-guard and the first thing I say is, "Play more." That is so dumb. I should talk about studying hard and volunteering more and not getting into fights but both Dr. Northup and Nancy begin to laugh.

I feel myself giving a tentative smile and say, "Life is too short."

"Indeed. It's been a pleasure to meet you, Ms. Joshi," says Dr. Northup.

"Yes, thank you for sharing so much about your life," says Nancy, smiling. "Good luck."

"Thank you for inviting me," I say. "I hope you feel that there's room for a student like me." Oh, shut up. Or else I'll find myself on my knees, begging.

We all shake hands and I leave the room.

I've bombed it.

And judging from the tepid smiles of the boys, it looks like it's been grueling for them too. Brandon looks cool enough, but Race has a bead of sweat trickling down the side of his face. We hang around in the lobby sharing our awkward answers to difficult questions, Race periodically using his handkerchief to wipe his brow. It looks like there were a lot of questions relating to personal beliefs. The fact that they interview you makes it so much more subjective. There is none of the small talk a couple of hours ago. The three of us bond over our emotionally draining interviews.

"C'mon, let's eat," says Race. "It's over and I'm starving."
He knows of a sandwich place a couple of blocks away. It's
his hometown.

The wind cuts through my billowy salwar, right down to
my bones. I cannot keep up with the boys' long strides. They
deliberately slide on the ice, whooping and hollering. When I
don't join them, they yell at me to take a chance.

"I have no balance," I shout out. And as if on cue, I slip.

Race and Brandon slide on either side of me, take my hand,
and pull me along. We are an unlikely trio—two boys in suits,
dragging a squealing girl in a salwar-kurta.

"I need to take you ice skating," says Race. "You'd love
it."

"Would you? I'm not leaving until tomorrow morning."
I've never felt so spontaneous before.

"Sure! Why not? Brandon, you want to come along? I
could pick you up too."

"No. But thanks. I'm taking the three o'clock flight to
Milwaukee."

"Oh, did you apply to go there as well?" I ask.

"Yeah, that's my home," says Brandon. "I'm only applying
in the Midwest, though. Family and all."

"Yup, Wayne is my first choice for that reason," says Race.
"I need to watch over my little brother, make sure he doesn't
drive Mom crazy. He's a punk." Race laughs. "Besides, I can
save money on rent by staying at home."

They don't seem to feel stifled or burdened by their
families. Brandon talks about being admonished for not
applying himself diligently. "I have to work hard for my
grades, but it's never good enough."

"Mom's always had two jobs," Race says, "leaving plenty
of time for my little brother to get into trouble."

"What about your father?" I ask.

"We only see him once a year," Race says without any bitterness in his voice, "for the Woodward Cruise."

"What's that?"

"Only the biggest car party on the planet." Race grins. "If you like cars, it's the place to be."

"Is that why you are called Race?" I ask.

"It's short for Horace," he says.

Brandon and I explode into laughter. Race—Horace—joins us.

I open up to them and share family stories along with Brandon and Race. I promise to show them some more of my scars because they've never seen a severely burned person. And I don't even feel weird about it.

We arrive at Blimpies. Great name. The little building with its green overhang lends brightness to an oasis of old, gray and weathered structures.

My pastrami sandwich is tasty. I eat Brandon's pickled peppers as he removes them from his sandwich. "Weenie," I taunt him.

He laughs.

~~~

We return for a tour of the medical school conducted by a second-year medical student. I can see myself here in a white coat, with pens tucked in the pocket, taking notes, following a doctor on his rounds. That image morphs into my own clinic in India, with children in comfortable cots, on the road to healing.

When it's time for us to leave, we exchange phone numbers and promise to let each other know about the results.

"Should I meet you back here or will you pick me up at the hotel?" I ask Race.

"Oh, the ice skating," Race says, slapping his forehead.

He forgot! And I'm such a dork for thinking he was serious about taking me. It was just conversation.

"You probably have to go home," I say in a rush, "and I'm beat."

"No, I was thinking we should probably go now. It'll be much less crowded."

"You sure? I don't want to be a bother, especially since you need to watch over your little punk brother."

"I have the day off," says Race, "and it'll be fun. So unless you want to rest your beat feet, let's go." He smiles and I can't help laughing in anticipation.

The two of us are completely overdressed for skating, but once I lace up, I no longer care. It's not easy walking, even on the carpeted area. How in the world will I glide on these unwieldy blades? But Race lends me his arm. At first I cling to him, but gradually I am only holding his hand. Still, I am not going forward from my own power, rather Race is pulling me along. He tells me to lift my foot off and bend and push the same way as if I were roller skating, but I have to tell him I've not done that either.

"Where've you been, girl? It's not like you just stepped off the boat." He laughs. "Well, it's never too late to learn."

He's right. I'm having so much fun; I wonder whether Spudnik, the old roller-skating rink in Moscow, Idaho, is still open. I remember Mom taking us there right before I got burned. I fell so hard and so often I had a bruised tailbone. And after, well, it was all a fight for life. Mom never took us there again, and I never asked to go.

I tell Race all this and so much more, and there's not a hint of pity in his eyes. I like that. I'm not a sorry little thing. And here on the ice, I feel like I can do anything.

Race lets go of me, going ahead. He faces me. "Come to me," he cajoles.

What a flirt!

I'm still moving so I extend my arms out and into his arms. He smiles widely and I imagine myself dancing with him like the old couple who have whizzed by us several times already. We do this a few more times until I'm moving on my own power. I'm terrified that I will fall but Race's fingers are always within reach, even when I have to go a longer distance to him.

He hugs me close and tells me to hang on to his waist. "Follow along," he says. And now I'm skating—fast. My chunni flies behind me and the cold air rushing by is exhilarating.

We spend the whole afternoon skating. I take numerous breaks just to watch Race. He looks like the devil himself in that suit, the way I'm tempted. Just once I'd like to glide into his arms and kiss him and twirl round and round. Images of Sheldon and me come unbidden. The kiss never happened. But that same craving tightens my chest.

But that's not what he's thinking of, I'm sure. He's just being nice and I doubt I'll even see him after the way I botched my interview. What was I thinking?

As soon as I step on the ice again, I forget about everything else. It's just Race and me. My stomach rumbles loudly and Race laughs. "I guess we'd better get some pizza."

"Let me treat you to an Indian meal," I offer, "for the excellent private lesson." I want to sit down where it's not so noisy with the music.

"Sounds good." Race checks his cell phone for places. "The Peacock's close by. I've never been to an Indian place, so I have no idea whether it's any good."

"We'll find out," I say.

~~~

After the raucous music of the skating rink, the droning of the sitar at The Peacock feels almost too quiet.

"Mmmm, the smells are so different," says Race.

It's a familiar smell to me, that of fried garlic, ginger and chilies, and I wonder whether it's pleasant for him or not. I have no time to ask because the waiter is ready to seat us. "Only two?" he asks.

"Yes," I say, slipping my hand into Race's. He squeezes it.

The waiter wrinkles his nose in disapproval. I wonder whether he'd do the same if I were holding Brandon's lily-white hand. Indians sure are color conscious.

Even before looking at the menu, I know it's going to be expensive with the dim overhead lights casting a glow over the white tablecloths, orange napkins, a real orchid and candle on every table.

A plate of *papad*—fried lentil crepes—arrives. Cumin seeds dot it. We break off little pieces and crunch thoughtfully.

"These are good," says Race.

I'm relieved. I order a South Indian style lamb curry with a bite of vinegar. I debate between eggplant and okra and decide to get both. I'm so glad because Race piles it on his plate. When he asks whether I know how to cook like this, I tell him how Joy and I pretend to.

We talk about our crazy families and our dreams for the future. I don't want the evening to end, so we sit in the parking lot of my hotel and talk about our interviews. Race has a theory that black professors have to be hard on people of color. "You don't want to get in school because of some racial quota that they have to fill. You want to get in because you deserve the spot," he says.

"True. Except my whole life I've never been given anything because I was female, dark-skinned, adopted, burned, or anything," I say. "I've had to slog for everything so I wouldn't mind if I got picked just this once for the color of my skin."

Race frowns.

"I'm kidding, I'm kidding!" I tell him.

Race smiles. "Good. Because this program is competitive. If you get in, it's because they liked what they saw." Race slides closer to me. "And I definitely like what I see."

"You mean what I show. I wonder what you'll do if you saw all of me." I unwrap the chunni from my neck.

Race reaches out. "Don't touch me," I tell him. I can't stand the thought of him feeling my leathery skin. Race drops his hands but takes in the sight of my twisted and puckered skin, the obvious patchwork, the uneven pigmentation, visible because of the street light reflecting all the snow.

"How far down did you get burned?" Race asks.

"I wore a one-shouldered pink dress with ruffles, decorated with cats. The entire dress burned into my skin. Not even a swatch was recovered. My worst burns are from my neck to mid-thigh." I will myself to hold the tears back.

Race puts his arms around me. He's taller than me and leans his head on mine. "I'm sorry, Rebecca." He looks right at me. "But you know what? Your inner beauty shines through."

"Inner beauty?" I ask. "Seriously? That's a euphemism for ugly. I'm not even plain enough to go out on a date or have a boyfriend."

"That's not true. You push people away so you can believe that," Race says softly. "You go on the offense so you won't be rejected."

I close my eyes. He's right. How can this boy who barely knows me be so perceptive? Without warning he presses his warm lips to mine.

I don't push him away to prove a point. I can smell-taste the cardamom from our rice pudding. He kisses my cheek, first on one side, then the other. He tilts my chin and plants a soft kiss on my leathery underside. Tears drip down into my hair and ears, and he kisses them away, on both sides.

These are my first kisses and they are so sweet, so healing. I always imagined they'd be from Sheldon, but he hasn't even managed to hold my hand.

"You're beautiful, Rebecca," Race whispers in my ear and for the first time, I dare to believe it. I dare to dream I can have a romance.

"Honest Horace?" I smile.

"Honest," says Race. "I don't go around kissing girls, you know."

"You should rent a movie called *Mississippi Masala*," I say, resting my head against his shoulder.

"I'd like to watch it with you."

I imagine the romantic scenes with Race and I in the lead. We sit in the car like that, close to one another, breathing each other's scent, and I'm aware how different I am after these kisses. This small knowledge of a boy who is struggling to make a good life for his mother and brother has changed me. I can't even imagine what making love must be like. It must be a shattering experience. Joy has changed, not just because she got pregnant, but because she had sex with a man. Oh, how I wish she could be married and experience the joy of raising her little girl as Mom and Dad did.

"If we both get accepted here … Thank you, Race, for everything, and my first kiss."

"My pleasure." Then like a gentleman, he escorts me to the hotel lobby where he gives me a goodnight kiss.

~~~

When I check my cell phone, it has twenty-two messages from Joy and one from Dad. He wants to know how the interview went. And he wants to make sure I'm okay. Wow! I didn't think he cared given that I had to fend for myself.

Well, there's no way I'm going to call him to tell him I bombed. So I lie and text him back: *Interview ok. G'nite R.*

I send Joy a text: *Busy day. Interview, no fun. Went ice skating. FUN. Will call tomorrow. Love, R.*

And I do. I talk to Joy and tell her everything minus the kisses. I promise to take her ice-skating in Spokane after she's had the baby. But who will watch it? Dad? It's not easy when I think of logistics.

I'm better prepared for Missouri and Florida, but I'll never get used to being scrutinized so thoroughly. My brain is mush after talking about burns and pediatrics and oncology and abortion and euthanasia and my suspension. But it's over. I am proud of myself for giving voice to my beliefs. It may not be the popular thing to say, but truth has set me free, just like Mom said.

On the long flight home from Florida, I go over this week, and despite the stress of having to interview, I realize I had a really good time visiting these places. I tried to get out and do something fun every day and the older students were great about directing me. I bring home seashells and shark's teeth and a stuffed toy turtle for Joy and the baby. My first real gifts for them.

I close my eyes and relive the tender kisses in Detroit. Race. Oh, how I want for both of us to be accepted there. I should've had my interviews in the opposite order, so that I could shine in Detroit, but then I wouldn't have met Race. I think of Rothschild's parallel universes; the possibilities are endless.

35

Dad and I argue about when to schedule surgery to correct my shoulder. We've put it off long enough and I've grown considerably since last year and the skin around my left shoulder has contracted. Dad wants it done before Joy's baby is born. I'd rather wait until summer so that I don't lose a week of school. He doesn't ever think about what's best for me. So here I am at Harborview again. I know the routine. Slice the contraction in my armpit, extend my arm up and over my head, and cover the exposed tissue underneath from a flap of meshed skin from my calf.

I'm thankful I don't have to have tissue expanders.

Joy is huge now, only a month away from delivery, and glowing. Her waistline was gone long ago, but now she looks like she's carrying a watermelon. Her belly bumps into my gurney as I wait to be wheeled into surgery. I already have an IV drip going.

"Will you be here when I wake up?" I hold Joy's hand.

"I promise." Joy is so much like Mom, caring and nurturing.

A nurse comes by. "How're you doing, Rebecca? Feeling sleepy yet?"

I manage to smile. "Uh-huh." I get wheeled. It's not unlike being in a train, except I'm strapped in, and train rides always make me sleepy.

The operating room is bright and Dr. Martinez peers down at me. Although I cannot see his mouth, I can tell he's smiling—his eyes are all crinkly. The anesthesiologist places a mask over my face. "You know the drill, Rebecca."

"Hundred, ninety-nine ..." I drift off to sleep.

~~~

I try to figure out where I am. Joy's whispering ... This is a dream. I tell myself to wake up. I can't seem to open my eyes. But Joy's voice is clear. She keeps saying, "*Sorry. I'm so sorry. Forgive me.*" I wonder why. "*They were going to kiss.*" How would Joy know this? I've never told anybody about wanting to kiss Sheldon. "*It wasn't fair. Rebecca was just a little girl.*" That's right. I was eleven. Her voice continues, "*I didn't know, Lord. I didn't know she'd get burned like this. I'm sorry. I'm sorry. Please forgive me.*" Joy is praying. "*I was so mad. I wanted to join my sparkler to theirs, but they were going to kiss. So I touched my sparkler to her dress for just a teensy-weensy second. I'm so sorry. Please, Lord. Forgive me.*"

I throw up.

I have no strength to hold my head up and so lay it down, into the bile. It bubbles up from my gut and I can't breathe.

"Nurse! Help!" Joy screams.

I'm fully awake from this nightmare.

There is so much commotion. Nurses prop me up, adjusting my sling so my left arm is at a right angle. My calf is sore too, from being the donor site.

I need to ask Joy about my dream. I can't forget.

"I'm here," says Joy, rubbing my hand. "You got sick."

"Ew." I try lifting my head up but can't. "Ow."

A nurse wipes my face and changes the pillow. "My hair," I gasp. I want my hair washed. But I can't forget the dream. "Joy?"

"I'm here," she says.

"Fire?" My throat hurts so badly but I squeak the words out slowly. "Did you set fire to me?"

Joy takes in a breath and squeezes my hand tighter. I scrunch my eyes shut. I don't want to look at her face. She did it. I didn't dream it.

My body instantly fills with rage. The blood pounds in my head. She could've killed me! She did kill me. I am no longer the same Rebecca. Why? Why? Why? I am exploding inside. I want to scream but no sound comes. I'm trapped.

No more. I'm getting the hell out. I'm never ever coming back. I wriggle my hand out of hers.

"It was an accident," Joy is saying in a small voice. "A terrible accident."

"We were *not* careless; you deliberately set fire to me." My voice is hoarse, bile rising into my throat. I swallow the bitterness.

"It wasn't like that. I... I... I..." Joy stutters.

"What?" I rasp.

Joy starts crying. "I wanted to touch sparklers. And ... and... and ... I just wanted to see what would happen..."

"You were jealous! So you lit my dress on fire. That's what happened," I whisper. My throat is so raw, every word hurts. I have to beg for water. Damned tubes. It's a miracle I even have a voice because of all the tubes that have been shoved down my throat all these years.

"I wanted more sparklers. But they were between you and Sheldon." Joy makes her sorry excuses. "It was an accident. I'm sorry. I'm sorry. Please forgive me." Joy sobs harder.

"Never!" I feel nothing but a rock in my heart. This is why she's always been so worried. She didn't want my death upon her conscience. But what about the way I look? Doesn't that *ever* bother her? I can't even rant at her because my throat is sore.

"You're upsetting the baby." Joy holds her belly.

"Then go away."

Joy stands still.

"Go away." I wish I could scream this into her ear, but since I can't I close my eyes to her stare.

Joy shuffles towards the door. Good riddance. Hot tears spill onto the fresh pillow. I want to die. My heart is dead. I finally made some peace when I was in India, believing I've endured so much suffering for a reason. I'm still suffering. And there's no reason. All this happened because Joy was jealous of a kiss that didn't even happen.

A nurse comes by. "What's the matter, sweetie?" She touches the wet pillow. She quickly fetches another one, checks my chart and says, "It's too early for your pain medicine, okay?"

I close my eyes. I don't bother to tell her that no medicine can melt the glacier lodged in my heart. I have no choice but to lie here and remember.

I can't sleep. I must talk to Sheldon. Has he known all this time? Mom? Dad? Colleen? Oh, God. How I wish I could go back in time and reverse that moment. Everything would be different. I'd be smart and beautiful, and Sheldon would be my boyfriend.

~~~

I must've dozed because the nurse is back telling me that I can have my pain medicine. She gives me a shot and within minutes my shoulder and head and heart quit throbbing. The nurse also changes the pillow. When I lay my head down, she strokes it.

"How're you doing?" It's Dad. "The nurse said you're in an awful lot of pain. I came earlier to check but you were asleep and I didn't want to disturb you."

"I'm okay," I whisper.

"Good. Let's hope this is your last surgery." Dad reaches out his hand to mine. "There was a time when I didn't know whether you'd even make it through the night, let alone the first surgery. You proved everybody wrong. You're such a fighter, Rebecca. We watched you fight for your life. Joy most of all." He comes back to the present. "Whatever's the matter with her? She's crying and saying sorry, sorry, sorry."

I try to shrug my shoulders but it hurts too much. I don't want to go into all this with him. He'll only try to defend her. After all, she's his real daughter. I'm just the adopted one. I was adopted for Joy, to be her companion.

"She's sorry," I whisper, pulling on Dad's hand. He brings his face closer to mine. "She's sorry because ..." I sob. "She set me on fire."

"No!" Dad recoils from me. I'm accusing his precious daughter.

"Ask her," I say.

"No!" he says again. "She wouldn't. She couldn't. She would've told us. How is it possible that nobody knew? We were all there."

"But nobody was watching Joy," I whisper. "Wawawai." That one word is enough for both of us to relive another terrible tragedy. There was a family picnic for everybody in the lab at Wawawai Park and although there were close to thirty people, a four-year old drowned because nobody was watching him. His mother thought the father was watching the child and the father thought the mother was watching. But they were too busy having a good time with all the other adults while we kids ran about and swam in the wading area. Nobody missed the little boy until another child noticed the floating body and screamed.

"Oh, no!" Dad says, his shoulders slumping as if he can't bear the weight of the truth.

My pain is dull now, but I feel Dad's.

~~~

The week drags, even with physical therapy. Joy stops by every day with stuff—flowers, books, a teddy bear. I ignore them. On the third day I snap at her. "Quit bringing all this crap into my room. I don't want it."

Dad is subdued. He tells me about the places he's taking Joy—the zoo, the aquarium, Ballard locks, the Pacific Science Center. I don't really care. I'm sure she's driving him crazy, but he should get used to it. I'm getting out. Out of Pullman and out of the Joshi family. Otherwise I'll blow up like Mt. St. Helens.

I decide to call Sheldon and ask him about that fateful day. Three messages later, he calls back. "Hey, what's up?"

I don't bother with the rejoinder. "Sheldon, do you remember how I got burned?"

Sheldon is quiet. I can hear him breathe. He's remembering. "I thought you wanted to put all that behind you," he says.

"I remember that we touched sparklers. Then we turned towards each other, and I remember distinctly that my sparkler was nearly out. I was going to kiss you, but instead, I was on fire and you pushed me off the bench."

"I had to push you away!" he says. "Are you mad about that?"

"Oh, don't be silly. I'm not mad at you. But do you remember *how* I got on fire?"

"No." His breathing is faster. "I ... I..." he stutters.

"Please?" I cry and cry on the phone.

"I was terrified," Sheldon says. "I thought it was all my fault because we kissed."

"We did?" Why don't I remember this?

He pauses as if sifting through his own memories. He says softly, "I remember our glasses clashed, our lips touched—yours were minty cool—then I smelled smoke. I pushed you off the bench."

"I forgot about the glasses." I begin to cry again because I hate that I don't remember my first kiss.

"They got knocked off your face. I picked them up later; they were bent. I still have them somewhere."

"Why?"

"I don't know. I thought you might need them, but then you were gone. I heard you went in a helicopter to Seattle."

"I remember so little. I never asked for my glasses. Somehow new ones showed up, but I didn't even know." Even though Sheldon is filling gaps for me, and I can picture a few things, the images do not come from inside me. "How come you thought it was your fault?"

"My sparkler could've started the fire," says Sheldon. "You know how I drop things. But here's the thing, our sparklers were stuck together, so I know I didn't drop mine on you. But I was still scared. Flying sparks can start a fire."

I find myself smiling. Yes, Sheldon stumbles and manages to drop almost everything he's holding. It's only in the water that he is smooth. I take a deep breath. "Joy confessed. You never have to feel responsible for what happened." I tell him everything Joy said.

Sheldon is speechless.

After a long while he says, "Kids were milling about everywhere but they never came into focus for me. It was like the whole world had disappeared and it was just you and me on that bench." I can almost hear him smile. "Joy didn't register at the time. She was a big girl, almost an adult."

"Except she never really grew up," I say.

"Maybe Colleen knows something."

"Yeah," I whisper. "Just once, when she got drunk, she said something. Remember?"

"Vaguely," says Sheldon. "Maybe she was protecting Joy. You should talk to her and find out."

Any moment now I feel I will burst into tears again. It's too much to process.

"I'm so tired," I tell Sheldon. "Nobody is ever going to love me. I'm too ugly." And the tears come. Again.

When I stop weeping, Sheldon says, "That's not true, Rebecca. You are so hurt, you don't let people get close to you."

What?

"This guy I met in Detroit said the same thing."

"You met a guy there?"

"Yeah, he was interviewing as well. We went ice skating and then had dinner together. He ... he ..." Oh, shut up. He awakened something inside me? I can't tell this to Sheldon.

"Whoa!" I can see him putting is hands up in the air. "I don't need details. So is *he* your boyfriend now?"

My face immediately feels hot as I relive the tender kisses, Race's. It's nothing like trying to imagine a kiss that you cannot remember.

"What do you care? You never even came to visit me, let alone hold my hand after I was burned. You ... you... you wimp!" Where are my Shakespeare insults when I need them? I don't know what's wrong with me. Why am I doing everything in my power to make Sheldon, my one true friend, mad?

"If you're done trying to make me jealous, let me set the record straight. My dad brought me to see you in Seattle a couple of times, but it was never the right time. You had treatments or therapy or had to have privacy," Sheldon says. "Once I saw you sleeping, all bandaged up like a mummy, with tubes snaking out of your nose and throat. I was terrified you'd die and it'd be my fault. And there was nothing I could do to fix it!"

Boys. They want to fix things.

"I've not been in the hospital forever, Sheldon. When I finally got home, I was bored out of my skull. You made all that effort to come to Seattle, but you never stopped by my house all these years just to see me."

"I was eleven!"

"I know," I say in a small voice. "We were both so young."

"Hey?"

"Hay is for horses," I say. Too bad he can't see me smiling.

"I'm here now," he says softly.

We talk more easily after that. Sheldon tells me one of the Friday lectures was on hyperspace, parallel universes, and time travel, but I tell him I already covered those in a private tutorial. It's something I've doodled in my notebook often, following different paths. We talk about his hopes of getting into Cal. Tech. and my hopes of making it in Detroit or Missouri, anyplace but Pullman. Of course, we both have an automatic admission to the Washington State University since we're faculty brats.

~~~

The drive home is anything but peaceful. Joy offers to let me ride up front, but I don't want to talk to Dad. Besides she can talk nonstop and I'm not up for her mindless prattle. I tell her "no thanks." We barely look at each other, but when I'm in the back seat, I stare at the back of her head and wonder whether she can feel how much I hate her as I shoot imaginary arrows into the base of her skull.

Dad looks from me to her and shakes his head. I think I hear him say "drama" under his breath.

We're barely out of Seattle when Joy says she needs to pee. Dad pulls into a rest stop and when Joy lumbers off to relieve herself, he turns to me and says, "You girls need to patch up, okay? You have every right to be angry for a hundred lifetimes, but in the end, it was an accident."

"She did it on purpose, Dad."

"But in her case, it's a like a child experimenting, not realizing the devastating consequences. You should be angry at me. I didn't watch over you girls, got busy talking to the neighbors."

Wow! He's accepting blame. This is new. "Okay, still she wasn't a five-year old. She was seventeen. And even if she's mentally incompetent, she knew she was doing the wrong thing. You can't make me patch it up. I don't want to. Look at what she's done to me!" I am almost in tears. "Don't ask me to forgive right now. I can't do anything right now. Maybe I need to go talk to Sellick."

"Rebecca, you've made so much progress over the years. Don't let this new knowledge eat you up inside," says Dad. "I hope Sellick can help you to let it all go."

"I'm already eaten up. Can't you see there's nothing left?" A sob escapes my mouth. "I cannot be with Joy anymore. I'm going to let it all go. I'm leaving!"

~~~36~~~

I don't stop by Colleen's to collect the house keys. The next few days I drive to school early because my shoulder is still too sore to carry the heavy backpack. After school I go straight to physical therapy.

Colleen stops me in the parking lot in the middle of the week. "Hey, where've you been? Did everything go okay? You never answered my calls."

"Why don't you check up on Joy instead?" I say. "She could really use a friend now."

"Huh?" Colleen's amber eyes narrow in confusion. "What's going on?"

"Look, I know what happened when I got burned," I tell Colleen. "It was Joy. How could you not tell me?"

"Because I gave her my sparkler," Colleen blurts out, tears filling her eyes. "I had so many."

I brace myself against my Civic to keep from falling but everything is clear. My voice feels like it comes from far away. "I'm so done with everything here." I leave her standing while I go to PT to do shoulder rotations.

~~~

I go into super study mode. I want to finish strong. But it's hard to concentrate on my school work with my future hanging in the air. I want those scholarships. In my dreams I relive the interviews, giving perfect answers.

I hole myself into my room. It's the only baby-free space in this entire house. I have to dodge a swing in the doorway and clear rattles and booties and stuffed animals off the table before we can sit down to eat. I didn't think Dad would allow

241

Joy to go crazy like this, letting her get a crib *and* a playpen, a swing *and* a bouncer, and so many clothes that we won't even need to do laundry for an entire month and by that time, the baby will have grown out of the stuff.

Joy still tries to appease me by buying more junk, but I feel nothing when I look at her. She's taking a three-month maternity leave and will be back to work in July. Tessa has arranged for daycare at the campus infant center. Dad does what I used to do—take her to the weekly appointments, go grocery shopping, coordinate things with Tessa—and I'm glad he's finally shouldering his responsibilities. I have no interest in Joy's small talk. We never, ever speak about what happened all those many years ago. Joy knows I'll be leaving soon and it makes her sad. But she has not asked me to stay even once, like she knows she has no right to ask anything of me anymore.

Dad has asked Meena Auntie to come during her summer vacation to help Joy with new baby stuff. I feel badly for Aji, but assuage my guilt with the knowledge that Sushila will be there with her little boy Deepak. Meena Auntie will get here in May after the baby is born. When Dad panics about the birth, I tell him that Colleen's mom will help us with the delivery.

I get a text from Race. It said: *I'm in. Partial scholarship. How about you? R.*

I ask for his email and write a big fat congratulatory letter. I'm so happy for him. Alas I'm still waiting, I tell him. I write about my surgery and recovery, but skip Joy's confession. I don't feel too hopeful about getting an acceptance. Shouldn't it have come already? They probably give notice to their first choices right away and make the rest of us wait.

Race writes back immediately: *Hang in there. Let me know ASAP. R.*

~~~

On Friday, Joy announces at breakfast, "The baby is coming today." Dad had taken her to her appointment the day before and told me Storck said it could be any day now. Joy holds her belly and asks me to feel it but I don't want to touch her. She begins to cry.

"Are you okay? Does it hurt?" Panic envelops me. We don't know even the first thing about having babies. "Should we go to the hospital?"

Joy shakes her head no.

"Then what is it?" I ask.

"Oh, Rebecca. I'm so excited," Joy blubbers, "and happy and scared."

"Me too." I lie. I feel nothing but dread.

I'm so terrified, I call Colleen's mom. She's here before I leave for school.

I can't concentrate on anything. Mr. Johnson reprimands me for day dreaming, and later Mr. Berry, for whispering to Sheldon. I wish I felt close to Colleen, so she could ditch her job at the fabric store to help me get through this, but I'm not ready for her sorries. I'm on my own.

I check the mail on my way home. I barely glance through the pile of junk, but my hands shake and everything falls to the ground except for the envelope from Detroit. It's very thin, which probably means I didn't get in. My hopes of leaving are dashed, but I open the envelope carefully. As I begin reading, it begins to sink in that I've been accepted with a partial scholarship and contracts and other information will be coming under separate cover. They offer me congratulations!

Oh, Lord! I am crying so hard because I've wanted this for so long, more than anything else in my whole life. And right by the mailboxes, on the wet pavement, I sit and re-read the letter. I slide the letter into my pocket and gather all the other flyers and advertisements— coupons for Pizza Hut, Taco Time, Corner Drug store, the spring sale at Woodlawn

Furniture, and even a sale of coffins and urns at Kimball Funeral Homes. I really get to leave this place and make a new life for myself. I can picture myself grabbing a sandwich at Blimpies. Without Joy. Without the baby. I don't know whether to laugh or to cry.

My future and my present collide as Joy comes waddling out of the house singing, "Tonight! Tonight's the night."

I get up, brush the dirt from my pants and walk the last few steps home with Joy dancing beside me. I'm sure it's not good for the baby, but Joy cannot be still.

"Joy is doing great," says Mrs. Mendoza, greeting us at the door. "She's been having regular contractions, about ten to twelve minutes apart, for the past couple of hours."

"Feel it," demands Joy.

I haven't touched her in a month, so when I place both my hands on the sides of her protruding belly and can feel how it becomes tense and hard, and how there's a new life growing inside, it makes me tear up.

"I'm going to run on home and cook up some food—you will need good nourishment. Call me anytime if you need anything." Mrs. Mendoza squeezes us into a giant hug. "Look at you two! I am so proud of you. This is one very lucky baby."

I wonder whether the baby will agree.

I dump all the junk mail into the recycling bin and go to my room. I stand against the door and re-read my acceptance letter. I'm in! I try to savor this victory but it's hard with Joy in the hallway, waiting for me. I slip the letter underneath my pillow.

I have really nothing to do once Mrs. Mendoza leaves because she's got Joy all packed for the hospital with clothes and books and music and even her stuffed wolf, Buck. All we have to do is go when the time is right. So I bring out a deck of cards to play War. We've not done this in ages.

Joy's happiness floods the entire house. When she wins a stack of cards, she yells, "Hooray!" After an hour or so, I tell her that we should cook some Indian food and take it to the hospital in the stainless steel tiffin-box. Joy loves the idea and so we cook like old times, Joy chattering away, me cutting up the chicken because she can't stand to cut up meat, and Joy chopping all the onions and garlic because the fumes make me cry. We consult each other what spices to put in as the onions and garlic are sautéing—a bit more turmeric, a pinch of cinnamon, another chili pepper, not too much ginger.

The chicken curry is simmering when Dad gets home. "How's my girl?"

"You'll be a grandpapa tonight," says Joy.

"Ah, then you should name her Kara for tax!" he says.

Joy and I are both confused. Is he crazy?

"You know, it's tax day today. Don't worry, I've filed everything, and I have nothing else on my mind," Dad says, the warmth in his voice real. "I remember what it was like waiting for you to be born. Your mother was just like you, cooking up a dinner."

Dad and Joy both laugh. I swallow a lump in my throat at these happy memories. My birth mother must've been alone and frightened. I get up to stir the pot as I listen to Dad.

"She had an easy labor and delivery. And daughters take after their mothers in this department, so I know everything will go smoothly for you." Dad kisses the top of Joy's head tenderly. He's changed in the last month, giving her the affection she needs since I've been so cold and dead.

As I breathe in the cinnamon and ginger in the curry, I think how Joy's labor is thawing my icy heart.

Joy is so excited, she can't eat supper. She takes small bites of rice and curry. No chicken. I give her an orange and that makes her feel better.

"This is the longest day ever," says Joy.

245

Indeed.

Labor is progressing nicely and for the first time, Dad is not busy with his journals and papers, but sits with us for a game of rummy after dinner.

It's well past nine at night when contractions pick up. They're five minutes apart, then three, and they last longer— more than a minute. I insist that we go to the hospital, but Joy tells me to stop worrying. "It doesn't hurt like the nurse said it might." She clenches her fists. "That's what it feels like." I believe her. She's not in any pain and simply enjoying her womanhood, her power to bring life into the world.

I'm grateful when Mrs. Mendoza stops by to check up on us and tells us that it's a good idea to go to the hospital now.

We rush out and it's only at the registration desk that I realize I've forgotten my scarf. But it no longer matters.

Tears fill Joy's eyes when she tells the night nurse filling out the paperwork that the father is Nick, that he has nothing to do with the baby or her.

"He doesn't know what he's missing," says the nurse. "You'll be fine. You have a very loving family."

If only she knew the whole truth.

We get Joy settled in her room. Dr. Storck is already there and beaming. Joy sings "Tonight's the Night" by Rod Stewart. The nurses laugh. Joy fingers the plastic bracelet on her wrist with her name and ID number. Dad goes outside to pace the hallway when it's time for Joy to get examined. Dr. Storck is quick and efficient. "You're doing great. Already six centimeters dilated."

Joy has an IV running for fluids. She's hooked up to monitors so that we can keep track of the baby's vitals. The baby's heart rate dips a teensy bit when Joy has a contraction. They are lasting longer, but still Joy shows no sign of pain. She even takes a little snooze. This is in such contrast to all the birthing scenes in movies, with the women wailing in agony.

An hour later, Mrs. Mendoza and Colleen join us. Dad is the odd man out.

Mrs. Mendoza fusses over Joy, adjusting the pillows and smoothing her hair. She even prays over Joy, which makes her feel very special.

Colleen asks to walk with me in the hallway. "I'm sorry," she says. "I blame myself. I should never have given a lit sparkler to Joy."

I realize, that just like Sheldon, Colleen has been bearing the guilt all these years. "It wasn't your fault," I say.

"But if I hadn't given her the sparkler, you would still be okay."

"Yeah, probably. In another universe."

"I had no idea Joy would ..."

"Exactly! I don't blame you. Never did. I'm just glad I know the truth."

"It would've killed Joy if you'd died," Colleen says. "It would've killed me too. Those first few days we were so scared, I thought we'd come apart. The fear was terrible. Joy and I made a pact that we'd never tell. The only other person who knew is the priest I confessed to. He said it was not a sin, but because your life was in danger, he said to offer up one Our Father, one Hail Mary and one Glory Be every day for you. And I'll never stop."

We pace the hallways quietly, each in our thoughts. Poor Colleen, only eleven years old and burdened with so much. But what a steadfast friend. I believe her prayers saved me.

Colleen breaks our silence. "Do you think you could've forgiven us if I'd told you?"

"Look at me," I say. "If you had my body now, could you forgive?"

"I don't know," says Colleen. "Probably not right away, but I hope eventually."

"Before you're all eaten up inside, right?" I finish her thoughts. "I have nothing inside me," I whisper.

"That's not true," says Colleen. "You still have a lot of love left in you."

"But who will love me back?"

"I do. My mom and dad. Your dad. Joy. Sheldon too."

I smile through the tears that are forming in my eyes. I'm not in love-love with Sheldon, but Race showed me I am lovable. I feel as though large hummocks of ice are falling off my chest.

We walk back arm in arm.

I tell Colleen about my acceptance to Wayne.

"I knew you'd get in," she says. "Did you tell your dad?"

"Not yet," I say. "Tonight is Joy's night."

Colleen hugs me hard.

Dad is stretched out in the comfiest chair ever, snoring with a *Human Genetics* journal on his chest. Mrs. Mendoza sits on the window-bench seat and crochets a baby blanket. Her hands are always busy, like Colleen's. I help her unravel the wool so she doesn't have to stop every so often to do it herself.

A loud POP startles us all. "Oh, no!" Joy screams. "Rebecca!"

"What? What happened?" I ask her, while buzzing the nurse.

"It's all wet." She grimaces and holds on to her stomach. "I can't stop peeing."

The nurse bustles in and checks on Joy. "Your water just broke. Things are going to move fast now."

I herd everyone out as Dr. Storck enters the room and takes her place between Joy's legs. I remember how awful it was to have people in the room when I had to have dressing changes. Mom was so good about protecting my modesty—she'd shoo everybody out and draw the curtains.

Joy cries out in pain. "I want Mommy!"

"Can't you give her some pain medicine?" I ask Dr. Storck.

"It's too late," says Dr. Storck. "The baby is coming soon, Joy. Push along with the contractions, okay?"

Even though I've been to most of the birthing and baby classes with Joy, I feel completely helpless to do anything to help her. "Please hurry," I tell Dr. Storck, as if that would speed up the birth.

I support Joy's shoulders as she bears down with each contraction. I bring a cup of water near her mouth in between contractions. I roll up my sleeves and wipe the sweat that trickles into her eyes. Joy cries out and pushes so hard, her face turns a deep red.

I don't know how long this goes on, but it feels like forever when Dr. Storck says that the baby is crowning. "Wait, breathe, breathe," she tells Joy. "Now, push!"

Joy obeys and it's the weirdest thing to see a head full of black hair sticking out between Joy's legs. The baby is covered in blood and some white stuff. It's easily the grossest and the most incredible thing I've ever seen. If I didn't want to be a trauma doctor, I'd go into obstetrics.

Dr. Storck wipes the baby's mouth and the rest of the body slips out in the next contraction.

The baby cries a pitiful cry and Joy falls back exhausted. I sponge her face with a cool washcloth.

"You have a beautiful baby girl," Dr. Storck says as the nurse whisks away the baby to be cleaned, measured, weighed, and wrapped.

The nurse lays the baby, who is wide awake, on top of Joy's breast. Her nipples are long and the areolae are darker and larger than I ever remember seeing them. The baby instinctively latches on the elongated nipple, her mouth covering the areola and sucking furiously. Joy can't take her eyes off the baby. I weep because it is the most beautiful sight.

249

Joy coos to the baby. She pries open the baby's tiny fist and she closes it upon Joy's pinky.

After Joy has been cleaned up, everybody gathers around her and the baby, nestled in the crook of her arm, content and peaceful. When they all leave, Dad, Joy and I have a midnight snack of rice with chicken curry. Joy is ravenous and breakfast won't be served until morning.

"She's perfect," I tell Joy. "What will you name her?"

"Ruthie." Joy smiles down at the baby. "Ruthie."

Yes, of course, Ruthie will be Joy's companion when she is old enough. Ruthie has unbound me, I realize.

~~~

There is only one couch, so Dad tells me to go home and get some rest. "I can keep watch," he adds. It is so gratifying to see him as I remembered him before Mom died. Ruthie's birth has changed everything. Where before he was doing things reluctantly for Joy, now he can't do enough.

"But I want to stay," I say, realizing it is the truth.

"Are you sure? It's going to be a while before Ruthie will sleep through the night. This might be your last chance." He grins.

"Then you take it."

Dad gathers me into a big hug. "I've been a bear, haven't I? But I promise to be here for all three of you. Don't you worry about a thing."

I nod against his chest. And I do trust him because his transformation mirrors mine. He kisses the top of my head and goes over to Joy to plant one on her gently without waking her. She mumbles. Last of all, he goes to Ruthie's bassinet and we cannot stop gazing at her, she is so beautiful.

"The power of babies," he whispers, touching his hand to his heart.

~~~

250

I spend the night on the comfy chair, with a pillow and extra blankets. Although nurses come in to check on us, they are quiet. In the middle of the night, when Ruthie awakens in her little bassinet, I pick her up. I snuggle her to myself and examine her by faint glow of the night light. She's got Joy's and Dad's round face. The gray-green eyes must be Nick's. I wonder if they'll change to a pretty hazel. Her plump little elbows remind me of Mom. Oh, how I wish Mom could see her. I know she'd love to be a grandmother. I kiss Ruthie's head, full of jet-black hair softer than silk. I stare into the depths of her eyes. She is utterly perfect and so terribly vulnerable.

Did my birth mother look into the black pools of my eyes? Did she fall in love with me like I am falling in love?

But she did love me enough. She wrapped me up and left me in a basket on a church doorstep. I look at Ruthie who is so calm in my arms, who just wants to be cocooned.

"You shall always know love," I whisper fiercely into her hair.

I splay open her tiny fists and plant a kiss into the palms. I dot her feet, her ears, and her darling little elbows with butterfly kisses. We doze together, content to just be.

It's still dark outside when the nurse turns on the light above the sink. She comes over to me. "Hi, sweetie," she coos to the baby. "You must be hungry."

We let Joy sleep while the nurse teaches me how to change her diaper, which is soaked. It also has the worst tar-like poop in it.

"That's meconium," says the nurse. "After this, she will have yellow stools that don't smell bad, that is, if Joy keeps breastfeeding her."

After the diaper change, we wake up Joy. She's ready to nurse Ruthie, who's eager. She makes loud smacking sounds and the two of them together make such a perfect picture, my heart melts and melts until it overflows like a river of love. Love for Ruthie. Love for Joy.

~~~

The next morning, a different nurse arrives and admires Ruthie. She has Joy give Ruthie her first bath, instructing Joy the entire time. Ruthie doesn't like it one bit and howls. But once she's dried off, bundled up and fed, she's content. Joy can't stop gazing at her.

Dad comes to pick us up in the afternoon. He carries the car-seat. Joy fusses over getting Ruthie nestled into it just right so that her head doesn't loll around.

When we come home, Joy erupts into great big shrieks at the balloons and big sign: "It's a Girl!" with all the vital statistics bordered by baby bunnies, chicks and bees. This has to be the work of Colleen, it's so fresh and pretty.

"Thank you," I tell Colleen.

"Hey, I'm an auntie too!" she says.

It's true. The Mendozas are family too. They've been a steadfast presence in our lives. Even now, the house smells rich with coffee and cinnamon bread. Mrs. Mendoza has been busy. I wonder how many lives she has saved with her quiet baking. She stays a while to help get Joy settled, assuring her she's just a few steps away.

After the Mendozas leave, I go to my room is to read my acceptance letter from Detroit. And I cry into the pillow. I want the security of knowing I will go to medical school. I want to be with Ruthie. I want Race. I want Sheldon. I want everything.

~~~

We quickly discover that there is no schedule that is valid for more than a couple of days when it comes to Ruthie. I tell Joy to take as many naps as she can with Ruthie since she is always hungry and has to be fed round the clock. Mel just loves Ruthie and her milky smell and is always near her, or on her blankets or baby seat. A home health nurse comes every day to give us tips as we discover our new life with Ruthie.

~~~

I've been going to school as usual, but I am tired from a week of waking up in the middle of the night to help Joy with Ruthie's diaper change. I do the changing and Joy feeds her. The crib is going unused because it's easier for Joy and Ruthie to sleep while nursing.

Dad and I take turns helping Joy at night but all three of us are tired. Taking care of an infant is hard work. But sharing the night-time duty has brought us all closer together. Dad is so tender with Ruthie and actually knows a lot about babies!

"Déjà vu," he says, grinning.

When Ruthie needs to be walked because her tummy is upset, it is Dad who holds her. She rests in his strong arms as he sings *Hush-a-bye baby*.

~~~

Ruthie instinctively turns towards whoever is holding her and starts rooting for a nipple when she's hungry. Barely ten days old, she starts rooting for one when I'm holding her. "There's nothing there," I tell her. After a few minutes, she starts howling for Joy. Her face is red and she looks exactly like Dad when he's mad!

Joy can't ignore her cries. "My milk is flowing," she says from the couch. I bring her to Joy and Ruthie calms down immediately. She knows exactly what she wants.

I don't want Ruthie to go hungry. I never want her to be deprived of anything.

~~~

Friday night, when Ruthie is two weeks old, we go folk-dancing. Everybody admires Ruthie and we all take turns holding her. Even when my arms get heavy, I realize how much I treasure the weight. Joy is tired from all the dancing and when we come home, she nurses Ruthie and promptly falls asleep. Ruthie is restless, so I pick her up and pat her little back. She gives the most enormous burp, surprising herself, and begins to cry. I keep rubbing her back until she falls asleep. I lay her next to Joy and slide down under the covers and fall into a deep sleep.

Mel's meowing wakes me up. Ruthie is awake, kicking her legs, disturbing the poor cat. I wake up grudgingly, change her diaper and bring her back to Joy.

"Oh, Ruthie," Joy murmurs, as she nurses her. "I love you. Don't leave me."

"I'm not leaving either," I blurt out. "How can I be a proper auntie if I'm not here?"

Joy's eyes grow big and round and her smile is so big her face might split. "But what about medical school?" She frowns a moment later. "I'm sorry about what I did," she whispers.

"I know." I hold her hand. My eyes rest on the maroon onesie that Ruthie is wearing. "I wanna be a Cougar too," I say simply.

~~~

Thin letters arrive from Florida and Missouri. I cannot believe my good fortune at being accepted to all three BS/MD programs. However, only Missouri has given me a full scholarship.

I show Dad the letters. "I'm so proud of you, Rebecca," he says. "It's obvious where you should go, right?"

"My heart is right here," I say. "That night at the hospital, when I said I wanted to stay, I meant it."

"Are you sure?" Dad's voice croaks. "You are so smart, so dedicated. You could go anywhere."

"I know," I reply. "But living here means I can have it all. My family *and* my training for medical school."

"Well, I hope you choose to live on campus, so that you have fewer distractions," he says, tears welling in his eyes.

"We can meet for lunch sometime. And the four of us can get together for games when you're not too busy studying."

I can't stop smiling as he draws me to him in an enormous hug.

I call Race telling him of my decision.

"I'll miss seeing you," he says. "But it sounds like you're going to have it all for a while."

We promise to stay in touch.

~~~

Sheldon comes by with flowers for Joy and a rattle for Ruthie. He admires her, holding her awkwardly until I wrap his other arm around her so that she's snug against his chest. I don't want him dropping her! After he gives her back to Joy, we take a walk up to the highest point of our hill to the water tower. I sit on a damp log.

Sheldon has gotten into the biochemistry program at Cal. Tech. He's shocked that I won't go to Missouri, since all I'd talked about was how much I want to leave.

"Don't give up on your dreams," he warns me.

"Oh, I won't." I lean closer to him. "I have plans, but right now they also include being near Joy and Ruthie." I gaze up at the blue skies. "Someday I will go to India, provide medical care to kids there, help them see their worth even when nobody else does." I slip my hand confidently into his.

"I may join you in that venture." Sheldon lets go of my hand and encircles me. Our knees knock. I tilt my head so that our glasses will not clash when his lips meet mine.

The End

~~~Gratitude~~~

The writing of this book would not be possible had I not had permission to borrow some of the life circumstances of my two lovely cousins, Sangeeta and Aradhana. Thank you both. I was able to finally give voice to that girl in my head who asked so many What Ifs?

I am indebted to Nancy Butts and the Institute of Children's Literature for giving me the book course. Nancy mentored me from the beginning to the end. She has been a solid rock against whom I could lean and bounce ideas off. Thank you for everything, especially "luminous."

My first reader, Jen Heger, spent innumerable hours at my kitchen table reading over the raw first draft. Without her waiting for the next chapter, I might have given up. She kept me true to my characters. Thank you, Jen, for your friendship and patience.

I've had the good fortune to have several astute readers who read the full manuscript and gave me much more insight. Molly Blaisdell, Ruthie Brouette, Bish Denham, Dominic De Souza, Amar Dhaliwal, Jorge Gomez, Marcia Hoehne, Faith Hough, Deana Lattanzio, Heather Mirman, Gary Ludlam, and Allyson Schrier—thank you for your time and willingness to discuss aspects of this story. Thanks to the children's writing community at the Blueboards (now the SCBWI boards) for the many years of shoptalk and friendship. It's been productive procrastination!

Thanks go to my family for giving me the time and space to write, for reading the full manuscript, for all the spirited discussions, and for putting up with all my idiosyncrasies. Your enthusiasm and belief in this story made it possible for me to continue working on this draft after draft. Thank you, Michael, Max and Dagny, Don and Charlanne, for loving me and supporting this wonderful writing life. I love you.

Finally, I sing Handel's *But Thanks Be To God*, who giveth us the victory through our Lord Jesus Christ (*1 Corinthians 15:57*). Deo Gratias!

Vijaya Bodach (June 8, 2018 on the
Feast of the Most Sacred Heart of Jesus).

Dear Reader, thank you for taking the time to read this story. If you enjoyed it, please consider sharing it with your friends and reviewing it. To learn more about me and my books, please visit my web/blog at **https://vijayabodach.com** or email me at **vijaya_bodach@yahoo.com**. I am constructing a sister site: **https://bodachbooks.com** to showcase BOUND and future books I publish.

Vijaya Bodach is the author of over 60 books for children, including TEN EASTER EGGS, and just as many stories, articles, and poems. BOUND is her first novel.

Made in the USA
Middletown, DE
22 October 2018